RAPE SEED

GEORGENE WEINER

ADAGIO PRESS
P.O. Box 276
Medfield, MA 02052
(617) 784-4084

This book is a work of fiction. Names, characters, places, and incidents are either products of the author's imagination or are used fictitiously. Any resemblance to actual events or locales or persons, living or dead, is entirely coincidental.

Printed in the United States of America

First Printing, September 1997
10 9 8 7 6 5 4 3 2 1

ISBN 0-9657804-0-6

Designed by Jonathan Sulkow
Cover photo by Allen Weiner

For Allen . . . whose constancy reminds me that
day follows night; that seasons change;
and that, like rain, tears cleanse

Acknowledgments

When ready to give birth, a woman places herself in the care of those whom she trusts, in professionals who are expert in delivering a child into the world. With this work, I experienced all the symptomatology of pregnancy, all the attendant physiological and psychological effects of "carrying" it to its moment of delivery. My early stages of labor were patiently monitored by Kathryn Deputat, editor and friend. Her insight and wisdom were like lessons in controlled breathing—they helped to sustain the contractions that were to come.

I wish to express my heartfelt gratitude to Annette Francis, editor—my literary doctor extraordinaire. Without her steadfast belief in the potential of my work, its birth would not have taken place. Without her exceptional skills and medicinal humor, all labor would have been in vain.

And to my husband Allen, I express my love for the encouragement, invaluable criticism, and technical support that brought my creation into being.

A secret is the sword of truth
sheathed in betrayal.

•1•

It was that precise moment in time and space when celestial bodies aligned in preparation for the great heavenly exchange. A waning crest of moon shimmered as a supernal command signaled the orderly segue to another day—imbued with hope, expectant with new possibilities lying nascent in the womb of chance.

Maxine Lane was somewhere she had not been before, somewhere between a dreamy here and a foreboding there—suspended and free-floating as a feather in a windstorm, impervious to the knowing or the not knowing of the perimeters of her physical being. There were no brackets to constrain the limits of her imagination. Low-hanging clouds muffled the distant ringing of a phone.

"Hello?" she thought she said.

"Hello, Max. This is your father." The voice that swept through the phone line on an icy wind, indeed, was Philip's.

"Dad? No, you've been dead for eight years! Who the hell is this?"

"It's me, Max. I've come to right my wrongs. Please listen to me." Philip's tone was hauntingly plaintive.

"The dead don't talk. Whoever you are, leave me alone."

"I left you alone before, Max. And, for your information, the dead do speak. You can trust the word of a dead man; he's got nothing to lose."

"What could you ever hope to gain, Dad? When you had it all, you blew it away; you gave me the royal finger. Please, go away. It's too late."

"All I want is some peace, Max. I'm a miserable excuse for a soul begging for rest. I can't be at peace until I ease my conscience. I need to tell you I'm sorry for what I did to your mother—I'm sorry for what she did to you. She'll try to destroy you, too, Max, and I have to warn you of it. Watch your back when it comes to your mother."

"Dad, how soon after dying did you start caring for me? The last piece of advice you gave me was when I was fifteen, that 'Don't sit on cold cement steps 'cuz you'll get hemorrhoids' crap."

"I saw what they did to you at my funeral. As usual, I was still thinking only of myself. I did nothing to stop it. By the way, that kiss-up rabbi could have tried to find something nice to say about me."

"He didn't know you, Dad. If he had, it would have made his task even harder." Maxie felt suddenly bold. "As long as you're here, answer me one thing."

"What's that?"

"Remember that Sunday afternoon at Sandy Beach—the day you decided to teach me to swim?"

"Max, that was thirty-odd years ago. Why dwell?"

"Oh, so you *do* remember!" Pressing harder, Maxie asked, "Why wouldn't you grab my hand, Dad? You let go of me in water way over my head. I sank, scrambled up, sank again. And you just let me think I was going to drown! Why?" Maxie remembered the taste of sea water as it filled her mouth, her nostrils.

"You just couldn't get it right," Philip stated matter-of-factly. "I lost my patience."

"You lost your *patience?* Geez, what about *me*? Did you *want* me to drown?" Until now, Maxie had not considered this last option.

A different kind of anger now gripped her. Contempt moved into her heart, pushed aside the old scorn.

"I'm sorry, Max." Philip sounded contrite.

"Sorry? No, you're not sorry—you're pitiful. You fished me out of the water, dragged me back to the blanket where Mom and Toby were playing cards. 'You're a lost cause . . . you're a lost cause'—that's what you kept saying all the way home."

"Don't you ever get over things?" Philip asked, deflecting.

"I don't think I'll ever get over *you*, Dad."

"I never could compete with your sharp tongue, Max."

"So you used your hands instead—is that it?" Maxie countered, wishing she could push fistfuls of Philip's gall down his throat. "You're still such a coward, you can't even show up in per . . . however you're supposed to look, damn you!"

Maxie wondered if it were possible to communicate the unspoken, if one's sadness and fury could cut through the tangled net that hung over the cave door of the unspeakable. "Why should I care about your peace, your eternal rest?" Maxie implored, wishing she could ask Philip, instead, if he had ever loved her. But a tinny click signaled that the line was as dead as the man she had heard on the other end. The receiver was still in her hand as she surfaced, breaking through the watery depths of her unconscious, tentatively opening her eyes.

Perspired and flushed, her heartbeat irregular, Maxie looked out her bedroom window and tried to draw the early summer morning to her—to wrap herself in the warm textures, the reassuring sounds, the constancy of what she knew. *Damn hot flashes,* she fretted, *now I'm having conversations with dead people. And with my father, no less! Good God, what next!* Still, Philip's warning about her mother Sarah's desire to "destroy" Maxie abraded her heart like sandpaper. It pricked her sensibilities with dread.

Maxie tried to reconstruct the features, the outline of her father's once handsome face—the chiseled, angular jaw, the salt-and-pepper mustache so meticulously sculpted over a pencil-thin line of upper lip. His cold, blue eyes never betrayed the shallowness of his character, forever darting, averting human contact. And his hands, so big—huge, really—out of proportion to his thin, wiry body. Maxie saw her father as the central figure in an El Greco painting—elongated, somber; but Philip lacked in spiritual grace, was devoid of that inner radiance of humility that made the painter's subjects so endearing. Philip easily could have died of his own sense of ineptitude, were it not for the cigarettes, the lethal white nails that sealed his coffin. A spiritual anorexic, he fed on his own failures. In any event, his wizened, hoary specter was what she envisioned behind the cold draft of words affecting her now. She shivered as the chill slithered up her spine. It was time to revisit the lake.

Hours later, Maxie sat on the worn, green park bench, swinging her feet back and forth like a fidgety schoolgirl. She kicked up mounds of sand with her toes, leaving heel tracks in the still damp uncovered layer, waiting for some revelation. It made no sense to her, a late riser, why anyone with no particular purpose or reason would choose to be up at 7 A.M. In the twenty-two years that she lived in Shafton, the placid waters had never quelled her aversion to the noisy crowds nor her disdain for the shrill, unrestrained exuberance of summertime children. Yet, for the last few weeks, she felt drawn to this place. Perhaps here, her deepest thoughts could flow to the water and wind their way to a greater source of understanding.

A few diaphanous patches of fog lifted gracefully from Lake Mattatuck, spiraling upward into oblivion. Luminous beads of morning shimmered gaily in the already brilliant sunshine. Whatever Maxie had hoped to see revealed she did not know. She left the bench, walked down to the water's edge, and let the cool wash over her feet. At that moment, she caught sight of a floating black object, a graduation cap that must have been jubilantly flung into the lake after the high-school graduation reveling of the previous night. Maxie had watched the ceremony on the local cable network; she remembered now that it had evoked from her an uncomfortable, dramatic reaction. She had thought that the tears that welled up in her eyes, the lump she had felt in her throat had been provoked by the joyful relief of the graduates, the pride and elation so visible on the faces of their parents. But no, she was hearing again the discordant strains of her own graduation march, wondering if those familiar chords were what led to the dream confrontation with her father. *You weren't there, you selfish fool; you didn't give a rat's ass about my pride, my honors, my prizes . . . me. You fucked up, Dad, and then, you died. How typically useless. And I'm here, feeling dead too, still hating you!*

Philip Kahn, fueled by suspicions of imagined transgressions, frustrated by the absence of joy in his own life, sucked the pleasures of Maxie's youth up a straw of cruel envy, slurping loudly as he reached bottom, emptying her. "You're not pulling the wool over *my* eyes," he would proclaim, each time she went out on a date; and with each accusation of fabricated misconduct, a smile would drain from Maxie's face like wet paint. Maxie remembered that neither she nor her older sister Toby could admit to each other the loathing and fear they harbored separately, secretly for their father. "Maxie," Toby had said once, with uncharacteristic insight, "you have to know a lot yourself about what you suspect in others."

Maxie could see and hear the power walkers, the joggers, all about now. Walking toward her, arm in arm, two older women exchanged complaints about their children. Each woman was trying to convince the other that she had endured the most punishment in her long-suffering role as a mother.

"My Rhoda," the first one said, hand over her ample, heaving bosom, "I gave her my life, my whole heart and soul. And what do I get for all those years of sacrifice, of going myself without, just so she could have dance lessons and learn to play the piano? What talent she had, my Rhoda! Now she tells me, get this, that I 'piss her off'! Can you believe she would say such a thing to her mother? I PISS HER OFF!"

Her companion, outdone, nodded and clucked appropriately. "You know, Martha," she said, "I sometimes think how we start out in life—alone and lonely. We marry, have children, live a little bit on our savings, and in the end find ourselves where we started, alone and lonely. Maybe that's just the way it was meant to be. Our birds leave the nest and fly off to their own loneliness. It's just that we can no longer protect them—or maybe they don't want us to. Maybe they *need* us to piss them off—so they'll leave!"

Maxie eavesdropped on this conversation for as long as the elderly pair was within earshot. She wished they had not walked away so quickly; their haste made her impatient, a little cross that she could not hear more. It was then that she became aware of her deep regret—a loser's excuse for being duped. *I should have seen it all coming. Maybe I did but just didn't get out of the way*, she admitted to herself, finally.

And now Maxie understood, clearly, that Cora Leib was the reason for her daily visits to the lake. She hoped that the two women would return tomorrow. Perhaps she would detain them, ask them: Did *they* know how a stranger can touch the heat of your pain but not be burned by it? She wanted to know how, in one simple act of caring, Cora Leib had replaced impostor emotions with something more enduring—something that kept Maxie from embracing, longing for death.

•2•

New England winters, like thieves, steal the breath away, leaving behind a feeling of violation. Penetrating gales lash at the windows of the psyche and creep into the bones. Maxie's first winter at Selby College had its way with her. She had arrived in Cambridge the fall of 1963, filled with a peculiar mix of anticipation and dread. Unsure of her choice of a small, liberal arts college with an all-female student body, she felt homesick and guilty. Maxie believed that her mother Sarah was either very sad or angry about her daughter's decision to abandon the tightly woven cocoon of home. Maxie had known nothing more of the world beyond Crocker Street, nothing more than what Philip had taught her: "The world is out to get you." At Selby, she was hearing, "There's a world out there to get!" Toby had flunked out of junior college, retreating almost peevishly to Sarah's nest, accepting with equanimity that her failure was preferable to the dangers of independence. Maxie instinctively took refuge deep inside her being where she could retreat while maintaining a physical presence.

Outwardly, she plunged into academic life, was elected class president, and was inducted into the prestigious Sapphire Key Honor Society. She successfully fooled everyone in her circumscribed world into believing that she was "fully realized," an expression then in campus vogue. No one would have guessed that a monstrous beast had begun to roar in her ears, searing her thoughts with anger-breath, poisoning her mind with suggestions of self-destruction. No one could have known that in that first college year oceans of tears would carry her out beyond the horizon where memories are tossed by waves of violent mindstorms. No one except Cora Leib.

Cora Leib's arrival at Selby coincided with Maxie's. As the new chairman of the foreign language department, she was to teach two sections of Conversational Spanish II and one section of Contemporary Spanish Literature. On the one hand, she welcomed the task of inspiring or enlightening new students; on the other, she wanted to be realistic in her goal of elevating the minds of some whose intellectual scope ended at the doors of Newbury Street boutiques. With enthusiasm and determination, Mrs. Leib held classes three days a week in a dreary classroom just above the old library. The "classroom" was a small alcove in a dreary Victorian home long vacated by its illustrious former owners. In the dark attic-like room, there were assembled two rows of one-armed desk chairs and a larger, well-worn desk that faced them, as well as a free-standing chalkboard. The single window on the back wall let in more cold air than sunlight. To compensate for this charmless chamber, Mrs. Leib came to class dressed in vibrant magentas, cerulean blues, sunset oranges. Raven hair worn loosely, in her own fashion, set off light, delicate skin; small facial features belied her Semitic heritage. Large, dangling earrings lent seductiveness to her modest femininity. Dark, deeply set eyes looked directly into Maxie's soul. Try as she might, Maxie could not avert Cora Leib's gaze—it penetrated the most durably cast superficiality; it flushed out any vestige of duplicity or subterfuge. Yet, her eyes beckoned, welcomed, and exposed her own profoundly romantic nature. To Maxie, Mrs. Leib's perfect diction, her regal demeanor, her insistence on correctness evinced strength and dignity; she was undeniably alluring. In fact, Maxie was embarrassed by the effect of Cora Leib's presence.

She was in awe—yes, she loved this magical, beautiful woman. She could feel her heart wanting to reach out with needful hands to embrace her teacher. *How weird this is*, she mused, *what is this wrenching I feel?* Unable to articulate her need for touch, Maxie thought she could get closer to Cora by excelling in her studies. Although duly acknowledged for her efforts, Maxie wanted more. She wanted what only Cora Leib could give her, and she knew it even then. In moments of fantasy, Maxie imagined Mrs. Leib as she would always address her, hearing plaintive sounds one late winter night and cautiously opening her front door. In a slice of moonlight, Mrs. Leib would discover a shivering lump—an abandoned animal that no one had had the courage to drown.

"Why, you poor little bag of wet bones," Mrs. Leib would say, kneeling down to scoop up her find, holding it with a gentleness unfamiliar to the rejected, "come inside where it's warm."

The sounds of children splashing and of mothers slapping brought Maxie's thoughts back to the beach. Pestered by the intrusions, she collected her things, searched in the pockets of her shorts for the car keys. With an audible sigh, she looked out over the lake, not knowing whether the bright sunlight was disturbing her vision or if her tears were distorting it. Sighing again, she left.

•3•

Maxie awoke the following morning to crackling booms of thunder and flashes of white lightning. Short, forceful gusts of wind blew fingernail-tapping drops of rain against the bedroom windows. The advent of inclement weather kept her from going to the lake, but she was not disappointed. Turning onto her back, pulling her downy comforter up under her chin, Maxie closed her eyes and lay very still, listening to the rat-a-tat of the intensifying storm. The sounds took her back in time to her early childhood, back to rainy afternoons spent with Aunt Belle. "Don't worry, child," Belle would say, "it's just the sounds of angry angels banging on their pots with silver spoons. Come, let's cheer them up with a story." Putting some water on the stove to heat, Belle would take Maxie into a cozy, nook-like corner of the living room in an apartment she shared with her disabled mother, Anna, and her two sisters, Frances and Dorothy. Heavily flocked velvet the color of ripened cranberries made the walls of this room appear to sag; gold damask drapes pulled apart by fringed tassels kept alive memories of Old World elegance left behind in Anna's precipitous flight from the advancing Nazi scourge. Settling beside Maxie on the cushiony velvet sofa, Belle would draw her favorite niece into her sturdy, cradled arms. Maxie luxuriated in the sweet, lavender scent of Belle's perfume; she felt the softness of Belle's pudgy, pink cheeks. Circles of rouge applied over an excess of pressed powder, curly dark hair, and mischievous brown eyes added childlike mirth to Belle's infectious optimism.

"Once upon a time," Belle would begin, snuggling Maxie even closer to her, "there were five bears."

"*Five* bears?" Maxie asked, already tickled.

"Yes," Belle said with conviction, "five *stupid* bears who lived in the forest. There was the momma bear, whose backside was so big she had to squeeze through the doorway of their little cottage! Then there was the poppa bear, an old poop, Maxie, who couldn't count on his furry black toes. And then there were the three little bears, so ug-guh-ly, I tell you, each face could stop an eight-day clock!" As Belle went on, improvising her outlandish stories about ugly bears or stupid birds, she sprinkled ridicule on them like chocolate jimmies on an ice-cream cone. With wide eyes and expansive gestures, she would pretend to be the clumsy, grotesque animals of the forest, and Maxie, watching the hysterical antics of her aunt, would have to hold her stomach where it hurt so much from laughing. The thunder and lightning would have long disappeared unnoticed. Through Aunt Belle, Maxie learned to appreciate the joy of her culture—its colorful language that had the power to evoke tears of laughter from the most self-deprecating jokes. The trick was to lessen the pain of ridicule by inflicting the cut yourself—to do unto yourself before someone else did.

Maxie smiled. She could still taste the fresh roll that Belle would butter, dunk into her creamed coffee, and hand to her niece. The sharing was like a kiss, only sweeter. And now, warm and snug under her billowy comforter, remembering those rainy days, Maxie's heart ached for one more story. Gone were the Sunday afternoon visits to her grandmother's apartment on Fuller Street, redolent with the smells of fried onions and cabbage soup made with marrow bones and large chunks of flanken meat. In this second-floor walk-up apartment, all the squabbling cousins assembled with their squabbling mothers and fathers. There they ate tzimmis, kishke, and gefilte fish together on Dorothy's crocheted tablecloth spread on the long dining-room table. Maxie missed the playful kicking that went on under the table and the confusion of everyone trying to talk at the same time. It was from this *poverty* that Sarah, Maxie's mother, had run to marry a dashingly handsome young man who drove flashy new cars. The years were gone and the faces blurred, but Maxie would always enjoy rainy days—they made her think of angels and silver spoons.

Although she would have loved to stay in bed all day, Maxie decided to call her friend Dawn. Rolling over onto her side, she picked up the bedside phone and dialed. Waiting for Dawn to answer, she looked at the clock on her night table and was surprised to see that it was no longer morning. Although a year had passed since their last conversation, Dawn understood that it was Maxie's self-imposed exile that accounted for the hiatus in their relationship. Dawn had been through an acrimonious divorce; Maxie had been struggling through bouts of depression. Each had chosen separate corners in which to lick their wounds. To Maxie's relief, Dawn welcomed the call.

"Dawn," Maxie began, tentatively, with a catch in her voice, "would you like to come over for some sugar?" referring to Dawn's habit of adding four teaspoonsful to her tea.

"Hey, thanks, old friend," Dawn replied without hesitation, "I'll bring the corkscrew." The offer was Dawn's affectionate referral to Maxie's propensity to draw wisdom from the bottom of a wine glass. Both were prepared to pick up the remaining pieces of their friendship, to move forward.

"I've got this really funny story to tell you," Maxie said, remembering Belle.

"Oh, good! Did your mother break her leg? Or was it my ex—the asshole?" Dawn's vitriol toward Rob was not about to dissipate any time soon. Still, Maxie feared that the wrong choice of words would pick at the scab that was trying to form over deep wounds.

"How are you doing with . . . everything?" Maxie's question sounded hollow to her own ears.

"Actually, I'm at that delicate stage of recovery where I have to make a serious decision."

"What's that?"

"Whether to slit *my* throat or *his*. Listen, Maxie, let me give you a little advice: If you should ever find out that Arthur's cheating on you, don't wait sixteen years to kick him out, as I did with Rob. Kick his ass so hard you lose your shoe. Give him something to remember you by each time he wants to sit down."

Maxie sensed that a few cups of sugar and several empty wine glasses would be needed to get both of them through this day.

"Come around two, if you can."

"That's great. When you called, I was just finishing up a poem I composed for the *schmuck*—it's called "Ode to a Turd." Pretty snappy title, don't you think? See ya later." *It's true,* Maxie thought, *Jews are the funniest sad people in the world.*

At exactly two o'clock, Maxie heard the sound of Dawn's car pulling into the front driveway and went to let her in. On opening the door, Maxie was surprised to see that Dawn looked so poised, so controlled. Neatly attired in a lovely peach silk pantsuit, she looked slimmer than Maxie remembered. Shortly cropped auburn hair and a golden tan accentuated her youthful appearance.

"Come on in, Dawn. You're looking just great," Maxie said, embracing her friend. "Just throw the umbrella into the stand over in the corner."

"Hi, there. Who were you expecting, Godzilla? Fooled you, didn't I?" Indeed, she had fooled Maxie. She was not gaunt nor pale; there were no visible pieces of her hanging by a thread.

Dawn closed the front door behind her, did as instructed with the soaking-wet umbrella, and followed Maxie into the spacious, modern kitchen that had been remodeled since her last visit. “Oh, I love everything you’ve done in here—all this glass and white cabinetry. It’s really gorgeous, Maxie. Do you wear roller skates to get around when you’re cooking?”

“It’s much bigger than what we had before, but I enjoy being in here—especially on days like this one. The water’s boiled for your tea. Want some?”

“Thanks, I could use a cup. Oh, and here,” Dawn said, extracting a corkscrew from her purse. Maxie went to the wine cooler and selected a bottle of Chardonnay. Returning to the table, she began to uncork it with great ceremony.

“I guess this is somewhat of an occasion, isn’t it? Shall I make a toast?” She poured the water for Dawn’s tea and sat down opposite her. Dawn began to shovel teaspoonsful of sugar into the cup, losing track of the number. Distracted, she looked pensively into her cup, forgetting to raise it to her lips.

“Hey, you OK?” Maxie asked, reaching out for Dawn’s hand.

“Yeah, I’m fine, or at least I think I’ll *be* fine. It’s my boys I’m worried about. Evan is vocal—talks all the time about Rob, albeit in expletives. He won’t answer Rob’s phone calls, but he’s getting the anger out. Paul, however, has totally shut me out and himself in. I think of him as the Silent Sufferer you’ll read about someday imploding in the middle of the Chestnut Hill Mall.”

“Are you going for help?”

“We’re all going for counseling. Frankly, though, I’d rather be doing something more constructive—like planning Rob’s funeral. I’ve already thrown out all the pictures, the slides, our wedding album—our memories.” Dawn was still stirring her tea.

“How do you throw out a memory?” Maxie was especially interested in the reply.

“You simply pretend it didn’t happen. Maxie, my life as I knew it is over—it's as if with one sweeping stroke that fraud erased twenty-five years of me and what I thought was us." Dawn got up from the table, walked over to the glass doors that gave unobstructed view to the backyard, and stood quietly for a full minute. As she sipped her tea in silence, the storm continued unabated, with conviction. Sheets of windswept rain blew across the surface of the swimming pool, barely replenishing what had evaporated over the last few days. "I can see your hubby still takes excellent care of the landscaping. Everything looks so fabulous, so manicured, so . . . *rich*," she said.

Maxie could forgive the bitter irony of Dawn's choice of words. Undoubtedly, she was thinking of child-support payments and legal fees. Maxie looked into her empty glass for something to say; finding nothing, she refilled it. "Would you like some bundt cake? I made it with apples taken from our two-tree orchard." *When there is nothing she can do,* Maxie thought, *a mother offers food.*

"No thanks, I'll just pour myself a little more hot water." Dawn removed the simmering kettle of water from the cooktop. Pouring, she chuckled at the white ceramic pot painted with black markings of a cow, "Cute pot." After retaking her seat at the table, she continued, relaxing the tightness in her face, the tenseness in her shoulders. "How's Sarah Dearest? You don't mind my calling her Sarah, do you?"

"You can call her anything you want; I would like to, but can't."

"Why? Still think you can kill her with words? C'mon, Max, I thought you'd be better by now."

"Because they say you shouldn't speak ill of the dead," Maxie replied flatly.

"Oh, my! I'm so sorry—I didn't know! When did it happen?"

"It didn't. She's just dead for me, that's all."

"Phew, I was about to choke on my big foot! Maxie, I'm going to get over this hurt with Rob, but what about you? Why do you still wear yours like a sweater?"

"Because it fits."

"You've got it so good. Can't you see how lucky you are? Sorry if I offend, but aren't you ever going to get out from under it?"

"Too many layers."

"So get rid of one at a time. Look, I've been deceived, too—and made a fool of. But do I look like I cry myself to sleep? Can you tell that I gag at the thought of food? No. I put myself together and try to appear in control. I don't want anyone to pity me, Max, even though I may never find someone to trust and love me again. I have to look as if I expect to. *I'm* the one with choices now." Dawn's eyes were focused, intense. "Hurt her back, Maxie. It must kill you not to."

"Dawn, a child, regardless of her age, should not hurt her own mother—simply because she *is* her mother."

"Still slinging the sanctimonious bullshit," Dawn grumbled. "I feel perfectly entitled to my anger. If I could, I'd hang Rob up by his balls over a snake pit somewhere in the Sahara Desert. Just the thought of it makes me feel better. You don't have to let your mother get away with whatever moves her. I'll never forget that afternoon when Sarah barricaded herself in the den of your last house and let Alden escape out the front door. Luckily, I was home when you called. Still can't believe it."

"I don't *have* to let her, but I do."

"You *choose* to, and that's the biggest mystery to me. Let me tell you something, friend. The only reward you get for biting your tongue is a sore tongue. For as long as I've known you, all you've done is think, analyze, obsess. Then you get depressed and run for your bed, where you think, analyze, obsess. You don't *do* anything. Don't you see? You've got to *act* in order to change your life. All you do is beat yourself up, damn it!" Silence hung in the air like dense smoke. Maxie put down her half-raised wine glass. She could feel her defenses called up on full alert.

"You've always been up-front with me, Dawn. I appreciate your advice," she lied.

"No, don't *appreciate* it, unless you think you need or even *like* the punishment."

"Do you actually believe that hurt feels good to me? How could I like it?" Maxie was stung by this last implication.

"Stop turning everything into an accusation. Nobody but you is out to get you, Maxie. You're your own worst enemy. That's all I'm gonna say. I didn't come over here to upset you. I'm sorry."

"I can take it. Don't worry." Maxie finished off the bottle of wine.

They continued to talk for more than an hour, catching up on the events of the past year. Dawn's humor was acerbic and unrelenting; her words cut, jabbed, and sliced like a boxer sparring in the ring.

"You remind me of something Cora Leib once told me," Maxie said, "that life is, at best, a joke."

"Do you still keep in touch with her? How is she?"

"She's still my Gibraltar. We talk and see each other often—more so in the last five years. Wish it could be more."

"It *can* be, Maxie," Dawn said, leaving the table and putting her cup in the sink. "Life may be a joke, but I don't see you laughing. Gotta go. Paul has an orthodontist appointment at four, and I have to pick him up at a friend's house first." Checking herself out in the dining-room mirror, she added, "Maxie, this little reunion was good for both of us. Let's do it again soon."

"Absolutely. Maybe breakfast at Joe's next week," Maxie agreed, accompanying Dawn to the front door.

"Call me." Dawn retrieved her umbrella, gave Maxie a warm hug. On her way out the door, she paused and listened to the grumbling thunder. Turning back to Maxie she asked, "Were you thinking about your aunt this morning?"

Surprised, Maxie answered, "Yeah, but how did you know

that?"

"Oh," Dawn said, suppressing a smile, "I just remembered you told me once her theory about silver spoons. See ya."

Maxie watched as Dawn walked out to her car and backed it down the driveway; there was a lone, dry spot where it had been parked. Maxie closed the door, leaned back against it, and closed her eyes. She wondered which had worn her out, the wine or the conversation. *I think I'll take a nap—one that could last a few days would be nice,* she sighed, then yawned.

•4•

The day after Dawn's visit was stifling hot. Maxie awoke at 7:30 to cawing crows and squawking birds. The cicadas added their shrill voices to the competition for authority in the treetops—a cacophony enough to hasten Maxie out of bed. Her husband Arthur had already left for his dental office; her twin daughters, Ashley and Rachel, had finally ceased their quibbling over whose turn it was to empty the dishwasher and had left for their respective summer jobs. Home for the long interval between high-school graduation and college, each tried to demonstrate imagined maturity. They were betrayed by their continual bickering and childish feuds.

Maxie reached for the remote control to her television and flicked on the weather station. Gene Kent, congenial weatherman with an obvious toupee, was predicting record-breaking temperatures and high humidity for the day. An advisory was being projected on the screen for anyone with respiratory disease: "Especially the elderly should try to stay indoors today," Congenial Gene was saying, "and, please, don't leave your pet locked up in your car without proper ventilation—hyperthermia is a deadly condition for them as well." Clicking off the television, Maxie made her way into the bathroom. After a cool, slow shower, she slipped into white cotton shorts and a black-and-white striped T-shirt. Within minutes, she was headed for the lake. A marionette on invisible strings, she was drawn to what she considered her thinking place. On her way down Temple Street, she heard a horn blaring at her from behind; her friend Susan was waving furiously, trying to get her attention. Maxie did not want to stop; she did not want to answer any questions. With a diversionary tactic she often employed, she rolled down her window, stuck out her arm, and waved. Susan would understand the evasion; at least, Maxie hoped she would.

Once settled into her place on the bench, she tried to pick up the threads of her thoughts from the last visit here. Relaxed, she removed her sneakers and thrust her feet into the still-damp sand, letting her mind float without purpose over the shining water. Feeling bold and daring, allowing for any possibility, she said aloud, "Come on, I'm ready for you." In quick succession, as if they were photographic slides from one of Arthur's carousel projectors, scenes from her first college year flashed before her. Mesmerized, she watched a slide show of her freshman year at Selby—in particular, a cold March evening that was captured by her mind's camera, preserved forever in the archives of her psyche. Maxie shivered as she once again experienced the chill of Dr. Leib's words: "My wife is in the hospital, Maxine. She's had a rather serious auto accident on the way to the airport, and she will not be able to resume her teaching duties here for a very long while. I will be taking over her classes in the evenings, after I leave my own responsibilities at the university." Like the stab of an icepick, his words were as piercing today as they had been that evening when they both stood in the dimly lit driveway behind the faculty parking lot.

"Oh, I'm so sorry," Maxie said, shaken by the news. Her knees began to tremble as she fought to contain her fear. "Yes, of course, I'll continue my studies with you. Would it be all right if I wrote a note? May I please have her address at the hospital?" Reluctantly, Dr. Leib wrote down the address on a piece of scrap paper Maxie had fished out of her pocket.

"I'm not sure that what I'm doing is the right thing," Dr. Leib confessed. "Well, maybe a little note might cheer her. Thank you, Maxine." They bade each other good evening, and Maxie watched him walk slowly down to his parked car, burdened by the weight of what he had withheld. As a WWII naval officer, Benjamin Leib had witnessed many courageous fights for life. He himself had been asked to be brave as they crossed the black water toward the coast of Africa; but the enemy had been tangible, and he had had formidable weaponry with which to destroy the menace that skulked in the darkness. His wife's condition required a more resolute courage—it demanded that he rely on hope and blind faith. That night he was not filled with either.

As soon as Dr. Leib was out of sight, Maxie bolted to her dormitory, gulping air, feeling nauseated. Something extraordinary was taking place. She did not know why she was so distraught, so overwhelmed by the news. When she reached her room on the second floor, she threw herself onto her bed and wept for what seemed like hours until she could weep no longer. *Dear God, please don't take her away from me. Please, I need her. I love her, but she doesn't know it yet. I have to find a way to tell her that I'm feeling something I've never known. I have to help her get well without appearing foolish, nosy, or insincere,* Maxie prayed. That week, exhausted and spent, Maxie felt nothing. She slept through her classes and remained in bed until she was able to clear her head, to plan her letter. Neglecting her studies, she quickly fell behind. Obsessed and hungry only for news of Mrs. Leib's condition, she ate little, slept less. Her concerned roommates urged her to seek counseling. Ignoring their advice, Maxie centered her thoughts on her evening class with Dr. Leib, her opportunity to find out whatever he was willing to tell her. For hours she composed letters, diligently avoiding gratuitous remarks or platitudes. Not wanting to sound sophomoric or jejune, she wound up crumpling the letters she started, tossing them into the wastebasket with despair. At night, with trembling fingers, she undressed, mindless of where her clothes fell. Depressed and immobilized, she was taken over by a force she could not identify, but one which drove her into a feverish weakness.

During those long, cold winter nights, Maxie began to see Mrs. Leib as a source of sunshine that had been absent from her life. She had become a lifeline to which Maxie had hoped to cling while making her way back to shore—away from the lies and deceits that blew her off course into the terrifying storms of panic and uncertainty. Somehow, she succeeded in conveying such feelings in letters of painstaking care and delicacy. Her efforts were rewarded one evening when Dr. Leib asked if she would remain for a few minutes after class.

"Maxine, are you feeling all right? You've been looking wan, rather drawn. Aren't you getting enough sleep?" Dr. Leib's questions caught her completely off guard.

"Oh, yes—yes, of course. I'm fine. I thought that maybe you'd be telling me about your wife. I just need to know if she's been feeling any better."

Dr. Leib's elegance and grace were not diminished by his sorrow, and when he was about to impart special significance to what he needed to say, he would draw his arms in closely to his compact body, bend them at the elbows, tilt his head backwards, then at a slight angle. Taking in a very deep breath, he would draw himself up to his full height, close his eyes tightly, and rock forward and back on his heels. In this one fluid movement, he projected a figure of imposing stature, of towering intelligence. The furrows of his brow would deepen, as he slowly, deliberately chose his words.

"Maxine," he began with much gravity, "my wife has developed peritonitis and is in real danger. I don't know when she'll return to Selby. Although I should prefer that you remain optimistic, you must consider the possibility of her not returning at all." Looking over the rim of his half-glasses to assess the impact of his statement, he continued. "Her spirits are low, but I do believe that your letters have been very comforting to her. She wants you to know how much she appreciates your concern, and sends her best wishes to you." After clearing his throat, he added, "I, too, am grateful for your efforts." To avoid betrayal by his own emotions, he did not wait for a response; he understood that his leaving quickly would obviate the need for any further, superfluous discourse. Neither of them wished to compound the sadness that resided in their respective hearts. Each wished to preserve the other's dignity of private grief. Words could only demean the exquisite pain they shared for the woman they both loved.

***

An approaching motorboat cut through Maxie's memories like a buzz saw, jolting her back to the already hot bench. Putting her hands up to her cheeks, she could feel the beginnings of a sunburn and considered the wisdom of leaving. Her watch showed nine o'clock and, as predicted, the humidity was already on the rise. Still, she wanted to continue her mental cruise back in time, riding on the undulating waves of reminiscence. Closing her eyes, she pictured herself once again in her dormitory, discussing the obligatory group meetings with her roommates Kate and Jenny. Jenny was waving a letter with a Selby letterhead under Maxie's nose.

"They're called T-Groups, Maxie, and they're obligatory," Jenny was explaining. "Everyone has to go, and your letter says for you to be there tonight at eight." Maxie had heard about these sessions run by the all-knowing, the seniors. New arrivals were asked to attend these "non-threatening" casual meetings and encouraged to discuss whatever problems they were having in their adjustment to "the rigors of college life."

"All right, I'll go," Maxie conceded, "but I think it's going to be a waste of time."

Maxie was not prepared for the invasion, for the attack on her privacy; she would always remember the words that penetrated those defenses that had kept her safe—weak, but safe. A friendly greeting had disarmed her, leaving her vulnerable.

"Come on in, Maxie. Make yourself comfy," a toothy upperclassman said, as she guided Maxie into a cramped, stuffy classroom and pointed out some folding chairs set out in a semicircle. Maxie could smell the lingering odors, the sensual mix of perfume and hair spray—reminders of the coquettes who were present in this room hours before. Serious students? She hadn't come across any yet. There was, in addition, that heavy odor of history, that overbearing aroma of academia that hangs in the air like stale cigar smoke. Ten or twelve other freshman girls sat, chatted amiably, relaxed and confident; others sat uncomfortably, appearing fidgety and self-conscious like herself.

"Now that everyone's here, let's get started. First of all, welcome to all of you. I'm Melissa, this here is Wendy, and next to her is Jane. We're here to help make your transition to college a smooth one. We also want you to know that we're your friends, here to help you succeed at Selby. Our philosophy," Melissa continued, "is that when people discuss their concerns in an open forum, a group of equals, they often see that their problems are not unique, and that they're not alone in their feelings of unhappiness or loneliness. Many of you will wonder whether you're up to the academic challenge—others will question your abilities to achieve social acceptance as well. We want you to know that these are perfectly normal feelings, but when these feelings get in the way of your studies, or when they keep you from functioning as you'd like, we urge you to come here and talk it out with us." Melissa's intense gaze settled on Maxie. Maxie looked over Melissa's bobbing head, concentrated, instead, on a complex mathematical equation left on the chalkboard. *How contrived and condescending,* Maxie thought, *but then, upperclassmen are known to take themselves too seriously.*

A second girl, also an upperclassman, her emerald-green cashmere sweater perfectly tight, took up the gauntlet. Her silky, blond hair was pulled back into a ponytail, exposing a creamy, porcelain-like complexion. The sparkling, blue eyes and effortless smile were meant to elicit trust.

"Maxie, if you don't mind, why don't we start with you? We've been advised that you sometimes don't feel very well—that you have, um, episodes of stomach pains and headaches."

"Who told you that?" A scarlet blush revealed Maxie's sense of betrayal.

"Your roommates have expressed some concerns about you to the faculty. Is there something troubling you?" Her smile looked almost wicked now.

"I thought this was a get-to-know-you meeting," Maxie said, trying to sidestep.

"That's exactly what it is. We get to know each other better through our sharing of feelings. Don't you agree?"

Sucked in, Maxie replied, "Well, I don't know. Maybe I'm a little homesick—you know, I've never been away from home before."

"Never?" Blondie asked, arching her perfectly penciled brows, thrusting her well-endowed chest into the dialogue. "How strange. So, how do you feel about having to 'cut the cord,' so to speak?"

"I may be feeling guilty or something. Right now, I'm feeling a little uncomfortable with these questions."

"Do you think you've done something bad?" one of the other students asked.

"Maybe good for me, but bad for Sarah, I mean my mother."

"Why is your going off to college bad for your mother?" Another voice was joining the interrogation.

"Because now she doesn't have me to take care of her—to look after her." *Why am I saying so much? What right did these people have to ask me such very personal things? And yet, I'm complying; I'm doing exactly what they want me to do. It doesn't make any sense.*

"Is your mother ill, Maxie, or an invalid?" The welcoming one seemed genuine.

"No, she just depends on me a lot. I guess I feel as though I've abandoned her." What *was* she saying!

"What about your father? Isn't he at home?"

"No. I mean yes—sort of. He's just physically there."

"You haven't mentioned anything about abandoning *him.* Doesn't he need you?" Who was making *this* judgment?

"Yes, I took care of him too."

"In what way? Who took care of *you*, Maxie?"

At that moment, Maxie's thoughts were spinning around inside her head as if in a centrifuge, colliding with the skeletal walls as well as with each other. She was confused by the sudden realization that what she was saying and what she was feeling were not the same. What she was saying was what she *thought* she felt. What she felt was what she was too terrified to think. A headache was mounting; the throbbing anxiety was urging her to flee. She felt quite nauseated.

"Please excuse me. I'm not feeling well and I need to leave."

"Of course, Maxie. We understand. This reaction is not uncommon to freshmen. Change is always difficult, especially when you don't comprehend the dynamics. We hope you'll come back, though. You obviously need to talk." The only obvious thing Maxie saw was that these self-important wannabe psychobabblers had performed more like a wrecking crew. That interrogation room should have been designated a hard-hat area. Grabbing her jacket from the back of her chair, she bolted for the exit door. Once outside, she felt the chill of the crisp, winter night—starless and inscrutable. Clouds of darkness hung low in the sky. Maxie could feel their weight upon her as she stumbled across the parking lot to the steps of her dormitory. Her once unequivocal devotion to Sarah was now galvanizing into a rock of anger and resentment. *Those trouble-making seniors put these thoughts into my head,* she thought. *Didn't they?*

Fumbling inside her jacket pocket, she began to cry. What began as a whimper, a little gust of hurt that escaped from somewhere deep within her, a little ache that began to swell in her chest like an inflatable balloon, expanded with every new breath until there no longer was any room in which to contain it. Before she could get to the door, that whimper exploded into a wrenching wail. Maxie crumpled and fell. Wedged into the corner of the old house, melting under the harsh glare of the gaslight fixture mounted above her, she tumbled down a steep abyss of depression. At bottom, chilled and frightened, she huddled in a dank corner of her mind and desperately tried to conceal her nakedness. A stench rose from the moldy hole as black water seeped from her inner walls. Rancid water inched up over her bare feet. She searched in vain for something to grab—something to hold onto.

But I've been good, Momma—just as I promised. Please, let me out! Rebuffed by the silence, Maxie screamed. *Can't you see that I'm trying, Momma? But where are the tears? Who will see them? This is so strange—you hurt me so badly, but I don't cry. Still, I must tell you that I love you—you make me say it. 'Louder, Max. Say it louder,' you order me. So I shout it. But you don't hear me. Is it because I really hate you? Can you hear what I* don't *say? Please stop, Momma. I'm going to die if you don't stop!*

Maxie awoke to her own shouting. Slowly she opened her eyes. She was relieved to be out of her hellhole. In the darkness she heard hurried footsteps, a familiar voice. Kate, on her way out for her nightly pint of chocolate ice cream, had discovered Maxie.

"My God, Maxie, what's wrong?" Kate shrieked. "Are you sick again?" Getting no answer, she leaned over Maxie's inert form, struggling to lift Maxie onto her feet. "Maxie, please help me get you upstairs. Lean on me as much as you need to, but try to walk. Can you do that?"

Maxie was still upset over the betrayal, but in no position to argue. Holding onto one of Kate's arms, feeling the strong comfort of the other arm around her waist, she allowed herself to be lifted off the concrete steps. Together the two girls made their way into the foyer, up the stairs, stopping twice to rest. Once inside their room, Kate led Maxie to her bed. Jenny, reading in bed, looked up, startled. "What happened? Did she get mugged or something?" Sliding off her bed, a cup of tea still in her hand, Jenny approached Maxie's bed. "I've told her so many times already not to go out alone at night. And where were *you* going by yourself, Kate?"

"Jennie, cool it. Just cut the mother stuff for now. She doesn't look hurt, just shook up for some reason—probably another one of those strange episodes. We have to talk her into getting some help. For now, let's let her rest." With that, Maxie's roommates removed her clothing and her shoes, covered her with a light blanket, dimmed the lights, and withdrew to the living-room study. Maxie fell into a profound sleep.

She would not attend any future T-Group meeting nor go on any excursions into territories booby-trapped with questions she could not answer.

•5•

Returning home from the lake, Maxie stopped to collect her mail. From among the stack of flyers and unsolicited catalogs, she extracted several bills, a postcard for Ashley, a letter for Rachel, and a notice from the septic tank company advising that it was again time for a cleaning. The thought of a backed-up septic system made Arthur nervous; his philosophy at home, as well as in the office, was to prevent things from becoming problems. Maxie added a call to the septic company on to her to-do list. Back inside the air-conditioned house, she started to feel better; her head ached less, and the tingling she felt in her fingers on the way home was gone. There was one message on her answering machine; it was from Arthur.

"Hon, if you get back from wherever you've been before noon, come meet me for lunch. It's just an hour, but I need some cheer after a very hectic morning. I'll do my best to get out of here on time. Hope to see you at Il Fiore's. Love ya."

Arthur's message lifted Maxie's spirits. Checking her watch, she saw that she had time to calm her morning agitation. Dawn was right, she thought. After twenty-six years of marriage, she did have it all—well, almost all. She looked forward to her date with Arthur, and in the cool, palliative shower, she realized that she could be both agonized and content at the same time.

After toweling dry, Maxie slipped into a sleeveless cotton sundress and sandals. She decided against makeup for her sunburned face, brightening her lips with a cool shade of coral. Before leaving the house, she set up an appointment with the septic company and took some boneless chicken breasts from the freezer to defrost for supper. She had more than enough time to get to Il Fiore's. Driving through Shafton Center, she pushed the button on the dashboard that allowed her to select a CD. She chose her favorite—Mendelssohn's Concerto in E Minor for Violin and Orchestra. No other musical work moved her as did this one; and it made her very sad to think about the composer's dying at the age of thirty-six. She remembered reading somewhere that he had enjoyed such a full, satisfying life—that he did not experience the melancholy, illness, poverty, or depression of many other composers of his time. Nonetheless, the deep resonance, the plaintive melodies of the second movement brought tears to her eyes. In what she imagined to be a dialogue between the violins and the orchestra, she sang the sorrowful, questioning strains, then waited for the measured advice, the understanding response, imparted with steady patience. Her body swayed, her head nodded until her entire being rose to the climax. "Yes, yes. That's exactly how Cora speaks to me—it's how she touches me to the core," Maxie said aloud, unaware of where she was. The ecstatic resolution left her drained. Pulling into a space in front of the restaurant, surprised that she was already there, she waited in the car until she regained control of her breathing. She entered the restaurant, still flushed.

"Good afternoon, Mrs. Lane," the young, redheaded hostess said, holding two menus to her chest, lovingly. "Would you like your regular banquette table in the corner?"

"That would be perfect, Sandy. My husband will be here shortly."

"Will you both be ordering your 'usual'?"

"Yes, thank you. If you don't mind, I'd like to have my coffee now while I wait."

"Sure thing. I'll get Linda to bring it right over. Maybe you'd like some iced coffee today. You look a little warm."

"No, hot is fine," Maxie replied, unaware that her flush was so noticeable. Sitting down at the banquette, Maxie made herself comfortable and surveyed the beautifully decorated dining room. The modern interior design, a classic statement of symmetry and contrast, shone with stark black tile that lined the walls and framed huge glass windows. Strategically placed beveled mirrors reflected one another, creating a sense of spatial infinity. On each black enameled table was a crisp, white linen cloth, folded napkins, and a single rose in a silver bud vase. Maxie felt secure in the sharp precision and orderliness of this room, reminiscent of the Art Deco interiors of the Sixties. Coffee arrived with the little silver pitcher of milk.

"Hi, Mrs. Lane," Linda chirped, "got a sunburn, do you?"

"Guess so. I was out so early this morning. I didn't think the sun would be a problem." She realized she wasn't making any sense; the forecast had been unmistakable.

"Well, you look great anyway. When Dr. Lane gets here, I'll bring out the salad and a basket of bread."

"Thanks. Let's hope he's not delayed. I'm starved." She wasn't starved at all, but thought that waitresses want to hear you say so—that it brought out the maternal instinct. Who knew? As she also pondered whether or not to bother Arthur with the morning's unraveling at the lake, he entered the room, his signature smile telling her how genuinely happy he was to see her. She saw him as he had been at nineteen when they had met—very handsome, sweet, and gentle. Of medium height and muscular build, with light-brown hair and gray-blue eyes that twinkled with mischief, Arthur was the only man she had ever loved, the only man in whom she had felt complete trust. A shy and humble man, Arthur guarded Maxie's trust with a great reserve of strength and fierce loyalty.

"Hi, hon. Sorry I'm so late. Got tied up with my last patient." Giving Maxie a kiss, he leaned back to appraise the sunburn. "Been out in the sun?"

"Hi, you're not so late, and yes, I should have paid more attention to the forecast. How was your morning?" Diversion is the art of deflection, not deception, she reasoned.

"Remember Mrs. Bryson, one of my *girls*?" Arthur asked.

"Sure, she must be close to ninety, right?"

"She's eighty-nine and adorable. In this heat, she brought me a dozen wild blueberry muffins. She baked them this morning. She and Mrs. Flaherty and Mrs. Jackson, they're just incredible ladies. Oh, and guess what? Alden called to say he'll be home for Thanksgiving. He sounds anxious to see us again."

"Fantastic," Maxie replied with the brightened smile and enthusiasm Arthur had fully anticipated.

Alden was a very special son whom they both adored. Throughout his uneventful high-school years, he had perfected an attitude of indifference, a disregard for peer approval and social intercourse. Although never sullen nor disrespectful, he could not be coaxed from what passed as nonchalance. Five years of private school had not only smoothed the few rough edges of adolescence, but also solidified his resolve not to be made in anyone else's image but his own. "It's as if we're all little cookies stamped out of the headmaster's mold," he had complained.

"I can't be what everyone expects, Mom," he had told her one night before dinner.

"Then be you, honey—be the you that *only you* can be." Something palpable happened at that moment between Maxie and her shy, vulnerable son. Alden studied her with tight-lipped seriousness; he appeared to be looking *into* her. Fighting back tears, he softly said, "Thanks, Mom," and gave her the most discreet little squeeze of her hand that said more than he could. Tall, darkly handsome, and occasionally brooding, he was self-conscious about touching, yet there was no mistaking that she had said what he needed to hear. Maxie was always grateful for that moment.

Arthur watched Maxie with concerned interest. He broke off a chunk of crusty bread, took a bite, and sat perfectly still, elbows on the table, his eyes fixed on his wife who had drifted out of the present. Abandoned, he concentrated on his meal. Ruminating on a mouthful of romaine lettuce, he scanned the dining room that had filled with the noisy lunchtime crowd of mostly young professionals. The women wore their importance with impeccable style; the men wore their hair in ponytails—some sported small hoop or diamond stud earrings. Their conversations were loud, intended to be overheard. Out of the corner of his eye, Arthur caught a glimpse of his friend and colleague Sam Bellenberg, waving furiously to get Arthur's attention. Sam was having lunch with his blonde secretary; she had very long, slender legs and a small, natural nose. *Why do short, fat men attract tall, firm gazelles?* Arthur wondered. Sam was motioning for Arthur to come over to his table; Arthur just waved his hand, which said, in effect, "How ya' doin', buddy?" Arthur already knew how Sam was doing; it was Sam's wife Lois who could not be faring as well.

"Dr. Lane," Sandy interrupted, looking at Maxie's plate, "are your salads all-right? Mrs. Lane?"

"Yes, yes, everything's fine, Sandy," Arthur said rather abruptly, aware that Sandy was now scrutinizing Maxie's face.

"Would you like some more bread or coffee?" Sandy asked, awkwardly.

"No, but would you be kind enough to tell Dr. Bellenberg that I'll call him later?"

"Sure thing, Dr. Lane," Sandy enthused, feeling useful again. Arthur was relieved to see her at Sam's table. Sam flashed a thumbs-up at Arthur; his secretary turned to flash more leg. Seeing Maxie still deep in thought, Arthur speared another pepper and watched a spindly spider crawl up the crease of tiles behind the adjacent table onto the mirrored surface; it stopped in frozen stillness, startled by the glazed repetition of itself.

"Hey, Maxie, where'd you go? Aren't you going to eat?" Arthur asked. His words reached down into the chasm of her thoughts, echoing, pulling her out of the well.

"Sorry. I was just thinking about Alden, missing him so much." Maxie apologized as she reached ground level.

"So, what's that little smile for?"

"Precious moments of honest feelings, that's all."

"What do you mean?" Arthur asked, confused.

"Oh, I just find myself reliving the past, that's all."

"Why would you ever want to do that? It's not like it was so pleasurable." Arthur was now chewing on a hot Italian pepper.

"Arthur, I don't know. Remember how I could never explain things when you came to my home in Rhode Island? Lately, I've been trying to reconstruct events, the whole experience. I feel as though there are pieces missing to a puzzle that gets more puzzling. Too many pieces, maybe."

"Wait a minute; back up. Which experience? What events?" Arthur furtively glanced at his watch, realizing that time was short.

"Starting with my first year at Selby, the year I couldn't hold myself together."

"Listen," Arthur said, taking Maxie's hand into his own, "I suggest that you need to see Mrs. Leib again. Let's take a few days off and drive up to Montreal. Seeing her makes you feel better. Besides, I could use a couple of days away from the office. Let's work out a date tonight, and then tomorrow you can call the Leibs to confirm."

Arthur's mother had died when he was eleven years old, and he felt the loss of his best friend and protectress well into his adult life.

Sarah once had held the promise of rekindling that special, tender maternal love; and, for a time, she had fooled him into thinking that she had something genuine to offer. Having lost twice, Arthur did not go to Montreal simply to please his wife; embraced by the Leibs, he, too, felt nourished and whole—loved, once again, without qualifiers. And the greatest gift they had given him was their love for Maxie, a profound caring that had prevented her suicide thirty years ago.

"Hon," Maxie said, looking down into her untouched dry tuna salad, "do you think there's something wrong with me? Be honest."

"No, Maxie, I don't believe there's anything wrong with you. I'm concerned that *you* think there is." Arthur's eyes had darkened.

"I didn't mean to ruin your day. I'm scared to death that I'm going to fall into that dark hole again." There, she said it.

"I have to confess that I'm starting to get a little uneasy with this disappearing into yourself that you do."

"I know. I don't like it either." It hurt to speak. She was so afraid to open her mouth, sure that she would vomit the pain in her heart.

"I've been watching you recede, slipping away from me at any given moment. Like just now. These last few weeks, especially. You sure you're not telling me something?"

Hearing Sam's lascivious laughter ricochet off the restaurant walls, Maxie moved in closer to Arthur. "Has he no shame?" she whispered. "Doesn't he think twice about humiliating Lois? It's such a small town."

"Probably not. Sam's the kind of guy who doesn't think at all; he just goes with whatever feels good to him at the moment."

"But doesn't he realize that he's hurting the woman who loved him all these years?" Maxie's annoyance had turned to resentment.

"You're avoiding my question," Arthur sighed.

"No, I'm avoiding the answer."

"Answer?" Arthur asked, perplexed.

"Why I feel this way—so sad, angry. What am I gonna do, hon?"

"Well, lets start with a little R and R. Call the Leibs and set it up." Reaching into his pants pocket for his wallet, he said, "Hate to leave you like this. I've got a patient scheduled for one o'clock. Do you want me to stay?"

"No, no, go ahead. I'll be fine. I'll have another cup of coffee." Seeing the worry in Arthur's eyes, she said, "It's all right, you can go. We'll talk more tonight." She smiled, aware of her transparency.

"You might want to have some of your salad too," Arthur chided. After paying the bill, he rose to leave; at the door, he turned back and waved. For the remainder of the day, he would worry about the vagueness that Maxie wore like insinuating perfume, a dab behind each ear.

Maxie accepted a refill of coffee, sat back in her seat, and let her thoughts drift back to joyful trips she and her family had taken to Montreal, to the horse-and-buggy rides around the Old City district on brisk autumn days. She envisioned the little puffs of smoke that would emerge from their mouths as they spoke. Pretending that his pen was a cigar, Arthur would delight the children with smoke rings. On one of their many horse-drawn carriage rides around the cobblestoned square, Edward the horse "took a dump," as Ashley had delicately put it. With her characteristic mix of revulsion and candor, she had blurted, "Oh, gross! Can't the driver at least pull over to the curb to let us out—until he's finished?" Despite the grossness and Edward's lack of modesty, they had laughed heartily and had enjoyed the day. Rachel and Alden had asked the driver for sugar cubes so they could reward Edward and pat his snout. After their ride, they walked to a lovely, flowered courtyard just inside the huge wrought-iron gates of Gibby's Restaurant. Here they stopped to have their pictures taken among the dozens of bright-orange pumpkins and strong-scented marigolds.

Arthur had found it challenging to take pictures of all three children together; invariably, one of them would refuse to smile. *It's like that, still,* she mused, *one up, one down.* After a quick stop for hot cider bought from a street vendor, they ambled along the hilly streets, peeking into the tiny storefronts of boutiques, bookstores, curiosity shops. When the requisite mementos were purchased—miniature Quebecois spoons, T-shirts, Inuit dolls, wood carvings, and scrimshaw bone engravings—they would pile into their car, exhausted and rosy-cheeked. At their hotel, they would rest, have some snacks, and watch TV. Arthur would doze on the bed, lying spread-eagle with his mouth wide open. Later in the evening, they would visit with the Leibs and drink in their goodness as if it were honey wine. The quiet time shared with Mrs. Leib was Maxie's sustenance; she experienced no physical hunger during these visits. In fact, she would suffer admonishments for not eating.

"Maxine, at least have some of this wonderful soup I made this morning. You don't eat enough, my dear." *I don't need food, I need you,* Maxie had almost blurted.

At the end of each visit, parting was difficult. "You tease us with such short visits, Maxine. Can't you stay a little longer?"

"I know—we feel the same way. I wish we didn't have to leave at all."

"Why don't *you* stay on with us, then? We have plenty of room, and you wouldn't incur the expense of a hotel room. What do you say?"

"Thank you, but the children need for me to be home. You know, carpools, music lessons. I seem to spend most of my time in the car." *Yeah, driving or waiting to drive—never* in *drive. Who am I kidding?*

"Well, I understand. Someday you'll have plenty of free time to do as you wish. I was being selfish, you see." Mrs. Leib sounded wistful.

Selfish! My God, I'd give anything to stay here with her.

And when it was time to leave on Sunday afternoon, "Come back soon" was what they heard the Leibs call out to them, waving and blowing kisses until the Lanes's car was just a speck in the distance.

Thank goodness, she came back. I wouldn't be here today had she not recovered and returned to Selby—to me. Maxie heard Sandy's concerned voice intruding. "Mrs. Lane, you haven't touched your coffee. If it's not hot enough for you, I can bring a fresh pot."

"No thanks, Sandy, I have to get going. Lunch was great." Leaving her seat, Maxie noticed that she had left her salad untouched. For her, edible food left her feeling more hungry. Cora Leib had nourished and sustained Maxie's wanting spirit. What Maxie yearned for was a touch, a kind word, a smile that said to her, "Maxie, you matter—you matter to *me*." The prodigious helpings of herself that Mrs. Leib gave to Maxie were enough to make her feel "full"; they filled the bowl of her life with love, even in her memories.

***

Driving home, Maxie could not resist thinking about Cora's return to Selby. The wait had been interminable; the separation, suffused with worry. Added to her anxiety then was the approaching spring break and her expected return to her parents' home in Rhode Island. Sarah labored for whole days cleaning their three-bedroom colonial on Crockett Street, polishing the furniture, sanitizing the bathrooms. Maxie never understood the cleaning ritual because the house was never dirty. All seven rooms oozed with antiseptic orderliness, and Sarah never invited company. Imagined dust clung to the crystal stemware displayed in the dark French Provincial breakfront; a full service for twelve of Royal Doulton china lay inside the cabinet, unchipped, undisturbed. Still, Maxie remembered the cooked-cabbage stink of loathing that fouled the air and made her stomach queasy. When, after two full years, Arthur got Philip's permission to sleep in that house, he would often find Maxie waiting for him on the front steps of the neatly trimmed front walkway, shaking her head, rocking herself gently.

"Is something the matter?" he would ask.

"It's not something I can explain to you, Arthur. All I can caution you about is that here, nothing is as it seems. Take nothing at face value, and try to be alert to all the smoke and mirrors. Eventually, you'll see what I mean. If it walks like a duck, quacks like a duck, and shits like a duck, it's probably a wooden decoy."

At home for spring recess, Maxie had been grateful to have term papers to write and exams for which to prepare. She had promised Arthur that she would keep busy and out of Philip's direct path.

"Try not to get under his skin, hon. You know how he gets when he's mad."

"I know how he gets even when he's *not* mad."

"Just keep your distance from both of them. Go to the library. Shop for underwear—anything!" Arthur counseled.

"I can't expect you to understand how impossible that can be. Sarah barges into my room at night—doesn't knock or ask if I'm busy—sits down on my bed and starts bitching about Philip. Once she gets rolling, there's no end."

"Tell her you've got cramps. Tell her whatever it takes to get rid of her."

"If the house were burning down, Sarah would sit and bitch until she had emptied all of her complaints on me."

"Maxie," Arthur said with impatience.

"All right, I'll try. Right now, I've got a whopping case of the zizzies. I'm all worked up even before I get there."

"Well, you know their track record. Your feeling shaky doesn't surprise me. But please, promise you'll do whatever you can to stay safe."

"I promise," Maxie said, knowing full well that promises are what you make when the stakes get too high. When you run out of options, you make promises.

She did try. But she worried continually that Sarah would read her thoughts—that Philip would see her disdain plainly visible. She wished that Sarah would be too self-absorbed and would not notice her. She prayed that Philip would stay calm. Within days of her arrival, however, Philip struck the first match. "You've changed, Max. Not for the better, either." Maxie did not respond. "So," he said, putting the second match to the fire, "you think you're pretty smart, don't you, Miss College-Girlie?"

"Dad, please," Maxie begged, "I'm not going to be home for long. Can't we try to get along?"

Boom! Bang! That was all it took. "Who the hell do you think you're talking to, girlie?" he ranted, slapping her face, leaving a red imprint of a full hand on her cheek. "Hot-shot, now that you're out of the house—sleeping around, too, no doubt. Well, you just remember who's paying for you to be such a big know-it-all! On Sunday, you'll go back to school in *my* car—with *me*—because I'm sure to embarrass you in front of all your pinhead *friggin' college* friends."

Philip's tirade had nothing to do with Maxie's putative life of freedom and sexual escapades, and everything to do with his own frustration of having to spend more time with Sarah. With Maxie as Sarah's constant companion, Philip's life had been simple, unfettered; he had been free to work twelve-hour days, to come home for dinner, to watch Jackie Gleason or John Wayne on the television before going to bed. On frequent occasions, he would find it necessary to remind Sarah who was "wearing the pants." Philip would sit down at the dinner table, gulp down a shot of Scotch, inspect the food, and commence the tantrum. "This is the same piss-pink salmon you tried to poison me with last time! You can't seem to do something as simple as buying the right thing twice. Or maybe you think I'm stupid. Get it through your thick skull: red salmon makes me vomit!" The salmon he liked was the one he insisted Sarah never bought. With the back of his hand—in one, swift movement—he sent the salmon onto the floor, along with whatever else lay in its path. Maxie would feel the sting of his words, absorbing them for Sarah, taking the blows herself in order to protect her mother. Slamming his fist on the table, he would continue: "I'll be damned if you're gonna give me this shit to eat! Eat it yourself, goddamit!" Within a minute, he would storm out the door, spewing further epithets and obscenities. Sarah would retreat to her bedroom, where she would stay for days. Maxie would wipe up the floor, wash the dishes, and seek refuge in her own room.

Arthur had guessed correctly that Philip had been storing his anger, waiting for spring recess. These episodes, and so many others like them, had been painful, yet strangely normal to Maxie when she had lived at home. As a matter of course, Sarah ultimately would emerge from her bedroom and speak cool, clipped words to Philip.

"Want coffee?" she'd ask.

"Got cream?" he'd answer.

There was never an apology. Things just returned to normal.

But Sarah's hurt and resentment hardened over the years to a steely bitterness that roiled in her gut and made her mouth taste sour. Seeing herself the long-suffering victim of an ignorant, violent man, she sought vindication through indifference and extortion; she knew that indifference could be lethal. Fur coats, diamond rings and brooches, new luxury automobiles were what she extracted from

Philip for her silence. “I’ll keep my mouth shut, because I know you wouldn’t want your brother Jake to know. Would you?” Jake made sure Philip had a job in his used-car business, a minor one in terms of responsibility, but not in public scrutiny. Jake would be incensed if it were known that Philip had moved out of the “master’s” bedroom when Maxie left for college. Sarah, however, enjoyed having the four-poster Martha Washington bed to herself; she luxuriated in the satin sheets she began to buy soon after Philip’s departure. She delighted in polishing the dark mahogany frame, the pineapple finials, running her hand lovingly over the smooth, strong finish—rubbing until it shone chaste and free of remembrances.

•6•

Back from spring recess to the reactivated Selby campus, Maxie immersed herself in the business of getting resettled. She welcomed the return of her roommates with joy, embracing them both, noticing that they did not demonstrate the same enthusiasm. Many of the girls had brought back lightweight clothing, anticipating—rather prematurely—the advent of warmer weather. Laughter and girlish squeals poured out of the dormitories as friends were reunited. Maxie overheard their lively chatter about vacation cruises, their ski-slope antics. They were happy to be over the March blues; she was happy to be over the insanity.

Unknown to Maxie, Cora Leib's recovery was more than a physical healing; it was an arduous exercise of mental fortitude that staved off the slightest suspicion of self-pity. Privacy was sacrosanct; the truth, her own business. Cora dealt with expediency the way a blind person crosses a busy intersection, taking cues from the ambient pulsations of the self-absorbed, moving forward on measured guesses, being fluid. The trick, of course, was to blend. She endured with seamless equanimity the fatuous cards—expressions of concern—as stiff as the recycled cardboard on which they were printed. It was LaRochefoucauld's maxim she kept repeating to herself: "Nothing so much prevents our being authentic as our efforts to seem so." She turned, instead, to philosophers and artists who knew more about truth and appearance. She sought the wisdom of Wordsworth, the inspiration of Puccini, the tranquillity of Monet. Trips to museums offered her more solace than the profane utterings of the bourgeois lightweights.

Cora's illness had taught her that what mattered was resolve. If only she did not have to wake each morning missing pieces of her heart.

She asked her husband only once, "Tell me, darling, what wretched act could we have done to anger the gods so?"

"My love," Dr. Leib had answered woefully, aggrieved, "we philosophers believe we have learned enough about life and death to ask the questions. The arguments, the answers, we leave to the theologians."

Cora Leib could have chosen madness, but decided that madness is not all it is cracked up to be; it is, she reasoned, another dimension of the mind, another facet of the psyche. Madness, she concluded, is just the flip side of sanity; if one keeps flipping the mental coin, the distinctions blur, the disparities fade. It's not glorious, simply melodramatic. Cora lay wounded beneath the rubble of collapsed hopes and mangled dreams, struggling with the inevitability of reengaging. She would tell no one the real cause of her prolonged hospitalization and patiently waited for the sorrow to lift. For Cora, surgery had been invasion, a theft that had altered the concept of self; the atoms and the molecules of her very being had scurried to realign, to make themselves into something new. Hoping that the demands of a daily routine would help her to refocus, she returned to her work.

Maxie did not realize how much darkness had enveloped her until light reappeared. Anticipation of the spring recess had worsened her spirits; the time spent at home had clouded her consciousness. When Mrs. Leib finally returned, appearing well and happy, Maxie felt well and happy also. But Cora Leib then began to detect a disturbing pattern of behavior in Maxie and, though cautious by nature, felt compelled to intervene. She knew Maxie to be a moody, preoccupied young woman prone to much inner reflection. What Cora now observed were manifestations of a more serious nature. Assessing the personal risks of getting involved, she doubted her own ability to absorb more grief, more despair. In all fairness, however, Cora had to admit that Maxie had no idea of what she herself had endured for six weeks. And, wasn't it Maxie who had reached out to her during her travails, unaware of the enormity of such investment, wanting nothing more in return than the assurance that she would see her language professor restored to good health? Cora could feel the destinies of two disparate lives coming together, forging an incontrovertible amalgam.

"Maxine," she said after class that first day back, "thank you for all your kind words of encouragement. Your letters were sensitively written, and your sincere expressions of concern for me are greatly appreciated. I'm sure they played no small part in my recovery." Cora paused, waited for some reply. Maxie lowered her head. Cora shifted in her seat, shuffled some papers on her desk, and continued. "Now, I've been thinking that practicing the language, orally, that is, would be of significant benefit to you. You need to incorporate new vocabulary and to get your ear used to the rhythm—syntax and grammar can always be corrected. It's more important to try to express your thoughts while thinking in the language. So, why don't you talk to me—about anything that may be on your mind at the moment, in Spanish, and we'll see what happens."

Maxie was astounded by this offer but too embarrassed to reveal what was, indeed, on her mind. *Where do I find the courage to say that her soft and gentle words are a salve on the open wounds I feel inside?* Maxie wondered. *How do I describe the demons that are raging in my head?* Maxie's thoughts were overwhelming her; she could not find words—Spanish or otherwise—with which to convey how Mrs. Leib's return was like a bright beacon of light lowered down the mindshaft of her misery. Ashamed, fearful of reproach, Maxie withdrew, feigning reticence and an inability to fulfill this assignment. Great waves of sadness washed over her, sapping energy, making her feel even more alone.

"I can't," was all she could force out of her mouth.

Seeing that her initial approach was not going to yield the desired fruit, Cora had another suggestion. "Listen, Maxine, I have another idea I'd like you to consider. How would you like to transfer from Selby to the university? I believe the curriculum here may not be challenging enough for you and that, perhaps, you are bored with the lack of more stimulating activities in which to involve yourself. If you say, 'yes,' I'll talk to my husband about trying to facilitate matters for you. Please promise to think about it."

More promises, Maxie thought, saying nothing, remaining transfixed. She responded in this dumbfounded way when she could not make her mouth work—when her tongue seemed paralyzed and her throat was tight, choked. Her experiences with words, with Sarah's words, had taught her to swallow or be swallowed. Sarah's words were like paper cuts swiftly, deftly executed to draw no blood, but to penetrate with maximum pain. Kindness can chafe the most calloused heart.

"Well, say something, dear," Mrs. Leib said nervously. Something told her that Maxie was uncomfortable with kindness.

If I speak, Maxie said inside herself, *I'll shatter like glass.*

"Well, all right, Maxine, I'll wait for you to think it over. Consult your pillow tonight and let me know your answer," Mrs. Leib said, getting up to leave, signaling an end to this most unusual one-way conversation. Silently, she vowed to convince Maxie to leave Selby, to get the machinery in gear as soon as possible.

***

Maxie did more than consult her pillow that night. Angry with herself for behaving improperly, for appearing ungrateful, she was determined to have an answer for Mrs. Leib within the two days before her next class. First, she asked her roommates for their opinions. Devoted, constant friends Kate and Jenny were often frustrated by their failure to coax Maxie out of her depressions. They did the next best thing—they gave her space and time to work out her problems.

"Go for it, Maxie," Kate implored. "I'll miss my cover story for breaking curfew, but I think it'll be good for you to make a change. You never really wanted to go into Early Childhood Ed anyway. Remember?" The color of Kate's hair reminded Maxie of the brilliant Titian reds of tropical sunsets. Her eyes were so blue against her pale, freckled skin; they were honest but mischievous eyes that held you prisoner to her merriment and often daring escapades. Like Maxie, Kate loved to sing, and sitting on their beds or walking to class, they would go through a Joan Baez repertoire, with Kate providing the bass harmony. Jenny would sit on the floor, legs crossed like a contented Buddha, munching on chocolate chip cookies and sipping tea from a Selby mug that seemed permanently attached to her hand. Gay's laughter was the comic relief they all needed after a long, tiring day of note-taking and dealing with demanding professors. Imbued with a surfeit of maternal instinct, Jenny did not always approve of Kate's circumvention of dormitory rules, but cared for her too much to report it. Jenny's shortness, her plain, trusting nature, played well against Kate's reed-like slenderness, her vibrant impetuousness. Maxie loved them both.

"Well, Maxie," Jenny advised, "I'd say that you shouldn't pass up an opportunity. We know you're not happy here, and we know you've been taking pills for anxiety. Maybe a change'll be good for you."

Maxie was touched by her friends' honesty; she was burdensome and relied too heavily on their good natures.

"Thanks for the input, you two. I know I've been a pain and sometimes a shit. But you know I love you, and don't mean to bring you down. I'll miss you, but, actually, I won't be going that far away. We could still see each other often. Right?" Maxie needed reassuring.

"Right!" both girls said in unison, pretending that things were going to work out as Maxie predicted. College had taught them all about skepticism.

Maxie left her roommates sitting on her bed and hurried off to call Arthur in New York. A biochemistry major, he was rarely in his room until late in the evening, having late classes and even later labs. She was delighted when he answered.

"Hello?" Arthur answered, sleepily.

"Arthur, it's me. Hope I didn't wake you. How're you doing?"

"Maxie! It's great to hear your voice. I've just been studying for an organic chem test tomorrow and was starting to feel sorry for myself. I bought a box of doughnuts and some orange juice to cheer myself up, but this is so much better. How are you?"

Without hesitation or preamble, Maxie jumped right to the point. "Arthur, I need your advice. Today, Mrs. Leib offered me the chance to leave Selby and all this Kiddie Lit crap. She said I could transfer to the university, and that maybe her husband could help. If they'll accept all my credits, I can transfer directly into the language department. I'll have mega work to do—a lot of literature and advanced writing courses in Spanish, but I think I can do it. What do you think?"

"Mrs. Leib said 'crap'?" Arthur teased. "And what's Kiddie Lit?"

"No, of course not. Be serious, Arthur. 'Kiddie Lit' is what we call Children's Literature. It's real lit shit."

"Maxie, it seems to me you've already made your decision. I'm certain you can do it, and considering how down you've been, maybe this is just the answer." Arthur tried to moderate his enthusiasm. He did not want to own responsibility for a decision that could backfire; neither did he want to raise her expectations.

"But how do I go about asking my parents?" Maxie asked, deflated by the realization that she would have to get Philip's consent.

"You don't *ask*, Maxie, you *tell* them what you're gonna do. They had absolutely no input, no interest in your admissions process the first time. They know nothing about you or college—they haven't the vaguest notion of what's involved. Just tell them that it's a decision already worked out between you and some advisory panel at the school, and that you'll take care of everything—that they won't have to do anything but visit you at a new location." Arthur took a bite of a powdered doughnut, chewed quietly while Maxie digested his advice. "Listen," he added, "they'll have all summer to *hock* you about the money. Tell them you'll apply to be a Resident Assistant in exchange for your room and board. Your father will do a dance!" Arthur had succeeded in convincing both of them when he was through.

"You always know the right things to say," Maxie told him.

"It works both ways, hon. You've helped me keep my head, 'while all others were losing theirs,' as they say."

"I've never done anything so risky, Arthur. What if my father gets . . ."

"Crazy? It's either you or him, Maxie. Just be tactful and natural, so he doesn't think you're trying to 'pull a fast one,' as he likes to put it."

"I really want to do this. No, I really *have to* do this. Wish me luck. And, thanks. I love you."

"Good luck, and I love you more." Arthur had added the "more" without thinking. He hoped it wasn't so.

Maxie hung up the phone feeling hopeful. With a newfound determination, she dialed her home in Rhode Island.

"Hello?" It was Sarah.

"Hi, Mom, it's Max." To her parents she was always "Max."

"Oh, Max, I was just sitting here in the kitchen trying to decide whether or not to call *you.*"

"Why? Is something wrong?"

"I had an appointment with Dr. Bizzuto today because I had some tests done last week. I wasn't going to tell you this, but he said that my blood pressure has gone sky-high, and so has my cholesterol. You know, I could drop dead on the street, just like Papa."

Maxie had thought that Sarah was going to say she had a terminal illness, and let out the breath she didn't know she was holding. However, her mother did have something to be concerned about. Mixed in with her concern was the knowledge that Sarah intentionally exaggerated her physical symptoms, using them to manipulate and attract attention; it was her craft. By playing up various illnesses, some of which she pretended to have, she could absolve herself of any wrong-doing, any responsibility for her actions, or her lack of them.

"Well, Mom," Maxie said tentatively, "did the doctor prescribe any medication? What about diet?"

"He gave me a prescription for something very strong, saying that he just had to get my pressure down. If you wait a minute, I'll go get the pills and read you what the bottle says." Her voice sounded nervous. As she waited for her mother to return to the phone, Maxie thought that perhaps this time the gods were playing serious poker with Sarah, and that maybe it was not the best time to mention the idea of transferring. Then again, she thought that Sarah might see the proposal as good news. "Maxie? They're called Lopressor, l-o-p-r-e-s-s-or," she said, spelling it out.

"Mom, I'm sorry to hear that you don't feel well. I'm sure the pills will help, though, and your pressure will go down to normal soon. Maybe you're upset about something."

"I'd say 'upset' is putting it mildly. Who wouldn't be 'upset' living with your father?"

Maxie had walked right into that one and regretted that she had let her concern overrule her reason. "I'll be home soon and we can talk, have lunch at the deli, and you'll feel better. Right now, I need to tell you that I'm going to be transferring from Selby to the university in Boston." Maxie held her breath again, unable to predict the reaction.

"You're doing *what*? I thought you were very happy at Selby. You've been doing so well too. Did something happen? You're probably overreacting to it, Max, you know how sensitive you are." Oversensitive was how she thought of her Max—no balls—not like herself, certainly not like her own mother, Anna.

"No, Mom. I just don't want to teach young children. I want to teach junior or senior high students, and I can't do that major here. I need to transfer to the university to do that." Maxie had thought quickly and carefully, hoping to land on her feet.

"When does this happen, and when are you going to do it?" asked Sarah, firmly laying the groundwork for her own uninvolvement.

"Actually, it's all worked out with the Dean's Office. There shouldn't be any problems with credits, especially if Mrs. Leib will write me a recommendation." As soon as the words were out of her mouth, she knew she had blown it.

"Oh, Mrs. Leib," said Sarah with just the right edge, with almost imperceptible sarcasm. She had been hearing that name much too often. "Is this *her* idea?"

"No, it's *mine*," Maxie lied. "Mrs. Leib would have to recommend me to the Spanish Department." Maxie was aware of Sarah's jealousy of Mrs. Leib; she knew that what Sarah disliked most was the possibility that Maxie might tell this woman things about her, things not necessarily complimentary.

"Then do what you want, Max. I'm sure you're getting good advice there. Oh, and give my best regards to Mrs. Leib. Thank her for me for being so *helpful*." There was no denying the intent of Sarah's last comment. She really did not want to be remembered to Mrs. Leib; she needed to *sound* as if she did.

"Thanks, I'll say 'hello' for you. Hope you're feeling better soon. I'll keep in touch and let you know how I make out. Dad's probably asleep by now, so just say 'hi' for me, OK?" Maxie crossed her fingers.

"I can't do that, Max—we're not speaking right now. The son-of-a-bitch won't even take me out for ice cream. So you'll have to tell him yourself about your plans."

"Mom, with high cholesterol, you're not supposed to be eating ice cream," reminded Maxie.

"Whatever. Good-night, Max." She hung up with no "good luck," no "I love you."

•7•

Ageless ingenue of the real stage, Sarah executed makeup with practiced artistry. Each morning, she inspected her cache of cosmetics, methodically lining up the lipsticks as if they were tubular soldiers. She arranged them in orderly rows of ascending vibrancy, beginning with the more demure mauves, ending with the siren reds. Pink was not her color, she had been told by some department store cosmetician; it "fought" with the natural dark olive skin tones and muddied her brown eyes. With calculating creativity, she penciled in her eyebrows—sometimes drawing arches of quizzical surprise; other times, long dashes of scorn and rebuke. By applying enough shadow, she could out-Bette Davis her Bette Davis eyes. By adding or subtracting rouge from her cheeks, she appeared either virtuous or vampish. Subtlety was not the desired effect. Countless bottles and jars of moisturizing cream, skin toners, and wrinkle-removing lotions camped on her dressing table. They were her Agents Against Aging. With theatrical pretension, Sarah would sashay over to her wardrobe to choose a costume for the day. First, however, she had to choose the character to play; she needed to select the script of well-rehearsed lines. And, of course, she had to target her audience.

Sarah bought her clothing at the finest boutiques and salons in New York, traveling to the city once a month—it took her twenty-eight days to siphon off the dollars from her weekly "allowance" for household expenses. Always inventive, she bought cheaper store brands of canned goods and smaller, less costly cuts of meat. All the suits and dresses were perfectly matched with coordinated accessories, fashionable shoes, handbags, and overcoats. She wore her jewelry, Philip's hush payments, like frosting drizzled on a cake.

Nonetheless, Sarah's most perplexing problem was that she had nowhere to go, nowhere to show off. Philip did not take her dancing, he hated the opera, and vacation was yet another word not found in his vocabulary. Consequently, Sarah—all five-feet-one inch, one-hundred-eight pounds of her—stood for hours at a time in front of her full-length bedroom mirror, dressed in her outfit of choice, practicing her faces of despair, surprise, indignation, or false pride; each emotion, she knew, could be controlled by a simple raising of one eyebrow, by turning a smile upside down. In fact, her best-honed act was illness; she could summon with amazing skill any variety of symptoms that ranged from migraine headaches ("Do you think I have a brain tumor, Max?") to a "nervous breakdown" ("My nerves are shot, Max. I'm out of control!"). With cold irony, however, the mirror reflected the real face of her sickness—the tragic need to act out her pitiful delusions. "Mirror, mirror, on the wall," she seemed to be imploring, "who's the cleverest one of them all?"

It would have been easier for Maxie to ascribe a verifiable medical diagnosis to Sarah's behavior—how else to rationalize the bizarre tears of jealousy that filled Sarah's eyes at the moment of anyone else's happiness. And Sarah's failure to convince herself of her own importance was the most caustic review of them all. The humiliated actress, vowing revenge, would turn defiantly on her heels to avoid the accusations in the mirror and exit in search of a new audience.

Sarah Minsky Kahn had been born into the lap of poverty, and had suckled on the petty jealousies that want and hard times spawn. Her father Max was a fun-loving, good-hearted man, a baker who worked nights, slept days, and kept his wife Anna pregnant. Both immigrants from Lithuania, only Max had considered it his duty to learn the language of his new country. Anna, a powerful Jewish dowager-queen, ruled the household of six daughters, a husband, and whichever "cousin" from the Old Country happened to take up residence in their apartment. Anna was the undisputed authority in that five-room apartment on the third floor of Mrs. Kafka's house on Fuller Street. She took great pride in her righteousness and strict adherence to laws of keeping kosher, and in her observance of the Sabbath—Hitler himself was not able to destroy the conviction that she was "chosen" by her God to inherit the land of good and plenty. Anna polished her silver candlesticks every Friday afternoon before the Sabbath, lovingly stroking them with a soft, cotton terry cloth, holding them tenderly as if they were the little children from her village, the ones who did not get out in time. On Friday afternoons, with the aromas of *challah* baking in the oven and chicken soup simmering on the old gas stove, Anna allowed herself to cry.

On the High Holy Days, although she did not fully understand why, Anna solemnly ascended the stairs to the women's section of the synagogue to sit behind the red velvet curtain that separated them from the men. On cue, Anna would beat her breast with a closed fist and confess her sins both real and imagined, acted out or unrealized. One had to purify one's thoughts and heart by professing repentance; all sinners had to beg forgiveness for their transgressions and beg to be inscribed in the Book of Life for another year. The louder the wails, the more fervent the sincerity of contrition. That the synagogue's Orthodox rabbi would eat at her table made her feel special, singled out for praise, accepted in her community. Her cousin Freida found it more rewarding and lucrative to refine her skills in making bathtub gin. While Anna sat beating her breast on Yom Kippur, Max would be indulging in a bacon, lettuce, and tomato sandwich at a restaurant conveniently located respectfully far from his neighborhood. He would never want to publicly humiliate his wife; that would be a sin.

The Depression hit the Minsky family with dispassionate cruelty; survival required ingenuity and discreet calculations in a tight budget. As a baker, Max was able, at least, to keep bread and pastries on the table. Poultry was a once-a-week treat; even the cheaper cuts of meat were reserved for special occasions. Anna found dozens of ways to prepare (disguise?) potatoes. With a few carrots, some onion leeks, and celery, there was always soup. For Friday evenings, they managed to scrounge up enough money to buy and prepare chicken, regardless of its miniature scale. Max would feel especially sorry for Sarah, whose allotted portion was one small wing; feigning fullness or indigestion, he would give her his own meager portion. The older sisters fretted and complained of favoritism. "Why doesn't Papa give *me* his piece of chicken?" Marion would whine. "Because he loves me more," is what Sarah would answer haughtily. It would be so until one fine October day, when the gnarly old oak trees that lined Fuller Street were ablaze with color and a tingling chill pawed at the necks of passersby. Having endured the indignities of wartime rationing and the vicissitudes of the Depression, Max fell to the pavement on his way home from the bakery and died of a massive coronary before an ambulance could be called. The police informed Anna that just minutes before his collapse, Max was handing out lollipops to the neighborhood children. Pregnant with her second child, Sarah prayed for a son she could call "Max."

Anna had come to America with her candlesticks and a three-year-old daughter clutched close to her hip, on the lookout for scurrilous deviants who kidnapped young children from under their mothers' coats for the purpose of selling them on the baby black market or into the notorious sweatshops of New York City. Anna learned all about the importance of projecting an image of strength;

with animal-like instinct, she was prepared to attack on a moment's notice. Sleeping little, keeping a constant, silent vigil, she was a formidable opponent, a force with which to reckon; although there was one foolish enough to test her fortitude, rumor had it that he did not continue to walk upright for the duration of the voyage. And, although she never learned to speak English, never became a United States citizen, she chose July 4th as her new birthday; it was for her a great act of patriotism.

Of Anna's six daughters, three married. The three who did not devoted their years to ministering to Anna's every whim, to every singular demand. They worked to pay the bills; they did the cleaning, the washing, the ironing, and the cooking. Sarah polished her candlesticks. Of the three who did marry, only Sarah and her younger sister Marion moved out of town—acts that Anna deemed traitorous, punishable by heavy doses of guilt. Like Sisyphus, Marion and Sarah were condemned to lives of futile endeavor, bringing gifts and tokens of homage, all of which were stored away in Anna's bureau, in their original wrapping, as bargaining chips in her daughters' bid for most-favored child. Their attempts to outdo each other registered quite well with Anna; she adored being showered with gifts of penance. Neither daughter stopped trying to win Anna's favor until she died—and she took her decision with her to the grave, leaving the two women to wonder if, in fact, she had ever really loved them at all.

Anna's was a perverse, wicked game in which Sarah and Marion had been unwilling participants—never allowed to win, never granted the satisfaction of knowing if they had made Anna happy. With this sense of betrayal, both daughters, still feuding for the spoils of victory they claimed due them, raised their own daughters. The skill with which they surgically sliced through any emergent bonds of sisterhood was remarkable in its duplication, shameless in the withholding of the love and approval that could have prevented their daughters from ever knowing each other as anything other than rivals. Now Maxie, after thirty years of balancing her fear of losing Sarah with her fear of losing her mind, resolved to break the twisted cords of psychic bondage. With twin daughters of her own, Maxie vowed to destroy Anna's legacy.

•8•

Home late from the food shopping which followed her lunch with Arthur, Maxie put the groceries in the cabinet and stocked the refrigerator with the perishables. She neatly folded the brown bags and placed them in a drawer. Her answering machine flashed three messages—from Susan; Brian, the carpenter; and her sister-in-law Julie. She made a mental note to call Susan later in the evening when both would have some quiet time to talk—it had been too long since their last one. Flipping off her sneakers, Maxie began to assemble the items she would need for a ratatouille—olive oil, zucchini, yellow squash, mushrooms, onions, celery, stewed tomatoes, and seasonings. As she poured a few tablespoons of the oil into a large stewing pot, she remembered Arthur's suggestion to call the Leibs. Checking her watch—it was a little after five o'clock—she estimated that they would probably be finishing their dinner and preparing for their "evening constitutional." Maxie poured herself a glass of wine, sat down on the stool next to her prep counter, and dialed their number.

"Hello?"

"Hello, Mrs. Leib, this is Maxine."

"Oh, Maxine, how wonderful to hear your voice. How are you? And Arthur? And the children? I hope everyone is well." She always asked for everyone at once.

“We’re all fine, thank you. How are you and Dr. Leib feeling?”

“Just splendid—keeping very busy, you know. As a matter of fact, we’ve just returned from an outstanding recital given at the university. I wish you could have been here to enjoy it,” she replied with her usual enthusiasm.

“I know we would have enjoyed it. I called to ask if you’ll be free next weekend. Arthur and I are thinking of driving up to Montreal to see you.” Maxie crossed her finger and sipped some wine.

“Absolutely, yes! How delightful it will be to see you again. By all means, make your plans. Darling,” she called out to her husband, “Maxine and Arthur want to visit with us.” Maxie could hear Dr. Leib saying something in the background. “He says that you must stay with us. You know, we have plenty of room, and, truly, it is no bother.”

“Thank you for the invitation, but, you know we like to stay at the Centre Towers. Please don’t be offended.” Maxie respected Arthur’s need for total privacy; intimacy would be out of the question if they didn’t stay in a hotel.

“I don’t understand why you insist on paying such outrageous prices, Maxine, but I won’t argue. What time shall we expect you for dinner then?”

“Oh, please don’t prepare anything for us. We’ll be arriving quite late on Friday,” Maxie said, hoping to discourage Mrs. Leib’s fussing.

“Nonsense. I will expect you for dinner regardless of when you arrive. Matter is concluded; case closed. We await your call with great anticipation.”

“All right,” Maxie conceded, “but please don’t fuss.” Dinner, she knew, would be lavish, but she would stuff herself on the sheer pleasure of their company, sharing their mutual affection, sipping sherry.

"I don't consider it fussing—just come. And I expect that *both* of you will eat," Mrs. Leib asserted.

"We'll see you then," Maxie said, ignoring the implication. "Take good care. I'll call as soon as we're checked in."

"Maxine," Mrs. Leib said in her gently probing way, "are you all-right? Do I hear something amiss in your voice?"

Surprised, as usual, by her own transparency and inability to feign lightheartedness, Maxie remained silent. Caught off guard, she did not know what to say; but neither would she lie. Mrs. Leib patiently waited for her reply. There was no fooling her when it came to Maxine.

"I've been having some difficult days," she said, faltering. "Some things have been on my mind lately, and, well, sifting through them has made me a little tense. Arthur thinks I'll feel better seeing you, and, as he puts it, 'refueling.'"

"We'll talk, Maxine, as we always have. Please don't let whatever it is get the best of you. Hold onto your thoughts. Maybe I can help you sift."

"You're the only one who knows me well enough to do that. I do need your help in reconstructing some events—that is, if you don't mind," Maxie said.

"You know that I don't mind; I never did. We've known each other a long time, my dear—too long bound for 'minding.' *Un abrazo fuerte, chica. ¡Recuérdate, siempre el ánimo! Hasta viernes. ¡Adiós!*" She was gone.

Maxie replaced the phone on the cradle, refilled her glass, and took not a sip, but a mouthful of the dry, oaky white wine. She was feeling shaky inside, and, although not certain as to the source of her discomfiture, was genuinely upset. She reasoned that if Mrs. Leib could detect something in her voice from so great a distance, she must not be too convincing in her attempt to hide it from others around her. Morning trips to the lake were rekindling the smoldering ashes of her anger, while setting afire a sudden passion for wellness. She was perplexed. *Do I have to put out old fires, just to set new ones? Could passion wear so many faces?* she wondered.

***

Expectant and upbeat, Arthur and Maxie set out for Montreal in the matinal stillness, talking in hushed, conspiratorial voices to avoid waking their sleeping daughters. They packed up the car with suitcases, gifts, and, of course, some wine to chill in the hotel room while they visited with the Leibs. Arthur slowly backed the car out of the driveway, stopping predictably to admire the pink, purple, and white impatiens he planted yearly along both sides of the brick walkway, and to check on the garden burgeoning with beefsteak tomatoes, fancy cucumbers, peppers, and red-leaf lettuce. "I hope the girls remember to water it," Arthur said, taking Maxie's hand in his. "Well, I'm off with my honey. I packed two bottles of Sauvignon Blanc, and we can get some cheese in Burlington. What else can we want?" He did not wait for an answer; instead, he drew Maxie to him and kissed her gently. Their time away from the demands of office and home meant peaceful moments together along the six-hour route; it meant unhurried lovemaking well into the early morning hours. Dinner with the Leibs would be intoxicating; it would lift their spirits. Later, they would drink more spirits and not let the night steal away with their joy.

After their brief stop in Vermont for gas, cheese, crackers, and some chocolates for Dr. Leib, they were back on the road. The Green Mountains glowed with majestic color. Omnipresent white church steeples rose high above the towns that lay in the verdant valleys below. Bucolic red farmhouses—reminders of another, simpler time—lush, rolling hills and sweet fresh air preempted small talk. As the natural beauty unfolded before them, tensions dissipated, flowing out and away as if by suggestion. The stiffness in their necks, the tightness at the corners of their mouths eased; they smiled at one another, sensing the ebbing of their concerns, the heightening of their desire. It was Maxie who broke the silence.

"Why can't it always be so peaceful? I feel so constantly afraid, hon, except for times like this. Right now, I'm so content to be sitting next to you. Why does it all change when I'm alone?"

"For as long as I've known you, you've been terrified, Maxie—terrified of losing what means the most to you. I can't imagine why you think that you're going to lose us." Arthur was driving too fast. "Nobody's going to hurt you again. Why don't you believe that?" The speedometer was registering eighty-five miles an hour.

"Slow down, Arthur, or you'll get another ticket. I don't want to sound dramatic, but I keep having these horrible feelings wash over me—mammoth waves of sadness rise up out of nowhere, and I think I'm going to drown. I can't seem to control it." Maxie turned her face away from Arthur. The delight and pleasure of the countryside faded completely from her eyes; her tone had been somber. As they drove, huge dark clouds like rumpled bedspreads rolled in over the mountain peaks, shadowing the landscape with long, accusatory fingers. A premonition slid behind its own shadow. Maxie watched in dismay as rain began to beat on the windows as it whirled by in gusts of wind, smudging the view like an oily cloth. The steady, rhythmic oscillations of the windshield wipers held Arthur's attention; he could think of nothing to say that might assuage his own loathing for Sarah Kahn, for the torment she bequeathed to her daughter. Troy's Helen would have met her nemesis in Sarah, whose strategy of assault on Maxie's self-esteem, her monomaniacal campaign of denial, had derailed Maxie's will for years—they became her invincible mind-war machine.

Arthur shivered and turned down the air conditioner. "Maybe it's time to see Dr. Weissman again," he offered tactfully, sensitive to the delicate issue. Maxie had been to see Dr. Weissman for short periods of time over the last ten years, experiencing a breakdown of courage each time she approached the most critical areas, especially the ones that might have ultimately freed her from her panic. Traversing Maxie's past was like tip-toeing through a deadly minefield; the landscape looked so innocent and lovely, much like what they were treated to today. Unfortunately, the topography was treacherously sown with potholes and booby traps into which Maxie would fall, unsuspecting and vulnerable.

Minutes passed as Maxie reflected on Arthur's suggestion; she had put her elbow on the side panel and covered her eyes with her right hand. "Yes," she sighed, "I've been thinking that too," she said, recalling the time she had indignantly run from Dr. Weissman's office. After the fifty minutes scheduled for her appointment, the doctor had made a deliberate gesture, turning the small table clock around so that she could not see the time. He did not dismiss her in the customary way, nor did he inquire about rescheduling. Instead, he rose from his chair, walked over to the window, turned his back to Maxie, and put both hands deep into his trouser pockets. "Maxie," he had sighed, "your mother is a bitch." Maxie had gasped, looking in disbelief at Dr. Weissman's back, waiting for a clue that would tell her how to respond. Seeing none, she rose, horrified by the truth, and fled from his office. He had been right, of course, but his words had cut too deeply, too soon. What she had told Dr. Weissman about her wedding and about Alden's birth could not have disgusted the unflappable, seasoned psychiatrist. Surely, she thought, he had heard worse. In any case, he had been moved to render his judgment, and it continued to ring in her ears.

"Maxie, we're almost to the Champlain Bridge. We'll be at the hotel very soon," Arthur observed. Thunder growled in the distance.

"Wake me when we're there, Arthur. I just want to close my eyes for a little while."

Maxie leaned back against the headrest and let her thoughts carry her back to her wedding night. Despite Philip's nasty innuendos about her virginity, Maxie believed that her virtue would insulate and protect her from his hurtful words. She could still hear the whining, the intractable demands, the spiteful protests of the feuding families.

•9•

They're not religious. We must have an Orthodox service," Arthur's family complained.

"They're too religious. Let them be grateful for the kosher caterer," Maxie's family protested.

"You haven't finished dental school. You should wait until you're thirty," Arthur's father insisted.

"What does it matter to you?" Arthur argued.

"Don't you dare think about inviting my sisters!" Sarah demanded.

"I'll send you to Israel for a year. You'll forget about her," Arthur's father tried to bribe.

With their patience worn thin, their stamina depleted, Arthur and Maxie decided to elope. Exhausted from wrestling with their families, Maxie and Arthur formulated a workable plan. They anxiously anticipated the coming of spring, its warm weather, and the rebirth of possibility.

"I know a rabbi in Milton who'll marry us in April, Maxie, just before you graduate. If we both can find part-time jobs, at least until you get a permanent teaching position, I think we can make it." Arthur had no savings, no means with which to support them. But he was determined.

"Where will we live?" Maxie pressed him. "Your father is going to cut you off at the knees. We'll be forced to crawl back for help."

Arthur wanted only to extricate himself and Maxie from Philip's remonstrations of poverty, from Sarah's sorcery; he could not picture himself crawling.

"Maxie," Sarah had said, calling her daughter to her bedroom where she lay in perfected lassitude, "my nerves are shot by all this bickering. Surely, you and Arthur can find a way to settle your . . . this mess his family has created." Maxie had found her lying on top of the white, knobby bedspread, half-covered by an ice-blue satin quilt. Her body was folded into a backwards N as she lay on her side, head turned away from the doorway. Sarah's right arm draped over her eyes, shielding them from Maxie's scrutiny; her nose was buried in the crook of her elbow that pointed up toward the ceiling. The stocking covered soles of her child-size feet stuck out from under the quilt.

"*Your* nerves? *His* family?" Maxie had shouted.

"Oh, can you hand me my Valium? I feel a migraine coming on," Sarah cried.

Max had fished into Sarah's night-table drawer for the Valium, displacing dozens of small plastic medicine containers, finding the pills that Sarah needed to enhance her credibility. "Thank you, Max. I'll need a little water from the bathroom." Maxie brought her mother a plastic cup of water, left the bedroom, and closed the door behind her. On her way down the stairs, she heard Sarah call out, "Your father will be home soon. Make sure he has some dinner."

With money borrowed against his college loans, Arthur bought two gold rings; and on a rainy Saturday evening in April, just before the Passover ritual of reciting the story of exodus and freedom, Arthur and Maxie stepped under a *chuppah* held up by four strangers and exchanged their vows. In a simple, white sheath dress found in Filene's Basement, a Jackie Kennedy-style "pill box" hat with half-veil, Maxie focused on a large moth hole in the rear corner of the faded, fringed canopy.

"You may now break the glass, as is customary, Arthur," the rabbi instructed, placing the white napkin-covered glass next to Arthur's right foot. Arthur lifted his foot and smashed the glass with a force that surprised even himself. Maxie heard the muffled sound of loss. For their honeymoon, they spent one night in New York City—Arthur's roommate was able to get free tickets for a Balanchine ballet.

For six months, Maxie worked as a recording secretary in the Social Service Department of the Massachusetts General Hospital, typing the reports of psychiatric social workers into patients' hospital records. From nine o'clock in the morning until five in the afternoon, she listened to the psychological evaluations that were stored on the Dictaphone and carefully incorporated them into the file. At five o'clock, Arthur picked her up outside the main entrance of the hospital and, fighting rush-hour traffic, delivered her to the front doors of the university at six, where she would attend class until nine. Arthur would again pick her up, and, finally, they would go back to their small but pleasant apartment in Mattapan. They struggled until Maxie's graduation in May. The summer went smoothly and Maxie got a teaching assignment for September. For almost three years, Maxie worked to keep them afloat, while Arthur finished his graduate work at Harvard.

Maxie was eight months pregnant when they arrived in Dover, Delaware. Arthur had entered the Air Force as a commissioned officer while the war in Vietnam was still raging. Maxie often saw the gruesome cortege of flatbed trucks stacked with the coffins of the sacrificed—slowly, solemnly rolling by. Sickened by the thought that the life inside her one day might be a soldier, too, she grieved.

Arthur and Maxie had endured the initial round of introductory and obligatory social events at the Officers' Club, delighted to return to their quiet, attractive off-base apartment. With thirty extra pounds of gained weight to carry around, Maxie was of little assistance to Arthur in setting up their new home. She had also been noticing increased swelling in her feet and hands, but assumed it to be a natural symptom associated with pregnancy. Maxie was relieved that, in her encumbered state, she was not expected to entertain, which was fine with her; they were happy to have made satisfying and compatible friendships with a few couples who shared her aversion to large parties and unavoidable posturing.

As the wife of an officer, Maxie was entitled to "special treatment" at the hospital. She was allowed to choose her own obstetrician, and, unlike the noncommissioned officers' wives, she would be assured of seeing the same doctor at every visit. In the days before her first scheduled appointment at the hospital, Maxie worried that all was not in good order, and, by the time that day arrived, her worry had blossomed into panic that something dreadful was going to happen—that all the dreams and hopes she and Arthur had shared during the last eight months were about to evaporate. Most of her maternity clothes were too constricting, forcing her to choose her largest, loosest-fitting jumper which she referred to as her "tent." On her feet she wore Arthur's unlaced sneakers, which pinched and made her ankles more swollen. Maxie's size and awkward gait depressed her. She did not like waddling, but she forced herself to think ahead. She would lose the weight after the baby was born and regain her normal appearance. She vowed to exercise.

Heaving her bulk behind the wheel of their 1967 Chevrolet, Maxie started the engine, carefully eased the car out of its parking space, and drove to the base. It was wise to have left early, as liberating herself from the car was more challenging than getting in. She had to pull the lever on the front end of the driver's seat that allowed the seat to roll far back away from the steering wheel, but this meant having to bend forward in search of the release bar. The mountain that once had been her stomach, which sat on what once had been her lap, made this maneuver nearly impossible. Once free of the wheel, she had to turn and hoist herself up and out of the seat, holding onto the door and frame of the car. With her pocketbook strap around her neck, perspiration staining the underarms and back of her jumper, Maxie closed the door and swayed into the clinic. She waited in the corridor, sitting on the front edge of a tiny, red vinyl chair and decided to suggest to the doctor a more suitable choice for the waiting room, one that did not add to one's already lowered self-esteem.

"Mrs. Lane, we're ready for you now," Dr. Davenport's nurse announced with starchy officiousness.

Maxie struggled out of her seat and made her way down the row of bulging bellies, taking care not to stumble over the protruding feet of the women who glared at her.

"Let's see what you weigh today, Mrs. Lane. Step up on the scale," the nurse instructed. "Oh, I see you've not been watching your diet! Tsk, tsk."

"Actually, I think I'm retaining a lot of fluid," Maxie said, intimidated by the accusation. *Nurse Ratchett, you've met your equal* was what she was thinking.

"Nonsense," the nurse declared. "We know when you've been cheating on salty foods and alcoholic beverages. Now, let's get the blood pressure." *These officers' wives are all the same* was what she decided. Releasing the Velcro strap on the pressure cuff, she admitted, reluctantly, "It *is* a little elevated, but if you watch that diet it should correct itself."

No one noticed the high levels of toxic material in the urine sample she gave before entering Dr. Davenport's examining room. Inside the room, she undressed and waited. The doctor breezed in without knocking, his lab coattails fluttering behind him. "How are ya feelin', Maxie?" he inquired. Maxie resented the familiarity, despite where he was going to be putting his hands in less than a minute. Tall and thin, with black wavy hair and seductive blue eyes, Dr. Davenport was a handsome young doctor. His bachelorhood made him most attractive, especially to those women whose husbands were away in some godforsaken jungle. Maxie wished he were older, less flirtatious.

"Pleased to meet you, Doctor," Maxie said, politely extending her hand to shake his. "I'm actually somewhat concerned about all this swelling I have, and the headaches too."

Dr. Davenport did not respond immediately. He shook her hand, placing his left one on top of her right, then turned to put on his examining gloves. "If you'll just put your feet into those stirrups and slide down as best you can. . . ." he said, positioning the bright light at the foot of the table, rolling his stool up close. Maxie could not see the top of his head over the mountain of flesh before her, but she did see his hand up in the air, waving, brushing away her concerns as if they were pesky flies. "Don't worry so much, Maxie," he said, rising from where he had disappeared. "All first-time mothers tend to be a little too—well, neurotic. Relax. You know, in some countries women deliver their babies in the bushes, without the benefit of modern science." Dr. Davenport tore off his gloves and flung them into the wastebasket. He was probably late for a golf match.

At each subsequent visit to the doctor, Maxie voiced her concerns. With regularity, Dr. Davenport assured her that she was "obsessing" unnecessarily. Although she was lightheaded and could wear nothing but Arthur's tennis socks on her feet, she tried not to behave like one of Dr. Davenport's stereotypes.

Four weeks later, on a chilly November midnight, Arthur rushed Maxie to the emergency room of the hospital where she was diagnosed as toxemic, severely preeclamptic. Blood-pressure readings were exceedingly high, and the risk of imminent seizure, coma and/or death so real, that she was whisked off to an isolation room. Secreted behind a drawn curtain, intravenous medications dripping into her arm, Maxie could have no visitors, no noise, no upsets. At the minimum, there was good reason to believe that she would deliver a stillborn child. Arthur talked Dr. Davenport into allowing him to visit, but before he could enter Maxie's room, he had to stop, calm his own fears, and disguise his fury over what was, without question, a result of negligence. His labor was in presenting himself with an encouraging smile. Maxie, he knew, would be asking him a million questions—that she would be looking desperately into his eyes for a sign of hope, some confirmation that she would be all right. As he held her hand tightly, he despaired of giving himself away, of falling apart under her penetrating stare. He was not a good actor; he was an even worse dissembler.

On the second evening of Maxie's confinement, the phone rang; against the rules, an ill-advised nurse handed it to her.

"Maxie?" a voice shouted.

"Yes," she answered, weakly.

"What the hell are you doin' in there? What's all this shit about?" It was her brother-in-law Stuart. Maxie disliked his vulgarity and pomposity.

"Stu, I'm very sick. I can't tell you what it's all about because the doctors and nurses aren't saying much to me. Are you calling for Mom?"

"Yes, and this thing of yours, whatever it is, has made her very nervous. When shall I tell her you'll be out of there?"

"Stu, you don't understand. I may *not get out of here!* Talk to Arthur." Maxie handed the phone to Arthur who had just entered the room. *Go away,* she thought, *just go away.* Arthur pulled the telephone over to the window and looked down on the busy parking lot below, reluctant to share any information with his brother-in-law.

"Listen, Stuart, yeah, hi. Yes, yes, I know that Sarah needs to know what's going on, but we don't know yet. Maxie has to rest and shouldn't be disturbed. If she goes into a coma, well, you know what eclampsia is." Arthur then turned his back to Maxie so that she could not hear what he was saying. "Stu, I'm asking you not to call again—wait till you hear from me. Yes, I'll tell Sarah. Good-bye." Arthur turned back to Maxie's bed, replaced the phone on the receiver, and smiled feebly. "He won't be bothering you anymore, hon. Just erase him from your mind."

Maxie remained under twenty-four-hour vigil for ten days. Lying in her bed, feeling the life inside her—sometimes strong, sometimes not at all—she wept, covering her mouth with a bedsheet to stifle the sobs. She did not want to bring the nurses scrambling to her side with their admonitions, their incessant attempts to calm her, to fool her. In the early evenings, she could hear the wails of newborns wafting down the corridor into her secluded corner; she could hear the jubilant voices of first-time fathers, the soft cooing of mothers, awed by what they had just brought forth. The thought of dying in childbirth had never occurred to Maxie; it's what happens to *others*, she thought. As she lay in her bed, disconsolate, the green-gall monsters in her head began to roar. They were angry at Stuart's callousness. But why were *they* so surprised, Maxie wondered; how could they believe that this time things would be any different?

Maxie knew that Stuart, a guy who grazed on his own guile, who considered human encounters as challenges to his manhood, would find a way to describe her illness to Sarah as a weakness. *How does Toby stand it?* she wondered. And *my mother . . . she just appeases his appetite for bullshit by feeding him some of her own. So, she calls it brisket . . . what's the difference?*

***

At the end of Maxie's four-week hospitalization, her condition stabilized and she survived the crisis. Dr. Davenport falsified the medical records that would have cost him his job. Arthur arrived to take her home—"if you promise to be good," he said, smiling broadly. "They say you'll be fine over the Thanksgiving Day holiday, as I'll be home to watch over you. The instructions are that you must stay off your feet. Can you manage that?"

Maxie opened her arms to Arthur and they embraced, dampening each other's faces with the tears of their relief. When Arthur pulled up to their front door, Maxie hesitated, unsure. "Hon, I know you've set up the baby's room, but I really don't want to go in there. I can't look at an empty crib."

"That's fine, I'll just close the door. Now let's get you inside." Arthur was unsure, as well. For Thanksgiving dinner, they dined on liver and onions; they felt genuinely thankful.

The next morning, Maxie went into false labor and reentered the hospital for observation. Left alone in a "holding room" with no one to talk to, she stared at a large black-and-white-faced clock which hung directly over the entry door, listening to the ticking of every second. Finally, Maxie's confinement abruptly ended, as two attendants barged into the room to wheel her away.

"Where are we going?" Maxie cried.

"We're going to have your baby, Mamma," one of them answered, grinning.

Twenty-nine hours later, a squealing, squirming Alden David Lane emerged, making the first of many statements on the world into which he had been so precariously thrown. A nurse lay the baby on Maxie's stomach, and she felt the warmth of his life on hers. It would always be so; he would warm her life with his goodness and his sweet innocence. Assured, drained from her ordeal, Maxie drifted into a deep, drugged sleep that would help to erase all the horrors of the preceding weeks. Arthur found a broom closet down the hall and, in the darkness, wept privately.

•10•

After five days in the hospital, Maxie was ready to go home, this time with her baby. With Arthur's help, she bundled Alden into a powder-blue bunting, leaving only his tiny, red face uncovered. He protested his confinement, squirming and kicking inside the fuzzy, blue bag. His face became pinched and wrinkled as an old man's as he lay on his back crying.

"It's OK, sweetheart, we'll be out of here in just a few minutes. Don't cry, Mommy's here." The sound of her own voice calling herself "Mommy" startled Maxie. *I'm a mommy now—me, Mrs. Maxie Lane. A mommy. Holy shit!* A pretty, young nurse with a long, blond ponytail entered Maxie's room with a wheelchair.

"We're ready to take you downstairs now, Mrs. Lane. Regulations require that I take you down in the elevator in this wheelchair, but you can hold your baby on your lap. It sounds like he's as eager to get out of here as your are," she said, good-naturedly.

"What do you want me to do with all these flowers and plants, Maxie?" Arthur asked, packing up Maxie's toiletries, bathrobe, and slippers. He had brought her a new "going home" outfit—black sweatpants and a black-and-gray sweatshirt. The pants had an elastic waistband that provided more than ample room for Maxie's expanded midsection.

"Maybe we can send the flowers over to the nurses' station," Maxie suggested.

"I'll take care of it, Mrs. Lane," the nurse offered. "Thanks."

"Arthur, I'd like to take the plants home though. Oh, and the stuffed animal you sent with the yellow roses." Maxie allowed the nurse to help her into the wheelchair; the pain medication made her feel nauseated and dizzy.

"You'll feel better once we get outside into the fresh air," the nurse advised, placing Alden in Maxie's lap and wheeling them to the elevator doors. Arthur followed, his arms full too. "Wait for me!" he called out as the doors swung open.

The ride to their apartment took barely fifteen minutes. Maxie sat in the front seat, holding Alden close to her; he had fallen asleep as soon as the car was in motion. Little puffs of baby breath tickled Maxie's nose as she bent over to kiss his forehead. Arthur was beaming.

"You're just bursting with pride, aren't you, . . . Daddy?" Maxie laughed.

"This is just too much, hon. I can't believe it," Arthur replied, blinking away the tears that had suddenly filled his eyes. "We're a family now—our own little family." Ten minutes later, pulling into the white parallel lines of their designated parking space, he announced, "And, we're home." As Arthur walked around to the back of the car to open the trunk, he heard the faint ringing of the telephone inside the apartment and rushed to open the door. In his haste, fumbling with his keys, he dropped them into a slatted mat on the stoop. By the time he got to the phone, he was breathing heavily.

"Hello," he panted.

"Arthur, I was just going to hang up. Why are you so out of breath?"

"Hi, Mom. We just got back from the hospital. Maxie's still in the car. I ran to answer the phone." Arthur inhaled deeply to steady himself.

"So, how's Max and the baby?"

"Fine, fine, although Maxie is really worn out from her ordeal."

"That's why I'm calling. I figured I'd come down there to help you out." Arthur felt as though his heart had dropped down to his feet; he hadn't expected Sarah to offer her help—he didn't want her to spoil things, as he knew she would. "Hold on, Mom, I'll go get Maxie and you can talk about it." Arthur left the phone dangling as he went outside to help Maxie out of the car. He took Alden from her, held him on his left shoulder, and extended his right arm to Maxie. "Once you're on your feet, take your time, hon. Take slow steps until you get to the kitchen. Then you'll probably want to sit down—your mother's on the phone, waiting."

"Has she asked you Alden's name?" Maxie inquired, pulling herself up on Arthur's arm.

"Not yet. She wants to come down here to help," Arthur said quietly. "Please don't let her, Maxie." Arthur never sounded so nervous.

"Shit," Maxie said, inching her way into the apartment, collapsing into a kitchen chair, reaching for the phone. "Hi, Mom. Sorry to keep you waiting so long," Maxie tried to sound cheerful.

"Well! I couldn't imagine what the hell you were doing all this time. Your father will have a fit when he sees the phone bill."

"It takes me a while to get going. I still have a lot of pain," Maxie explained.

"I heard you had a pretty rough time of it. I was very worried about you. Stu said we weren't *allowed* to call you in the hospital. Did Arthur tell you I'd like to come help you out?"

"No, he was too busy helping me *in,* but it's nice of you to offer." Maxie groped for time to think of a way to discourage Sarah's visit. "Can you wait just a bit, Mom? I'm not exactly good company right now."

"I don't need for you to be good company, Max. I'd like to see my grandchild . . . that is, if you don't mind. By the way, what's his name?"

"Alden," Maxie answered, proudly.

"Alden? What kind of a name is that?" Sarah asked, displeased by the choice.

"It's a beautiful name. We used the 'a' from Arthur's mother's name—you remember, Adina?" Maxie was struggling to keep her answer from sounding defensive, although it was how she was being made to feel.

"What I mean is, why couldn't you pick something more . . . Jewish?"

"Mom, his name is Alden. He's been circumcised by a rabbi and he'll be named in a temple." Maxie's patience was thinning.

"No need to get testy, Max. Does that mean there'll be no *bris*?"

"That's right. It would have been too much for us to handle right now." Changing the subject, she asked, "Can you come in, say, about a week?" Arthur had taken Alden out of his bunting and had put him down in the crib to nap. He was surprised to see Maxie still on the phone with Sarah after unloading everything from the trunk of the car. "What's happening?" he whispered. Maxie put her index finger to her lips to keep Arthur from being overheard. In return, Arthur stuck out both hands, palms out, to indicate to Maxie that he did not want Sarah to come. Taking a bottle of club soda out of the refrigerator, he emptied it in one, long gulp. "Stall, Maxie," he whispered pleadingly.

"Are you saying you don't want me? Is that what all this hemming and hawing is about? Because if it is. . . ." Sarah raised her voice in wounded anger.

"No, of course not. If you think you're up to it, then sure—just let us know what airline and what time to pick you up." Maxie relented.

"Stu will drive me down on Wednesday, his day off," Sarah declared. *Queens get driven, Maxie, dear, don't you know that yet?*

"Drive? Why not fly? It's a six-hour ride!"

"Because Stu said he'd take me. I don't argue with someone who wants to do me a favor." *Silly girl, whatever made you think this was going to be easy? She will come thinking she should, even though she really doesn't want to.* Maxie frowned, and Arthur pulled a chair up close to the phone. Maxie tilted it slightly away from her ear so that he could hear the rest of the now-worsening conversation.

"What time shall we expect you on Wednesday then?" she asked, rubbing her forehead. She was feeling dizzy again.

"Whenever we get there. Stu says he can't stay too long. He's being such a dear to take me all that way, don't you think?" Arthur rolled his eyes.

"Sure, Mom, a real dear."

"Now, Max, don't start. See you Wednesday."

"'Bye. Have a nice trip." As Maxie replaced the phone on the hook, Arthur put his arms around her and hugged her. Maxie was furious with herself for letting this happen, for nibbling at the bait. *"Don't start,"* Maxie muttered, "she tells *me* not to start. She tells *me* when she can come. And with that pimple-faced prick!" Maxie seethed, resting her pounding forehead against Arthur's shoulder.

"Calm down, hon. She's got you on the ropes again and there's nothing you can do about it now." Arthur wished Maxie had been more forceful, but he also knew that Maxie would forever blame herself if Sarah had a sudden heart attack. He had tried so many times over the years, to no avail, to convince her that people don't *give* others heart attacks.

"I still can't challenge her, Arthur. I can't confront her, no matter how little sense she makes—no matter how she infuriates me.

Don't start . . . geez!"

"Maxie, don't let her upset you. Today's supposed to be so happy for us. Come on, let's go see what it's all really about. He's in his crib, and you haven't even seen his room all wallpapered and painted. I stuck a gigantic, shaggy green dog in the corner; I hope it doesn't scare him." At the door to Alden's room, they stood together, holding hands.

"I want so much to be a good mother," Maxie whispered, giving Arthur's hand a gentle squeeze.

"You will be, hon. No question."

***

Novembers in Delaware normally are pleasant and mild. The late summer smell of decay in the marshes lingers; the few, leafy remains of corn crops sway to the soft rhythms of gentle breezes. November mornings beckon you to walk along the miles of wheat and barley fields, to push a baby in his carriage, to smile at the sun in a cloudless sky. Maxie, weak and drawn, could only watch out her bedroom window as Arthur took Alden for daily outings. She watched, in dismay, as the blue carriage kept time with Arthur's bouncy, jaunty stride. She watched them disappear together down the parking lot, around the corner, out of sight. Her jealousy brought on weepy moments of guilt. "It must be the postpartum depression I hear about," she had told Arthur during one of those inescapable moments.

Arthur took a few days' leave from the dental clinic to care for his wife and son. Much to his surprise, he enjoyed doing the household chores, sterilizing baby bottles, warming formula, and being able to hold Alden in the crook of his left arm, feeding his son with his right hand, tilting the bottle as Alden slowly emptied it. Arthur loved the little sucking sounds that Alden made as he drew from the nipple; he delighted in the soft, tender touch of tiny fingers on his own. Maxie lay in bed feeling miserably inadequate as a mother, burdensome as a wife.

•11•

Wednesday came too soon. Maxie wasn't ready to have Sarah see her so dependent; she wanted to show Sarah how well she could "mother" her new baby. "The thought of having Sarah take care of me, as if *I* were the baby, really sickens me," she told Arthur on Tuesday night. "She's going to love my needing her."

At exactly noon the following day, the doorbell rang—then rang three times more. Arthur hurried to the front door and opened it to find Sarah, half-smiling at him. *Take your pick which half,* it seemed to say. She was dressed in a black gabardine wool suit, a white silk blouse with red trim on the collar. A gold belt with red leather buckle circled her small waistline, accentuating her full bosom. She held a black Gucci bag on her left arm; black pump heels and sheer nylons completed the "look." In her right hand was a box of candy, which she offered to Arthur. Stuart came up behind Sarah carrying two suitcases, obviously heavy, considering the dark rings of sweat on the underarms of his shirt.

"Hi, Mom. Stu. Come on in where it's cool. Here, let me help you with the bags." Arthur smiled and stepped aside to let Sarah pass; she gave him her cheek, which Arthur kissed obligingly. As he took the bags into the living room and put them behind the sofabed, he asked, "So, how was the trip?"

"Just as you'd expect," Sarah answered cryptically.

"Traffic was a bitch on the New Jersey Turnpike as usual," Stuart complained.

"Where's Max—and Aldron?"

"*Alden*, Mom. He's asleep, but you can go in to see him if you like. Maxie's in her room, waiting for you." Arthur turned his attention to Stuart; Maxie had asked him to be a good host. "Want a cold beer?" he asked.

Beads of perspiration still clung to Stuart's upper lip. "Yeah, sure. Is there any other kind?" He followed Arthur into the kitchen, running his finger along the console of the new stereo system Arthur had bought from his upstairs neighbor, a fighter pilot. "Nice," he said.

"Thanks," Arthur replied, handing Stuart a mug with a bottle of beer.

"I can see you're not a beer drinker, Artie. *Real* beer drinkers slug it down from the bottle—like men." Smirking, Stuart threw his bulk onto the sofa and put his feet up on the coffee table. "Listen, Artie, I understand that Maxie called Sarah and begged her to come today. I had a golf match scheduled at the club, but Sarah said Maxie was adamant."

"That's not the way it was at all, Stu," Arthur protested, not sure whose lie it was, Sarah's or Stuart's.

"In any event," Stuart continued, ignoring Arthur's comment, "she bitched the whole way down here."

"So, what else is new?" Arthur could not resist.

"She's fighting with Philip again. They're at each other's throats all the time."

"How come?"

"You know, same old shit. He won't take her anywhere, they have no friends, he's so cheap he squeaks when he walks—same old shit. But, of course, you don't have to deal with any of this—you're away from it all." Stuart emptied his bottle, belched loudly, and helped himself to another beer. A bullish man, Stuart was already overweight at thirty-two years of age. His face was pock-marked, acne-plagued. Having lost most of his hair by the time he was twenty-six, Stuart now wore a wig—one of those ink-black jobs that sat on top of his head like a wet rug. Stuart repositioned himself on the couch, grinning broadly. Out of habit, Arthur inspected Stuart's teeth; although perfectly aligned, they were dirty. Arthur expected to see two menacing rows just inside the lower jaw. "So, what I'm saying, Artie, is that Mom has been having a tough time and needs some calming down. Don't upset her."

"Wait a minute, Stuart. Sarah offered to come here to help *us*. As you can see, Maxie is in no condition for more stress."

Stuart took out a pack of cigarettes, tapped one out, and put it to his lips. Striking a match, he looked around for an ashtray. "Got something to flick this in?" he asked, holding the match.

"We don't smoke, Stu. You know that. Why don't you have your smoke outside on the back porch?" Arthur thought of a better place for flicking Stu's cigarette.

Stu blew out the match. Leaning forward, his tone confidential, he said, "Listen, Artie, I wonder if you'll do me a little favor?"

"What can I do for you?" Arthur hedged.

"Well, there's this week-long convention in Las Vegas I'd really like to go to, but Toby doesn't want to go." Stu struck another match, lit his cigarette, and took a long drag. He blew a thick, gray cloud of smoke toward the ceiling. "How's about if you and Maxie invite Toby down here for a little visit?"

"And how's about if you put that cigarette out?"

"OK. OK." Stu stuffed the butt down the neck of the beer bottle.

"Thanks. Now, when is the convention?" Arthur leaned back in his chair, crossed his legs.

"Beginning of January. I'd really hate for her to stay home

alone. She's never done it before. Gets kinda nervous, you know."

"Couldn't she stay at Mom's? Or maybe Mom, with her?" Arthur knew he sounded obvious.

Stu lowered his voice. "Toby needs to get away from Sarah. They're *too* close. And, she needs some time for herself, away from . . . the kids too. She still won't get on an airplane, so she says she doesn't mind if I go without her." Stu was squirming, talking very fast.

"Have Sarah and Philip agreed to watch your children?"

"I don't *ask*, Artie—I tell. Only way to handle 'em."

"Well, sure, Stu. Tell Toby she's always welcome here." Arthur knew that Toby would not visit. She never went *anywhere* by herself—never left her house, except to shop with Sarah, or to go with Stuart to their country club.

"Great. I'll tell Toby you've invited her—that way, she won't think it's *my* idea."

"No problem. I'm sure she'll be calling. We'll ask her then."

"Does Toby call here a lot?" Stuart's voice was suddenly edgy.

"No, quite the contrary. I just figured she'd want to know more about the baby. It would be nice to hear from her."

"Oh. Yeah. Well, you know how it is with these sisters—always something."

Stuart rose from the sofa in slow motion, pulling himself up to his full six-foot-two height, scratched his beer-bloated stomach. "Gotta go; thanks for the brew. Where's the can? Always have to pee after a beer." Reaching into his shirt pocket, he took out a folded check. "This is for what's-his-name, Aldron. Toby sends her regards."

"Alden," Arthur corrected yet again. "And thanks. The toilet is across the hall from Maxie's room. You can say your good-byes while you're down there."

"Yeah, better hit the road. Got an early morning patient coming in for a neck adjustment. He's the town dog warden and I owe—want to return a little favor. You know how it is—you scratch my back and I'll scratch yours. Ha!" With that, Stuart was off to the bathroom. Arthur gladly threw three empties into the trash can before wiping up the ring of condensation Stuart's bottles had left on the cocktail table.

Stuart emerged from the bathroom, checked his zipper, and hiked up his pants. As he entered Maxie's room, Alden began to stir, working up to a cranky complaint. "That's my cue," Stuart said, leaning over to kiss Sarah on the forehead. "Can't stand the smell of baby shit. I'm outta here." He patted Sarah's hand, whispered something in her ear, and winked. Sarah smiled. Stuart then leaned over and planted a sloppy, wet kiss on Maxie's lips. "See ya, kiddo. Better hurry and get out of that bed. Artie's apron strings are starting to show." Stuart breezed out of the apartment, chuckling to himself. "So long, Artie," he called over his shoulder. Was Arthur hiding? Neither of them could tell. The front door slammed shut, frightening Alden. Arthur waited in the kitchen until he heard Stuart's white Mercedes pull away from the complex. When he heard the gunning of the motor as Stuart turned at the street corner, Arthur let out a very long sigh of relief and went into Alden's room. Sarah was holding the squirming infant. "Arthur," she chided, "you shouldn't let him scream like that. Look at him, poor thing. He's probably soaking wet and getting a rash."

"He wasn't screaming, Mom," Arthur defended. "If you give him to me, I'll change him."

"Already you're contradicting me, Arthur. He was screaming, and that's not good for a newborn. I never had boy babies," she said, wistfully. "You can do the honors." Sarah handed a quieted Alden back to Arthur. "Be careful, now. I'm sure the cord is almost ready to come off." Thoughtfully, she added, "That much I remember."

Sarah headed back to Maxie's bedroom and sat on a small rocker. "Do you have any coffee, Max? A bulkie, maybe? I'll make a pot, and then think about what to fix for supper."

"There's coffee in the cabinet. Help yourself. But don't worry about dinner—Arthur will get some take-out." Sarah was massaging the back of her neck, slumping into the chair. Her shoes were off, and she began to rub her swollen ankles for Maxie to see. On her left hand she wore a new diamond ring. "Why are your ankles so swollen, Mom?' Maxie asked, hooked.

"Must be from sitting in one place for so long. And besides, it's time for my diuretic. That bald bastard wouldn't stop for a rest. And I had to pay for all the tolls!"

"I thought he was such a dear."

"Some dear. He can rot in hell for all I care!"

"Who are you talking about, Mom?" Maxie was confused.

"His vile mouth wouldn't stop saying things about my Toby." Sarah was still rubbing her feet.

"Like what?"

"Oh, that she's a . . . he's . . . *ach*, never mind. Do you want some coffee too?" Sarah had dropped the charge into muddy waters; she'd wait for a propitious time to detonate it.

"No, but I wouldn't mind falling asleep for a while. The pain is coming back."

"How much longer do you plan to stay in bed, Max?"

"Another day, maybe two. That's all," Maxie assured her, feeling accused.

"Well, listen, Max, I need to talk to you about your father."

"Can't it wait until tomorrow?" Maxie asked wearily, eyeing her mother's new ring. *She's not wasting a precious heartbeat, is she? And look at the size of that new rock on her finger. Their last fight must have been a humdinger!*

"I came down here to get away from him. I hate him with every inch of me. I want a divorce." Sarah, on stage again, paused to see if she had acted well, if her lines were spoken with the right pathos.

"I thought you came to see your grandson," Maxie answered, hurt.

"Yes, yes, of course I did. And he's darling. But in the meantime, I need to find a way out of this hell I live in. I have no life, no joy, nothing." Sarah sniffed.

"What about Toby and Stu? What about us? I wouldn't call that 'nothing.' "

"I knew you wouldn't help me, I knew it!" she cried.

Maxie had learned over time that she was expected to observe, to absorb Sarah's anguish, to hate Philip as much as her mother did.

"What do Toby and Stuart have to say about all of this?" Maxie asked, wincing as sharp pain flared along the line of her episiotomy.

"That *putz* is afraid he'll lose his inheritance. He can't fool *me!*"

"How would you support yourself? I mean, Arthur and I can help a little, but we're not exactly rich." Maxie imagined Arthur's reproving words on hearing this suggestion.

"I'll get a job. You know, I used to be a very persuasive saleslady before I married your father. Everybody loved me—nobody would buy a dress without my approval." She smiled, remembering her successes as a single girl, the five-dollar "bonuses" her employer would put into her paycheck envelope for "moving the merchandise," as he called it. "Your miserable father didn't want me to have money of my own. He was afraid that I'd leave him if I did. He was right."

"Maybe you can do it again," Maxie said, stifling a yawn.

"You know, Max," Sarah sighed, "I've tried. I had a second child, thinking that if I gave him a son, that boy would save my marriage. Well, obviously, you weren't that son. I'm glad you've had one, though. Men want sons. Yours, at least, will have a loving father. Take a nap for a little while. I'll wake you at suppertime."

Sarah left Maxie's room, bypassed the nursery, and went to the kitchen to make coffee. Standing in her stocking feet, staring into the refrigerator, Sarah called to Arthur. "There's nothing to eat in here, Arthur. How did you expect me to prepare dinner when there's nothing to make it with? What have you been eating?"

"Liver and onions, Mom. There's still some in the freezer, left over from Thanksgiving. Want some?" Arthur was trying to be facetious, but Sarah took him seriously.

"You know I have high blood pressure. What are you trying to do, poison me?"

"I'll get some Chinese food to take out. What'll I order for you?" Arthur refused to answer the question; he didn't want to lie.

"See if they have egg foo yung and some fried rice. Haven't had that in so long. I'll treat myself, just this one time."

Philip called at six thirty. From her bedroom, Maxie could hear Sarah shouting, "No, she's not well enough to talk to you! It looks like she's going to need me to stay much longer than I planned. So, do you miss me?" A long pause preceded her thunder: "Well, then, you can kiss my ass!" After slamming the phone down on its hook, she stormed into Maxie's room. "That was your very concerned father—so concerned that he sends me with that son-of-a-bitch Stuart. I asked him, 'Do you miss me?' And, believe me, Max, I was just kidding around with him. 'I'll have to think about it,' he says."

"Maybe he was just kidding around with *you,*" Maxie reasoned.

"Like hell he was. He's going to kill me, I swear it!" Holding her hand to her chest, she added, "I need to go lie down. Have Arthur make up my bed, will you?"

***

Despite the two tranquilizers she took at eleven o'clock, Sarah could not fall asleep. Although weary from the long ride to Delaware and of Stuart's insufferably boorish conversations, she tossed and turned, doing battle with unrelenting night sweats—those assaults of internal combustion that reminded her, mercilessly, that she was losing ground—losing whatever precious control she thought she had over nature, her own destiny, to the hungry worm of time. The steady hum of the refrigerator kept her company; the punctuated clicking of the kitchen clock ticked off the last of her performances onstage—her last curtain call before the lights dimmed, went out. Sarah could hear the skipping beats of her heart, feel her pulse quickening, as she rode each wave of heat and flush, dampness, then chill; her burning cheeks struggled to find a cool, dry spot on the sheets of her lumpy sofabed. Sarah ran the back of her hand across her forehead, wiped the back of her neck, her throat, the groove above her lips where drops of moisture collected. Reaching under her blue satin negligee, she felt the wetness on her body, touched the give of once-firm skin, the now slippery looseness of aging flesh. Using her nightgown, Sarah mopped the beads of perspiration that trickled down between her breasts.

Slowly, inexorably, Sarah's hand reached down to rest where no man had been for twenty-five years, and she moaned. Holding herself, she rolled over onto her stomach, aching not with desire, but with the memory of it. And as she did so many times before, Sarah wept and trembled, until there was nothing more to feel—nothing left but her constant shame.

Late into the night, Sarah rose from the bed, her nightgown clinging to her like a blue blotter, her hair matted, sticky. Guided by the dim night-light in Alden's bedroom, she groped her way in toward his crib, looked down on her grandson, in innocent sleep—his pink toes peeking out from under his yellow terry cloth gown, a bubble of saliva on his baby lips. Sarah breathed in his clean smell of soap and baby powder. She was moved by such freshness, marveled over the little life so fragile, so untouched by the dirt of living. Leaning over the side rail of the crib, Sarah tenderly stroked Alden's fuzzy head and whispered, "Sleep, my sweet, beautiful boy. Had you truly been mine, things would have been different. *You* would have protected me . . . loved me." Sarah squeezed her eyes shut, hoping to hold back a flood of tears. Alden stirred, and Sarah withdrew her hand. "You will come to hate me, too," she said, her voice low and raspy, her heart trapped in a tightening vise, "just like all the rest. It's just a matter of time. They think they know me. They don't know diddly squat!"

At that moment, Sarah sensed that someone else was in the room. Turning to the door, she gasped, brought her hand up to her throat. Caught in her anguish, she sucked in the air that had held her words.

"Mom? Is something wrong?" Arthur asked. "I thought I heard Alden whimpering."

"No, no—nothing's wrong," Sarah protested, modestly turning away from the light and Arthur's view of her so exposed. "I was just checking on him, that's all."

"Well, OK. Good-night, then." Arthur yawned and retreated into the darkness.

"Good-night," Sarah said, relieved that the show would go on tomorrow as scheduled.

•12•

The next morning, Sarah was up early, making noise in the kitchen. Arthur was due back at the clinic and was up early anyway. Maxie would have preferred to sleep a little longer—it was going to be a long day, for sure. Arthur declined breakfast, telling Sarah his stomach was upset from last night's meal. "I offered to make you supper, but you wanted Chinese. Here's a list, Arthur. On your way home this evening, stop at the commissary and pick up a few things for the rest of the week." Arthur was all too glad to leave for work. Kissing Maxie, he gave her some warning: "Don't promise her anything, honey—just listen. We'll discuss 'the divorce' when I get home. Can't wait!"

"Wish I could go with you," Maxie smiled wanly.

Surprisingly, Sarah did not talk about Philip for the whole day. Instead, she busied herself in the kitchen, dusted and vacuumed the apartment, fielded phone calls from Maxie's friends, brought meals to Maxie's bed on a tray and tended to Alden when he cried. Her mood seemed to have improved. Maxie could hear her singing along with the radio, washing the dishes. Later in the day, Maxie asked Sarah if she would bring Alden to her for a while.

"Let him be, Maxie. He needs to sleep." Sarah advised.

"Mom, tell me. Why do you hold Alden only when he cries or wants his bottle?" Maxie asked.

"Oh, Max, you know I'm not very good around babies, especially boys," Sarah admitted.

Whom are you good with? Maxie wondered.

Arthur came home loaded down with groceries. Sarah's list had been specific. Canned tuna had to be "solid white," no store-brand mayonnaise. As for the chicken, it had to be a "pullet that's quartered for soup." Sarah and Arthur unpacked the bags together, putting all the items on the cabinet shelves or in the refrigerator, exchanging pleasantries as they worked. "How was your day, Arthur? Was it difficult getting back into the routine?" Sarah asked.

"Actually, everything went fine—no problems. And yours?" Arthur was testing, not sure about his read on Sarah's softened mood.

"Just fine too. We all had a good day. Maxie will be up and feeling much better once I get some of my homemade chicken soup into her. She'll be 'good as new,' as we say." She was smiling; Arthur was suspicious. "I'll be back in a minute, Mom. I want to see Maxie and Alden."

"Sure, sure, take your time. I've got what I need to keep me busy here. Holler if you need anything."

Arthur entered his bedroom to find Maxie holding Alden, looking content. "Hi, hon. Am I dreaming, or are things really going as well as they appear?" He took Alden from Maxie and put him up onto his shoulder, patting the back of his pajamas.

"I'm as surprised as you are, Arthur. I don't know what caused the sudden turnaround, but who's complaining?"

"She's making chicken soup and brisket. Maybe she's calmed down and reconsidered." Arthur was sounding hopeful, but he was feeling anxious—the way he did whenever Sarah abruptly changed course and threw him off balance. "Well, let's enjoy it while it lasts!"

It lasted until after dinner. Sarah had worked hard and had prepared a delicious meal. "Nobody makes chicken soup like Sarah

Kahn," she boasted, as Arthur leaned over his bowl and spooned up the last drops of soup and stray noodles.

"You outdid yourself, Mom," Arthur complimented Sarah, as they cleaned up together. Sarah then went to get Maxie's tray. She, too, had enjoyed her first good meal in weeks.

"Thanks, Mom. It was delicious. I'm feeling better already," she fibbed.

Maybe it was her wry little smile; maybe it was the cold, glassy look that suddenly crept into Sarah's eyes; maybe it was Maxie's imagination. A change had taken place in Sarah's demeanor. She appeared to stiffen, to harden. "When I finish in the kitchen, Max, I want to talk to you and Arthur about my leaving your father. I've had the whole day to think about it, and, with or without your help, I'm going to get rid of that worm—once and for all." Sarah turned on her heels and left with the tray. Maxie's mouth remained open, but no words escaped. *I shouldn't have said I was better, damn it!* She scolded herself.

True to her script, Sarah summoned Arthur to Maxie's side and pulled the rocker up close to the bed. Looking genuinely fatigued, Sarah began to outline her plan of action. "First," she said, placing her right index finger against the left one, "I need to find a place to stay. Second, I need to find a job. Third, I need for you to get me your lawyer friend Ken to tell me what my legal rights are and how to go about this thing." Arthur and Maxie were struck by the lack of emotion, the absence of expletives, and, by the cool, methodical presentation of her thoughts as she let her right finger rest on the third finger of the opposite hand. There was no great drama, no theatrics. A rational plan had been set forth; a convincing argument had been made.

Arthur looked at Sarah intently, trying to detect a ruse. "We'll do what we can for you, Mom, but you have to be serious about going through with all the legal technicalities before I bring Ken into this."

"Arthur, do you think for one minute that I *enjoy* begging for your help?" Sarah shot back.

"No, I don't suppose you do," Arthur reluctantly agreed.

"Are you still going home on Sunday?" Maxie asked.

"Yes, I need to take care of a lot of loose ends. I'm determined to do it this time. We can take care of business over the phone, all right?" Appearing satisfied, mission completed, Sarah got up from the rocker and prepared to leave the room. "What time will you be taking me to the airport, Arthur? I have to let Philip know. Wouldn't want him to be suspicious of anything."

"Your flight is scheduled for two o'clock. We need an hour or so to get there, so let's plan on leaving around noon. Will Philip be picking you up at the airport in Rhode Island?" Arthur was still reeling from Sarah's rapid-fire delivery—the dispassionate, set-in-stone expression on her face.

"Yes, he knows not to ask Stu to do it. I've made that very clear to him. Good-night." When Maxie was certain that Sarah was out of earshot, she said to Arthur, "Has she been talking to Philip all this time? When did she tell him not to ask Stu?"

Arthur shrugged, fell back on the pillows, closed his eyes, and groaned, "Who knows?" Maxie leaned her head against the backboard, folded her arms across her chest, and tried to figure out where she could find a genie to grant Sarah's three wishes. Alden was whimpering in his sleep and starting to show signs of colic.

***

As arranged, Philip was waiting for Sarah at the airport baggage claims. He had promised himself that he would be patient, that he would ask Sarah calmly why Maxie refused to speak to him when he called. Chain-smoking in the airport lobby, he watched the monitor that would signal the arrival of Sarah's flight, that would bring back the woman he both loved and despised.

"You have no idea what a mistake I made going down there, Philip," Sarah began, almost as soon as she closed her car door. "They treated me like a servant, giving me orders to cook this, to clean that, to wipe up their kid's messes!"

"So why did you stay so long?" Philip asked.

"And they give me this bumpy pull-out bed to sleep on, expecting me to get up every time the baby whimpered in his sleep. Maxie sat on her ass and let me do everything. You'd think they'd at least offer to pay for my airfare back!" Sarah's tirade lasted all the way home. Philip never got an answer to his question—not that it really mattered.

•13•

As Arthur pulled up to the side entrance of the Sheraton Centre Towers, Maxie rubbed her eyes, stretched and yawned. "Hon, wake up—we're at the hotel." Arthur was weary from the six-hour drive. "It's three o'clock. Want to grab something to eat before we go upstairs? Don't forget we have our own wine too," Arthur pointed out.

"No, I'm not all that hungry right now—just a little tired. But the wine sounds like a good idea. If I know Jacques, he'll have something for us to snack on."

Jacques, the doorman, recognized the Lanes immediately, and they him. With quiet efficiency, he took immediate charge of their car and luggage. Separatist agitation in Montreal was having a serious impact on tourism. Americans, in particular, found the French-speaking service employees both rude and arrogant. Jacques, however, disassociated himself from this campaign of exclusion and was protective of his special relationship with the Lanes—he was courteous and gracious. Arthur was appropriately generous with tips. Tall, thin, with delicate features, except for a sharp, bird-like nose, Jacques was an attractive young man who practiced his functions like a diplomat. His small, oval mouth and rosy cheeks reminded Maxie of the wooden soldiers in the *Nutcracker Suite*. All Arthur and Maxie had to do was to find the elevator. Jacques took care of everything else, including the bucket of ice he sent up to their room. Arthur slipped the key into the slot and opened the door. Putting her purse on the king-size bed, Maxie spied a small basket of fresh apples, pears, and bananas set out on the bureau with fine linen napkins and crystal stemware. A little welcoming note from the management was tucked inside the basket.

From the large windows that faced the stately Laurentian Mountains, Maxie looked out on the panorama of a city she loved—a city where old-world charm blended with fashionable, modern elegance. The political climate notwithstanding, Montreal to her was like a good marriage, where past and present respected each other's freedom of and need for expression. Maxie swung her suitcase onto the baggage stand next to the closet and began to unpack. Arthur, exhausted from driving, had other ideas. Uncorking a wine bottle, he poured two glasses and set out some of the cheese and crackers they had purchased in Burlington. He then went over to the bed and pulled back the floral chintz bedspread, draping it over one of the armchairs near the window. "I'm lying down for a few minutes," he informed Maxie. "Want to join me?"

"As soon as I get these things out of the bags, Arthur. They're probably all wrinkled by now." Maxie answered over her shoulder, not turning around to see that Arthur had already undressed. Struggling with the suitcase zipper, she was unaware that he was lying on the cool, white sheets—his head propped against oversized pillows.

"Come on over here, Maxie. That can wait. I can't," Arthur called from behind her. He sipped his wine impatiently. "Can I interest you in some wine and some other goodies?"

"Arthur, this zipper just won't. . . ." She turned and blushed at her own stupidity. "I'm such a jerk, Arthur." Seconds later, her clothing lay on the carpet where it fell, leaving a trail that led to Arthur's side.

"That's not like you," he teased.

"Maybe it's more like me than you think."

"I don't want to think. I want to love you." Time and space melded, as their love blurred, then erased the invisible line between what is and what would be.

Later, still entwined, they exchanged the same question and answer that had become ritual. "Where would I be today if we hadn't met and fallen in love?" Maxie asked, the possibilities still nibbling at her.

"I'm sure I don't know that," Arthur said. "What I do know is that we did—that's all that matters." Rolling out of bed, he reminded Maxie, "The Leibs are waiting for our call." Before ducking into the bathroom, he blew her a kiss. Maxie dialed the Leibs's phone number.

"Maxine, you've arrived! We've been waiting impatiently for your call, hoping you weren't all tied up in traffic," Mrs. Leib said, relieved. Not waiting for an explanation for what she considered a delay, she added, "So, you'll come as quickly as possible then?"

"We can be there in about forty minutes, maybe less. We're sorry to have worried you. The traffic was pretty heavy. See you then." Maxie hoped she sounded convincing.

Wrapped only in a towel, Arthur emerged from the shower still damp, smelling faintly of after-shave—his broad, muscular body a statement of strength and discipline. Maxie was able to survive her persistent panic attacks, her frequent bouts of depression, enveloped in both. Arthur's strength flowed into her like a potent current of hope and validation. Maxie hugged him tightly.

"Careful there, sweetheart. I don't want to take another shower just yet." Maxie released him. "All right, my turn. We're expected within the hour."

***

Jacques was waiting with their car, protective and officious in his gray flannel uniform, his gray and burgundy cap tilted slightly to the right. Silver buttons shone like medals on the front of his jacket; light reflected off the polished black surface of his shoes. Opening the car door, he smiled warmly, "*Bonsoir,*" he said. "*Merci,* Jacques," Arthur replied. "We'll be back late tonight. Hope to see you then." Pleased, Jacques bowed and waved them off. Once onto Avenue René Lévesques, they were able to make the drive to the Leibs's west-side condominium in less than ten minutes. In the antefoyer Maxie picked up the house phone and dialed the code number.

"Is that you, my travel-weary friends?" Mrs. Leib asked.

"We're here," Maxie responded.

"Come on up. We'll be waiting at our door."

Inside the spacious, mirrored lobby, Maxie and Arthur turned right at the marble columns and stepped inside the elevator. As they ascended to the third floor, they smiled at one another, knowing what to expect. Alighting from the elevator, they spied Dr. Leib at the entrance to his apartment, his arms opened wide, beaming with genuine pleasure. Dressed in a tan linen jacket, dark-brown trousers, and one of his trademark bowties, he called out to them, "*¡Saludos, hijitos!* Come in, come in!" As the Lanes approached, "Papa Leib," as he referred to himself, embraced them, planting kisses on their cheeks in the European fashion. Within seconds, Mrs. Leib joined them, wiping her hands on a colorful hand-woven apron from Chile, smiling effusively, and taking her turn to embrace her guests. Maxie handed Dr. Leib a large box of assorted chocolates bought at a candy factory in Burlington. For Mrs. Leib she had bought preserves and some Vermont maple-mustard.

"Again you bring us gifts, Maxine. You really must stop spoiling us!" Mrs. Leib protested. Dr. Leib had already opened his chocolates. Licking his lips, he winked at Maxie.

"Come in, please," Mrs. Leib insisted, motioning toward the living room. "How good it is to see you. Why, you look just splendid, just marvelous, both of you!"

"You look equally splendid," said Arthur.

Always the philosopher, Dr. Leib asked with a twinkle in his eyes, "Do you know the three stages of life, Arthur?"

"No, I don't," Arthur replied, although he did.

"First, there is youth. Then, there is maturity. Then comes, 'you're looking good!' So thanks for the compliment, my boy!"

They all laughed and entered the large living room. A golden ribbon of rippled sunlight bathed the room in fluidic peace. All about were articles of memorabilia brought back from years of travel abroad. The paintings, artifacts, sculpture, all spoke to the fascinating worlds the Leibs had explored together. As a renowned scholar and lecturer, Dr. Leib could not keep up with the constant requests for personal appearances at universities and academies worldwide. That he would make the time to spend with Maxie and Arthur was as much an honor as it was a tribute to their unique friendship—a testimony to the endearing qualities of a man of great humility, a man never altered by his fame. "Fame," he had said, "does not select you—you must want to seek it." Some of the most distinguished writers, essayists, and outstanding thinkers of their generation—from North America, Latin America, and Europe—had sat in these same seats that Maxie and Arthur were about to occupy. And, for Maxie and Arthur Lane, the tenor of the Leibs's hospitality would be no less indulgent, the scope of their generosity no less circumscribed.

"May I offer you some sherry?" Dr. Leib asked, guiding his guests to the sofa.

"Thank you. I'd love to join you." Arthur sat down on the sofa, crossed his legs, and straightened his tie. Maxie shook her head in the affirmative to indicate her desire for the sweet, redolent sherry, undoubtedly from Jerez, Spain. Mrs. Leib scurried off to the kitchen to bring in the *tapas*, a variety of little snacks and appetizers.

"Oh, no thank you," Maxie said to Mrs. Leib's offer to try the guacamole dip. "I'll need to save my appetite for dinner."

"Are you still eating like a little bird, Maxine? Don't you know that you need nourishment to subsist?" Mrs. Leib asked.

"I'm not as active as I should be," Maxie explained, "and I really do have to watch what I eat." *I'm starting to fill up already. Who needs food?*

Leaning back in her chair, pressing two fingers to her right temple, Mrs. Leib arched her eyebrows and gave Maxie a disapproving look. "So, tell us, what's happening with Ashley and Rachel? Are they looking forward to college? And what's Alden up to these days?" she inquired.

"They're all doing fine," Arthur stated, "this week."

"Don't be surprised if the girls begin to try your patience," Dr. Leib counseled. "I'm sure they feel a little anxious about the unknown."

"I think they're a little apprehensive," Maxie answered, adding, "ambivalent about leaving, I guess." She wondered about her own misgivings.

As they continued talking about children and the age-old challenges of raising them, Mrs. Leib asked, "How do you manage to escape the inevitability of being blamed for the consequences of every poor choice they make?"

"We don't," Arthur said. "We just hope for a time when they'll own up to their mistakes and take responsibility for their actions."

"Spoken like a true but idealistic parent," Dr. Leib remarked.

"What I always say is: expect the worst, and hope for the best!" Mrs. Leib's comment was said in jest, but Maxie detected something more subtle—a tinge of skepticism in her voice perhaps.

Dr. Leib's reproving gaze was quick, furtive; but Maxie saw the intent and immediately caught the nuance of his stiffening. "Is dinner ready, my love? No doubt our guests are ready to sample your culinary treasures this evening."

"I'm ready whenever you are. Please, everyone, be seated at the table." Mrs. Leib's tone was affable, no less enthusiastic; she had gotten the message. "I'll serve the gazpacho. Maxine, would you care to help me?"

Maxie cleared the napkins and glasses from the marble cocktail table. Arthur carried the dip and crackers to the kitchen, making a mental note to ask Maxie later if she had picked up on something unusual in Mrs. Leib's demeanor. Mrs. Leib handed bowls of the cold tomato soup to Maxie. "Gazpacho is nutritious and delicious, Maxine. I expect you to have seconds!" The twinkle returned to her eyes. Maxie could relax again.

After dinner, the men adjourned to the living room. Maxie helped clear the table as Mrs. Leib squirted some detergent into the sink and ran the hot water. As Maxie handed her the dishes, Mrs. Leib submerged them in the sudsy water. Rolling up the sleeves of her ruffled, long-sleeve blouse above her elbows, she plunged her hands into the sink and began to wash the dishes. Maxie stood to Mrs. Leib's right side, dishtowel in hand, observing out of the corner of her eye. There was a long silence during which Maxie watched, and Cora Leib hummed some Gershwin melody *sotto voce.* Steam rose from the sink as Cora scoured the stubborn residue from a roasting pan; a strand of raven hair slipped down in front of her eyes and hung like a long, black question mark. Beads of perspiration trickled down her right cheek, turned left at the corner of her pursed mouth, and came to rest in the tiny hollow of her upper lip. She turned, wiped her forehead with her right forearm, and caught Maxie staring at her.

"What? Oh, I'm sorry, Maxine. I lost myself in the warm bubbles!"

"I didn't mean to stare. It's just that. . . ." Maxie stopped short. She, too, had gotten lost.

"Just what?" Mrs. Leib, asked casually.

"You are . . . so . . . beautiful," Maxie whispered, turning away to conceal her embarrassment.

"Oh, come now," Mrs. Leib laughed, flattered nonetheless. After shutting off the faucets, she wiped her hands on a dishtowel.

"I've wanted to tell you that for years," Maxie confessed. "Just now, I . . . needed to say it." Maxie sat down at the small kitchen table, shocked by her brazen confession.

"Well, thank you. I'm flattered." Mrs. Leib was blushing as she sat down at the table and patted Maxie's hand. "Maxine, tell me what's on your mind. Is it your mother?"

She knows already, Maxie thought. "It's been over six years," she answered, tentatively.

Mrs. Leib had thought about how she would broach the subject since her phone conversation with Maxie. She had decided that she had to tread lightly, to move slowly. She was not going to serve up Maxie's past on a platter—small bites at a time might make the details more digestible. "You seem absorbed, distracted, my dear. What is it?"

"I'm having trouble putting things into perspective, I guess. And something keeps gnawing at me from inside. I feel a queasiness almost all the time."

"Are you worried about something?" Mrs. Leib tried.

"Not exactly. I mean, I want to get on with my life, but can't—something is holding me back."

"Like what?"

"Actually, I was hoping you could tell *me* that. Whatever it is, I'm scared."

Mrs. Leib got up from the table and poured herself a glass of water. "You were always plagued by attacks of fear and self-doubt,

Maxine, no matter how illogical. Do you remember way back, right around the time you were finishing up your studies at the university? You put in a desperate phone call to my office, but I was teaching a class at the time. The word that reached me was that you were so distraught, you feared what you might do."

"I remember calling you, but nothing after that," Maxie said, trying to picture that day in her mind.

"You don't? Well, frankly, that surprises me. I dismissed my class, ran to phone you, and insisted that you meet me on Commonwealth Avenue—immediately. I drove there in a frenzy, worried, but trying to control my own anxieties." Mrs. Leib took a long swallow of water, wiped her lips with a napkin. "You were in quite a state when you got into my car, and I honestly didn't know what to do."

"I don't remember anything."

"I just kept driving up and down Route 9, trying to calm you, trying to get you to open up."

"Did I say much?" Maxie could not imagine that she would have.

Mrs. Leib sat down next to Maxie and continued, "All you kept saying was, 'I'm so afraid—I think I'm going to die.' "

Maxie held her breath. She didn't want to move, didn't want Mrs. Leib to stop.

"I took you to our home, insisted you stay with us. All night you kept saying, 'The sharks are going to get me.' What did you mean by that, Maxine? Do you remember, now?"

"No, but my guess is that I was feeling pretty threatened." Maxie rubbed her chin thoughtfully. "I never felt any other way, come to think of it."

"It took me most of the night to calm you down. You wouldn't eat anything, wouldn't drink. You cried until you finally fell asleep in my arms. Now do you recall?" Cora pressed, searching Maxie's eyes with her own. She looked away, remembered how strong her arms had been for this child in danger.

"It's all a blur, so mixed up in my head, really."

"Listen, Maxine, there is more we should talk about. Perhaps you could get away by yourself for a few days. Come up here, and we'll address whatever may be concerning you. This may not be the right time." *When is it?*

"I wish I could, but I've never left Arthur alone. The girls will be going off to school in a few weeks. There's a lot to do."

"I suspect that right now you are feeling some sense of impending loss, my dear. We must address that as well." Cora Leib sounded wistful.

"I'm not sure I understand what you mean by 'loss,'" Maxie replied.

"Well, you know that when the girls leave for college, you're going to be alone again. They are at the same age you were when you first began your still unfinished odyssey into adulthood." Mrs. Leib got up from the table to wipe up the remaining drops of water around the sink, then hung her dishtowel over a wooden peg on the wall.

"Yes, I see," Maxie said, slowly realizing the connection, "but they are going off in far better shape than I did."

"You didn't understand your feelings at the time. You thought everything was the way it was supposed to be—until you got away from the sharks. Are you afraid that your daughters are going to suffer the same agonies you did? Be honest."

"I want them to be happy, that's all."

"Well, that's not within your control, is it? If what we want for our children simply comes true, how will they know what *they* want? Try to relax. Let life happen, my child." Hearing the words, *my child*, Maxie's eyes began to tear. "Maybe this is a good juncture at which to stop. Let's put on some water for tea and join the men.

They seem to be having quite a bit of fun out there." Smiling, she took a reluctant Maxie by the hand and led her into the living room.

In fact, the men were regaling each other in an exchange of familiar, unflattering Yiddish expressions—outrageously insulting epithets used by a generation of immigrant parents. The transition to festivity lightened Maxie's heart. Before anyone realized it, midnight had slipped by them; it was time to part. With the promise that they would return the next morning for brunch, Maxie and Arthur said *adiós*, hugged, kissed, and hugged the Leibs again. They were still waving to each other as Maxie and Arthur stepped into the elevator.

During the silent ride back to the hotel, Maxie savored the afterglow of the evening. Arthur chuckled as he remembered a joke told by Dr. Leib. Later, well into the night, Maxie lay awake, watching the sheer curtain swaying in the breeze of the open window. Without warning, she began to cry. Unable to stem the flow of burning tears, she tried to stifle her sobs by burying her head in her soaked pillow. Feeling wasted, Maxie turned on her back and stared into the darkness with her only clear thought: *I need help.*

•14•

Monday mornings were meant for new beginnings and resolutions. This would be the day for starting again, but not necessarily over. It had been ten years since her last visit with Dr. Weissman. Dialing for an appointment had been difficult—it was the affirmation that Maxie could no longer keep at bay the powerful and destructive forces that were fulminating within.

Choosing what to wear did not seem of primary importance to Maxie, but she wondered if Dr. Weissman would ascribe carelessness to her lack of interest in looking "put together." The only observation he would make, undoubtedly, would be of her now salt-and-pepper hair, actually more salt than pepper. The black-gray areas, though not unattractive, correctly underscored her ambiguity—and, perhaps, her self-contradiction. Light olive skin, though still unblemished, hung more loosely, especially around the mouth. What lay beneath large hazel eyes remained protected; perfidy and betrayal hid behind a bolted gate of denial. The demons stood as sentinels.

As she began to apply her makeup, sparingly and without much thought, she recalled being admonished by Sarah for not using enough blush, for not selecting a vibrant shade of lipstick.

"For heaven's sake, Max, put some color in your cheeks! Liven up that dreary lipstick!" Sarah would criticize. Maxie was feeling a delayed impulse to rebel by forgoing the makeup altogether. More importantly, she was struck by a new thought: *Hmmm—she named me Max and tells me to look more feminine. That's a good one.*

The drive to Dr. Weissman's office provoked tenseness. *Will he see through my calm exterior? Will he eventually succeed in cutting through my defenses? Will I "break" and cry? Will my intellectual agility fail me in time to stave off the deluge?* Maxie was still wondering as she pulled her late model Cadillac into the Medical Center parking lot. Drawing a ticket from the automatic dispenser, she sighed, resigned to letting it happen.

At exactly 2 P.M., Dr. Weissman opened his door and greeted her. He offered his hand in welcome and smiled—warmly, genuinely pleased to see her.

"Come in, Maxine. You're looking well. How nice to see you again."

Maxie smiled, extended her hand to him, and repaid the compliment. Trying not to be conspicuous, she took in the familiar surroundings. With some very minor additions and a new coat of gray paint, the room was comforting in its sameness. The long, graceful mahogany desk was where she had last seen it; the carpeting, though clean, was a little worn. She speculated on how many pairs of anxious feet had carried desperate souls across this carpet. She remembered how often she crossed and recrossed her long legs, sometimes sliding them forward and back, forward and back. With some surprise, she saw that the ten years had not been so kind to Dr. Weissman; but, Maxie found comfort in the one constant—he was still short.

When both were seated—Dr. Weissman behind his desk and she in a comfortably upholstered floral armchair positioned before him—he merely sat back, arched his fingertips in a tent-like fashion, and waited for her to begin. "Anytime you're ready, Maxine," he said.

"Dr. Weissman, I'm here because I simply can't get out from under this leaden pall of sadness that has descended on me. I feel obsessed with some nameless fear, and . . . I cry a lot," Maxie almost blurted out.

While listening, Dr. Weissman would half-close his eyes, appearing indolent and about to fall asleep, only to startle his patient with a keen alertness to nuance or evasiveness. "Can you try to pinpoint when you first became aware of this 'pall?'"

"I've been spending countless mornings at the lake, drawn there by a strange magnetism. I find myself thinking about my past. I become agitated and angry." She wondered if this sounded clinically routine.

"Tell me about your family. How are the children? Arthur?"

Maxie was a bit surprised by what seemed like circumlocution. "Arthur is quite fine, very busy and content with his work. Our marriage is still strong. He's supportive of me, still incredibly patient. Although often he cannot understand my state of mind, he does try to validate my feelings. As for the girls, well, they're off to college in September. We're both dealing with the ambivalence of our feelings, knowing how much we'll miss our daughters, while somewhat guiltily looking forward to being alone. Of course, we're concerned about the transitions to a freer, less controlled lifestyle, but we're resolved to deal as we're dealt. Alden is happily ensconced in a new government job, entirely classified, so I couldn't begin to tell you what he does. I simply don't know." A perceptible little smile formed on Maxie's face. The tight lines around her mouth relaxed; the furrowed brow and the hard edges with which she had entered were softening, as they invariably did when she thought about her children.

"I'm delighted to hear that your family is doing so well, Maxine. You've worked hard, I'm certain, to ensure stability and wellness in your children. Of course, we don't always succeed, nor are we given any guarantees. What matters always is the trying. The hard and often unrewarding work that goes into parenting doesn't always yield the expected results. I suspect you know what I'm getting at. It was when we talked about *your* mother-child relationship ten years ago that you precipitously bolted from this office." Dr. Weissman sat forward and pushed his tortoise-shell half-glasses further down his nose, almost to the tip. He looked at Maxie over the rim, locking her with a penetrating gaze, testing her.

Maxie had wondered not *if* but *how* Dr. Weissman would get around to her cowardly disappearance. He was not admonishing her, thank goodness, but neither was he wasting any time in moving toward what they both knew had been the catalyst of her breakdown of courage.

"I'm ashamed of my immaturity. When it came down to fight or flight, Doctor, I chose the easy way out," Maxie apologized.

"I want to stand for the reality," he said, leaning even more forward, resting his arms on the desk, "that despite your keen intelligence and ability to analyze, there are dimensions to your psyche that, at present, you cannot scrutinize properly. Your inner vision is colored by your fears, and there's considerable risk in trying to go through life behaving in ways that are the consequence of faulty assumptions. The need to protect ourselves from further hurts often supersedes our need to know the truth. That is why you come here." Dr. Weissman removed his glasses and lay them on the desk. "I can't protect you from the hurts, Maxie, but I can help you to accept the realities of them and, hopefully, to encourage you to break your bondage to those faulty assumptions. There's nothing to be ashamed of. Your coming here is a courageous step toward wellness. You owe that to yourself." Dr. Weissman was not playing around.

Maxie was looking into a face that was intent and earnest. Dr. Weissman did not soft-pedal. His reputation for directness was well-known and often criticized within the medical community. She knew, however, that dancing around the campfire of her issues was not her style either; duplicity and misrepresentation had driven her back to this room. She appreciated his honesty.

"I'm here for the duration, Doctor," letting him know she understood the meaning of his words. "I'm committed to finding some peace, even if it requires some fierce mental warfare. I'm prepared to do battle." *And what a battle it's going to be,* she told herself.

"Good, then. Why don't you pick up where we left off?"

Unexpectedly, spontaneously, Maxie began to talk about her second pregnancy.

"Dr. Weissman, of the various and sundry ruses, capers, and plots that Sarah has devised, all of them clever and calculated to hurt me, there are two that I cannot get beyond. My anger toward Sarah is destroying me—it makes me feel that I've lost my mind. There are moments when I wish either she or I were dead." Having confessed, Maxie felt the heat rise up from her neck to her face; she was flushed. Observing her color, Dr. Weissman injected, "Maxie, often things lost become more precious to us and are worth the pain of rediscovery. Free up the truth and allow that anger to flow in a more appropriate direction."

Maxie, calmed by his reassuring voice, began the unpleasant task of relating her story.

"When I discovered I was pregnant for the second time, I called Sarah to let her know. I figured she'd be thrilled, but would tell me not to reveal the fact to anyone before I was fully three months into the pregnancy. The little superstitious request wouldn't be too much of a burden to me. When Sarah answered the call and I told her my news, she demanded to know why I had gone and done something 'so stupid.' I asked her why she wasn't happy for me. Her answer was that *she* wouldn't have gotten pregnant again, considering all the problems of the first pregnancy. Then she asked me why I couldn't be content with just one. I was outraged, but I kept my disappointment to myself. I promised not to say anything about my 'condition' to anyone before three months had elapsed. After warning about the perils of salt—what she believed was the culprit behind the toxemia—she informed me that her blood pressure was 'sky-high,' and that her doctor was concerned about her escalating cholesterol levels. I knew how regularly Sarah cheated on her so-called low-salt, low-fat diet, but decided not to antagonize her."

"That was probably judicious," the doctor offered.

"I just told her to keep doing whatever her doctor recommended and to be careful. Sarah begged off, with a 'gotta go now.' She said she was getting a migraine, and did I want her to tell my father about the pregnancy. Seeing no reason why Sarah would ask this, I told her 'by all means.' She reminded me that Philip was peculiar about 'these things.' I let it drop. She could tell him if she wanted to. I really didn't care what his reaction would be."

"You didn't?" Dr. Weissman asked, puzzled.

"No, Philip didn't like to talk or think about sex as it might apply to his daughters. I think he thought that Arthur slept in the bathtub, or something stupid like that." Neither Maxie nor the doctor could repress their smiles. He leaned back in his chair and put the heel of his left shoe on his right knee; Maxie privately admired his stylish, patterned socks. "As you know," she continued, "I fell in my fourth month and tore the ligaments in my pelvis that are supposed to support the fetus. Painful at first, it soon became imperative that I stay off my feet. By the sixth month, still not knowing that I was carrying twins, I was no longer able to walk nor to lie flat on my bed. I was given an ultimatum by my doctor: stay put, preferably in a reclining chair, or be admitted to a hospital. I was fitted with a type of girdle that restrained movement, yet provided support—much-needed support for the weight I was carrying. I agreed—no, solemnly promised—that I would leave the chair for bathroom privileges only. It was set up in our living room, and it was from that chair that I said 'good-bye' to Arthur every morning at seven o'clock, and from there that I greeted him every evening at 6:30 when he returned."

"Seeing you confined like that must have been difficult for Arthur," Dr. Weissman interjected. "Did he ever complain or share his feelings about that with you?"

"No. Arthur never complains, Doctor. He would just smile and kiss me, but I could see the sadness in his eyes." Arthur's sadness distressed her more than her own. She could still feel it.

"Go on, Maxie."

"Sarah, in an uncharacteristic gesture of goodwill, came to take care of me, Arthur, and Alden. Looking back on it now, I can see that as difficult as it was for me, my limitations gave Sarah an opportunity to feel useful and needed. My dependence also provided her an unprecedented six weeks away from Philip, now an apparently unessential factor in her life. With a grand display of martyrdom and sacrifice, though delighted to be free of Philip's daily annoyances, Sarah arrived. She cooked, cleaned, and tended to Alden, who was then three years old. Practically speaking, the arrangement worked well—until that sixth week.

"On a very cold afternoon in March, approximately two weeks before my anticipated delivery date, I heard Sarah and Alden in some kind of argument. Alden was begging Sarah to go outside to play with him. Sarah never played with her own children, so this was already contention in the making. There was snow in the backyard and the front walk was very icy, so I fully understood Sarah's rejection of Alden's proposal. I could hear strained, raised voices, and could sense that Alden was being unreasonable—as a three-year-old can be. Sarah flatly refused Alden's demands. 'Max, your son wants to go out, and I don't want him to. It's too cold,' she said. I pleaded with my mother not to argue with the child and suggested she offer him something else to do. Hearing my reply, Sarah turned on her heels and said, 'Then *you* deal with him—I've had enough!' She went to her bedroom, slammed the door, and took to her bed. It was then that I heard the front door open, and knew that Alden was on his way out. You must understand that we lived at that time on an old, but busy country road with no sidewalks. There was nothing to keep Alden from running into the street and into the path of oncoming cars. A chilling fear coursed my body as I struggled out of the chair. Supporting my sagging midsection with both hands clasped beneath it, literally carrying it in my hands, I cautiously made my way to the door. I watched Alden making his way down the driveway toward the street."

Dr. Weissman picked up his gold Cross pen and began to turn it over end to end, tapping the desk nervously. "You must have been very anxious," he opined, shifting his weight in the desk chair.

"I screamed to Alden, begged him to come inside. But he was adamant. He wanted me to play with him—outside. Doctor, I don't think I've ever been so afraid. My heart was pounding furiously, and my legs felt like wobbling Jell-O. I felt a sudden tearing somewhere in my stomach—a pain so searing, I envisioned both babies dropping out of me, hanging by their cords—dead. With tears stinging my eyes, I pleaded with my son to come in. Then I thought of something that might persuade him. I promised to call my friend Dawn to see if she would come over to play with him. At that time, Dawn had no children of her own. She loved Alden and he adored her. The few seconds that it took to deliberate this final offer seemed an eternity; I felt lightheaded from holding my breath."

"Excuse me for interrupting, Maxie," said Dr. Weissman, "but could your mother hear all of this desperate conversation between you and Alden?"

"Yes, absolutely. We were right outside her bedroom."

"And she still remained holed up in her fortress?" There was disbelief in his voice.

"Yes, she stayed in there for the remainder of the day and evening. Alden agreed to come in, and Dawn did come over, thank heavens. She got me back to my chair and stayed with Alden until Arthur came home. The episode was more traumatic than I realized. That night, with Sarah still behind her locked door and not answering Arthur's entreaties with anything more than, 'Leave me alone,' I went into labor. Arthur had to call Dawn and her husband to watch Alden. He then whisked me into the car atop a pile of towels. Hearing what was transpiring, Sarah emerged from her hiding place and said feebly, 'Good luck.' Forty minutes after arriving at the hospital, the girls were born. I almost lost them, Doctor."

"It seems to me you could have lost all three in one day!" retorted Dr. Weissman.

"I've never gotten over the fact that she *knew of the danger* to my son—yet chose to act so callously. I'll never understand that."

"Well, considering her behavior, is it not conceivable that like her, you wouldn't have had a son, either?"

"What do you mean?" Maxie was breathless.

"Did you not tell me once that Sarah said you were not the son she had wanted—the son that was going to save her marriage?"

"Oh, my God! Could that be true? I thought she was just displaying her usual egotistical, irrational behavior! Then, she really did despise me for failing her!" Maxie was nearing a state of near hysteria, which Dr. Weissman monitored closely; but he wanted Maxie to understand the ramifications of this seemingly deliberate act.

"Maxie, Sarah does not appear to behave rationally. Her actions, however abominable and incomprehensible to you, may originate in an unhealthy mind."

Maxie thought of Anna and all the sisters that Sarah loved, then hated; she had heard so many bitter stories of jealousy and spite.

"So, what happened after the delivery?"

"Arthur called her to tell her that she had two beautiful granddaughters, and, that if she wanted, he'd take her to see them in the morning. Sarah waited until I was being discharged to see my babies. She came, she said, because she would be needed to hold one on the way home. She did exactly that. She held one, sitting stiffly and withholding any emotion. As we arrived home, we spotted Toby's car. She had come to take Sarah home. Sarah had called her the night I went into labor and told her to be at our house to take her home. She had complained that she had been abused—that she needed to be taken to Rhode Island immediately upon our arrival home. Moments after the babies had been placed in their cribs, Sarah said her frigid good-byes, gave me a look of disgust, and left—slamming the door behind her."

"Whew!" exclaimed Dr. Weissman. "Did you have anybody besides Arthur to help you out?"

"Arthur and I were left to do it all. I still couldn't walk without holding onto the wall or onto someone. I had no idea how I was going to manage three little ones when Arthur returned to work. Doctor, would you believe that Sarah called later in the week to let me know that she and Philip would be coming up to visit?"

"Did you allow that?"

"Unfortunately, I didn't think I had a choice. I felt that I should allow my father to see his grandchildren. Who knows why? When they arrived that day, Alden went to the door to greet his grandparents. Sarah brushed by him, went directly to the cribs, picked up one of the girls in her arms and asked, 'So, Max, which one do you love more? You know, every mother has her favorite.'"

Dr. Weissman checked his watch and saw the hour was well past. Bringing the session to a close, he leaned forward, resting his chin on the interlocking fingers of his hands. "Maxie, we must stop here. You've revealed a great deal of what has been giving you pain. Now, allow the anger to rise to the surface. Feel it again—only this time, try to see that Sarah's punishment of you has nothing to do with your deserving it. Let's pick up on that note the next time. Is Thursday all right with you, same time?"

"Yes, fine," she said, rising unsteadily. She was glad to have this session over. She was extremely agitated and wanted to know more about this woman she had called "mother." Dr. Weissman had been right; she *was* a bitch. Leaving the office, she smiled wanly. "See you then. Thank you, Doctor."

"Maxie, if you think you need to speak to me before our next session, please call me. You have my home phone number."

"I'll remember, thank you. Good-bye."

Maxie left the building, but remembered nothing after that. She did not remember how she got herself home, how she had navigated through the sea of cars on the highway, nor how she drove the long, circuitous route that led her through a congested intersection, and, finally, to her driveway. She shuddered, thinking that numbness had guided her home—an act of Providence had spared all the others on the road. Numbness had been her chaperone. She had gone into auto-pilot many years ago, letting some greater force propel her forward onto a path that had no destination, no end point. *It has always been this way,* Maxie said to herself, *around and around. I keep chasing some illusive promise that there will someday be road signs and danger signals that I can spot.* Recently, her daughter Rachel had said, "Mom, I just don't get it."

Maxie had asked, "What is it you don't get, honey?"

"Well, I just don't understand life," Rachel had said, not fully appreciating the magnitude of the generalization.

"Honey," Maxie had answered with delicacy, "there really isn't much to get. Life is, that's all. Sometimes it's wondrous, and sometimes it just plain stinks. There's nothing to be gained from analyzing. What you need to *get* is that we must make every effort to open ourselves up to life—even if we don't happen to like the import of the moment, even if we don't understand what it all means." This exchange with her daughter now weighed heavily on her consciousness. She wondered how much of her own rhetoric—indeed, her sermonizing—placated her or salved her own festering wounds.

Maxie sat in her car for a half-hour before she was aware of a bruise on her right hand. It was turning dark red-blue and was swollen. She must have slammed her fist against the wheel. Frightened by what she had done, she hastened to get out of her car and into her refuge—her home. Depositing her handbag and keys on the kitchen desk, she ascended the stairs to her bedroom. *Truth really wears you out, she thought,* collapsing on her bed. Closing her eyes, she pictured herself standing again at the doorway, pleading with Alden to come in. Suddenly, the profound anger she had not been able to express then ascended as fury. Remembering Dr. Weissman's advice, she allowed the hostage-held feeling to break out of its inner prison, to rise to the surface of her senses. *My mother could've killed my son! . . . This is sick! . . . Punishment . . . her obsession, her only weapon!* A heavy curtain descended before Maxie could ask herself more unanswerable questions. As she slid down the dark shaft of sleep, Maxie heard Dr. Weissman's words echoing: "You were not the son she had wanted . . . like her, you would not have had a son, either." *But I didn't lose him—you lose, Mother—he lived, and made his covenant with God—the God of Abraham, Isaac, and Anna Minsky.*

•15•

Alden's covenant, his Bar Mitzvah, was scheduled for Sunday, the first day of Hanukkah. He would have the honor of lighting the first of the eight candles on the menorah as part of the early-morning ceremony. During the three days that preceded that December 12, fate played a mischievous game; the weather was so exceptional as to be portentous. Temperatures climbed into the high sixties, and sunshine warmed even the most obdurate of hearts. Cloudless skies moved Arthur to joke, "I think I'll take a lounge chair out back and sit by the pool. This is like June in January! Well, December." Sarah Kahn, however, chilled the air around her; a draft of cold air, she snuck under the doors and gave everyone goosebumps.

Alden had studied and rehearsed his chanting of the *Haftarah* for three months with Cantor Lewis. The idea of standing before the congregation of invited guests, of singing the ancient melodies as required by the Scriptures, filled him with the awe for which such ceremony was intended. He had to be coaxed, prodded, cleverly enticed to sing loudly enough to be heard; he was self-conscious and concerned that his voice might make too much of a statement.

"You need to project your voice, Alden," Cantor Lewis insisted. "It's a very lovely voice, and you must not deprive your family and friends of hearing your chanting. Come on now—turn up the volume knob. I promise you your voice will not crack." Cantor Lewis knew thirteen-year-old boys well. Patting Alden on the back, he winked at him, one man to another. For this was the day Alden was to become a man, a newly inducted member of the adult congregation who would have the honor of being counted in the *minyan*—the tenth man on the prayer-team.

On the evening before the event, everyone was ready. Parts were learned, dresses and suits were on hangers hung over the bedroom doors. Shoes, socks, stockings, shirts, ties—even the underwear—were set out so that there would be no morning "Where's my this? Where's my that?" The caterer was set to transform the function hall into a burst of festive color; royal blue tablecloths, striped with red, yellow, and green, would drape fourteen round tables, each accented with balloons of corresponding colors. For the head table, Maxie had chosen white roses. On all the other tables would be mixed arrangements of red anemones; yellow and white hardy mums; birds of paradise; and red, white, and yellow roses. The orchestra had been given a list of "preferred favorites"—Maxie wanted "Gloria"; Arthur chose themes from *Fiddler on the Roof.* There would be the traditional round of dance to "Hava Nagilah" and Alden, man of the hour, would be hoisted up high on a chair held by four strong men. It was meant to be a day of rejoicing and merrymaking.

Although every minute detail had been scrupulously taken care of, Sarah arrived in Shafton a few days early "to help," her euphemism for stirring things up. Actually, she wanted a Saturday afternoon appointment with Maxie's hair stylist, and she needed a "few little things" like pantyhose and cosmetics. She and Philip had flown to Toby's house in Rhode Island for Thanksgiving. Philip, Toby, and her family were to drive up to Shafton on Sunday morning, eschewing the more rational suggestion that they come on Saturday to eliminate the potential for last-minute glitches.

After dinner, stirring her cup of coffee, Sarah began slowly.

"Max, you have no idea how much this affair is hurting me. I'm trying so hard to be happy for you, but for some reason, you and Arthur have decided to stick a knife right through my heart."

Maxie was at the sink, cleaning her wedding band with ammonia and a toothbrush. "What?" she blurted, whirling around to face her mother, her eyes wide open, aflame with disbelief.

"Stu says I have to have my bags packed and be ready at the side door of the synagogue. He says we'll all leave as soon as the ceremony is over." Sarah did not look at Maxie; instead, she studied the wallpaper, as if counting all the blue polka dots in between the vertical rows of pastel irises. "You've done a terrible thing, Max. We were all thinking that maybe we wouldn't come at all."

"What? What did I do? Not come? *All* of you?" Maxie was dumbstruck. She could not move from the sink. Her hands were shaking and she felt like throwing up.

"You invited my sisters. You know I didn't want them here. You know how much Stuart detests them." Sarah was now looking straight at Maxie from behind narrow slits of accusation; her hands were on her hips, demanding, defying Maxie to engage.

"They're your *sisters*, Mom. Why would I not invite them, just because Stu had a falling out with them years ago? What does that have to do with *us?*" Maxie was feeling self-control seep out from every pore. "There's no way I wouldn't invite Aunt Belle—and the others! And, besides, when the invitations went out, you were speaking with them, you were getting along. Why didn't you say anything to me?"

"Things have changed since you sent out the invitations. Stu is my ride back to Rhode Island. We're staying in his house and have to do what he says."

"That's a coward's way out! You knew about all this way before tonight, didn't you?" Maxie's wave of nausea was cresting; the stranglehold of anger tightened around her throat. Arthur entered the kitchen just as Sarah sprang from her chair. He saw and heard the slap she delivered to Maxie's face. He watched in horror as a red blotch appeared where her hand had struck his wife's right cheek.

"Don't you ever talk to me like that!" Sarah screamed. "You're still not too big for me to cut down to size!" Wiping invisible tears from her eyes, she spat, "You're just like your father!" The mother of all insults. Seeing Arthur in the doorway, unable to move, she turned her wrath on him. "I want to go home. I'm not going to take this abuse from you or anyone else. Call me a cab, Arthur."

"I'll do nothing of the kind," Arthur said through clenched teeth. "Home?" he asked. "Isn't that where the heart is supposed to be? Stuart is 'home' to you?—a warm, loving place?"

Sarah swept by him without answering, without glancing at Maxie who stood by the sink, still holding her hand up to her burning cheek.

"We'll deal tomorrow, hon. She won't get away with this, I promise you." He took Maxie by the hand, shut off the kitchen lights, and guided his stunned wife up the stairs.

"What happened, Arthur?" Maxie asked, weakly.

"I haven't got the vaguest notion," Arthur answered, "but, then again, I never do when she acts like this. We should have expected a scene." He suspected there would be more.

They went to bed, but neither slept. Both of them tossed, turned, and punched their pillows. At 6:15 Sunday morning, the phone rang. Maxie answered with trepidation, "Yes?"

"Maxie, it's Toby. There's just no way we can come to the Bar Mitzvah." She was not feigning disappointment.

"Why not, Toby?"

"Haven't you looked out your window? There's a blizzard going on. Dad doesn't want to risk the two-hour drive."

"Is it Dad, or Stuart?"

"Maxie," Toby lied, "we all got up at five to dress—so we could get an early start. But there's a furious storm out there. Didn't you hear the weather reports last night?"

"No, we were thinking more about the storm inside."

"I'm sorry, Max. My kids were really looking forward to it."

"No, they weren't, Toby. You knew you weren't coming long before the storm. Well, fuck you. Fuck all of you. Your mother wants to leave here as soon as possible. You can pick her up tomorrow."

"Are you upsetting her again, Max? Leave her alone, will you? She's a sick woman!" Toby shouted.

Maxie slammed the phone down. Arthur, fresh from the shower, raised the shade. "My God, Maxie, it's snowing like crazy! Where did *this* come from?"

"Toby just called. They're not coming." Sitting down on the bed, Maxie put her head in her hands and began to cry. She wondered how Toby could have learned so soon about her scene with their mother.

"It's all right, hon. Honestly, we'll have a better time without them. Who needs them anyway—those troublemakers. Maybe the storm is a blessing in disguise. And, besides, the Leibs will be there—you can bet on that." Arthur sat down on the bed and took Maxie's hands away from her tear-soaked face. "Better pull yourself together. We both owe it to Alden."

Arthur was the first to come down into the kitchen and, to his amazement, he found Sarah, dressed and ready, sitting at the kitchen table where the previous night's imbroglio had been initiated. She was staring out the glass slider, watching the white curtain of snow that whipped the window in gusts of howling winds. Arthur studied Sarah from the doorway. *Look at her, that witch! I sometimes prefer her anger—if nothing else, it's a feeling.* She had decided to go to the synagogue where she did not know or care how to pray; she would not have to ask forgiveness from a God who, she was convinced, had abandoned her years ago.

"Didn't expect to see you in here," Arthur said, registering his surprise, dispensing with amenities.

"I'll be ready to leave when it's time," Sarah answered, never taking her eyes off the storm.

"Do you want some coffee?" Arthur asked, an incredible twisting in his chest. He had hoped to mollify this woman who could, and probably would, he thought, bring the whole day crashing down on all of them.

"No, you all can have what you like. I'll be in the den. Call me when you're ready." Sarah got up from her chair, pushed it back into place, and walked past Arthur. Premonitions clung to the glass slider window like condensate, chilling the air. Arthur shivered. When Maxie came down, tentatively approaching the kitchen, she asked, "Who were you talking to? I thought I heard voices."

"Your mother. She's ready to leave with us. I offered her coffee, but she said she'd be in the den, waiting." Arthur saw that Maxie's efforts to conceal red, puffy eyelids had failed. There were dark circles under her eyes; she was clenching her teeth. "Let me make you some coffee. We still have some time, in spite of the weather."

"Did she say anything about last night? Is she going with us this morning?" Maxie wasn't quite sure she could get herself to speak with her mother.

"I guess so," Arthur replied, serving Maxie a mug of hot coffee. "Let's just play it by ear. Let her call the shots. The last thing we want is a spectacle in the sanctuary."

Maxie sipped the hot coffee slowly, her eyes focused on the snow. "I'm really tempted to leave without her, to tell her to stay home."

"If you do that, her absence becomes *your fault*, hon. That's the name of her game, remember—put the monkey on someone else's back." Arthur had seen Sarah manage guilt chips like a croupier at a craps table. At that moment, the children entered the kitchen and Arthur changed the subject.

"Good morning, kids. Don't you all look fabulous!" Maxie's cheerfulness seemed hollow, even to herself.

"Mom," Rachel said, "are you, I mean, is everything. . . . What were you and Grammy shouting about last night?"

"This is not a good time for me to explain it, honey, but I promise that I'll try tomorrow. Let's just all put smiles on our faces and do our best to forget about last night."

After coffee, juice, and shared bagels—no one was particularly hungry—they all left for the synagogue. Sarah sat in the back seat with the children, silent. To Arthur's relief, the parking lot had been plowed, the stairs shoveled. He was able to drop his family off at the side door. Nevertheless, covered with the rapidly falling sticky snow, they had to shake their clothing and stomp their feet on the large, black doormat. Maxie's hair was wet. Tight curls were springing up around her hairline, but she did not care what she looked like. Sarah, holding herself erect, undaunted, left to hang up her fur coat in the coatroom. "She's such a bitch," Ashley whispered to Rachel. Rachel gave Sarah the finger behind her back.

Entering the vestibule, Arthur shook the snow from his hair, hung up his coat, and gave the girls a little push toward the sanctuary. "Let's have none of that," he chided. "Here, Alden, put on your *yarmulke*." Arthur put on an identical white sateen skullcap, and both "men" wrapped themselves in the traditional, fringed prayer shawls, reciting the appropriate blessing in Hebrew. Inside the dark, solemn sanctuary, Cantor Lewis was waiting to assist Alden with the laying of the *tefillin*, the wrapping of the hand, forearm, and head with leather straps that held two small boxes containing holy Scripture—one container rested on the center of the forehead, the other was bound in place on the left forearm, close to the heart. *And thou shalt bind them upon thine hands and upon thine heart, and they shall be for frontlets between thine eyes.* Alden smiled at his father as he performed his first act of Jewish manhood. Sarah sat alongside Maxie in the polished oak pew, front row. She did not even look over at her grandson, but instead took out a compact and, ostensibly unimpressed by what she considered an archaic ritual, powdered her nose.

Maxie bit her lower lip, furious at Sarah's indifference. *I just can't believe her! Not even some pride for her grandson. She's hiding behind that damn mirror—too bad she can't see herself.*

As the men took their positions on the *bimah*, relatives and guests began to arrive. Many came over to wish the Lanes *mazel tov* and to extend their best wishes to Sarah as well. She accepted their kind words with a polite detachment, a politeness that caused Dawn to whisper into Maxie's ear, "The Ice Lady cometh?" Maxie grimaced. Sarah's sisters approached, kissed Maxie and the girls, and tried to speak with Sarah.

"*Mazel tov,* Sarah," Belle said, attempting to embrace her sister.

"Get away from me—all of you! I can't believe you would come here to disgrace me!"

"We came here to honor Alden, and to show Maxie and Arthur and the girls how much we love them too. This is their celebration and you're trying to ruin it for them, aren't you?" Belle's disgust was evident in the curl of her lip, the glare of her eyes. "I'll deal with you later," she said, stalking off.

Rabbi Silverstein came forward to the first lectern on the raised platform facing the congregation. Behind him stood the Holy Ark, draped in gold velvet—the lamp containing the Eternal Light hung low, down the center, between two tablets that were a replication of those Moses received at Mount Sinai. Each tablet contained one vertical row of five Hebrew letters, representing the first word of each of the Ten Commandments. At the center of the *bimah*, between the two lecterns, was a basket of artfully arranged, sunny yellow and white mums—a sorely needed touch of warmth on this gloomy day. Alden had taken his place on the altar, settling into the huge, high-backed oak chair with scrolled arms. He looked like a child-king on a throne much too big for him. Dressed in gray wool slacks, a burgundy blazer with matte gold buttons, a white shirt and a tie of geometric designs, and burgundy loafers ("but no argyle socks, Mom, they're too preppy"), Alden sat with both feet planted firmly on the carpet, simultaneously stoic and vulnerable. Looking down to his left, he caught his mother's eye; his were on the verge of a sadness he could not truly understand. Maxie winked at her son, and he forced himself to smile. To Maxie's left sat the Leibs, excited, animated; they smiled, waved, and blew kisses to the family. Maxie noticed that Mrs. Leib had not approached Sarah. *Strange,* she thought.

Rabbi Silverstein looked down at Maxie from behind his lectern. They exchanged a silent, though powerful, moment. His eyes did not seem to be saying, "Rise above, Maxie," or "This, too, shall pass, my child." No, his look had more to do with disbelief than belief, everything to do with being human and feeling another's anguish. He looked at Sarah too. She was studying the tips of her shoes, wet from the snow—expensive shoes that were now ruined and would have to be discarded. She was impassive, her heart set like a steel trap caught in a house of worship that reminded her too much of Anna, too little of Max.

"*Chag Sameach,*" the rabbi greeted the congregation. "Happy Hanukkah to all of you. Please turn to page eight of your prayer-books as Arthur Lane, father of our Bar Mitzvah, Alden, leads us in the morning service." Arthur looked at Sarah, more worried than ever that he would not be able to concentrate on his task. He fought hard to expunge his thoughts of retribution while invoking the name of the Lord.

The storm weakened by ten o'clock. Most of the guests arrived on time, including those from distant states. Alden's voice did not crack once; Arthur's did. To Maxie's chagrin, Sarah did not go up to open the drape of the Ark when called. *Leave it to Sarah to decline such an honor!* Maxie could hear the shock ripple through the rows of whispering guests. Belle stepped forward to silence the whispers, to minimize the disgrace she knew Sarah was causing. Passing Sarah on her way up to the platform, she said under her breath, contemptuously, "You witch!" Sarah smirked. And when the rabbi bestowed the concluding blessings on her grandson, Sarah fled from the sanctuary. Whipping her coat off the hanger in the coatroom, she bolted for the side door to a waiting taxi—an arrangement she must have made sometime during the night. Mrs. Leib watched her running down the corridor and started after her. "Mrs. Kahn, where are you going?" she called out to her in dismay. "You!" Sarah shot back, her word like an icy arrow. As Sarah pushed the heavy side door open, a blast of snow and cold air nearly blew her over. Regaining her balance, she drew the collar of her fur coat closer to her neck and, shoulder to the wind, made her escape.

Maxie did not see her mother leave. She assumed that Sarah had gone to the ladies' room to freshen up. When Sarah did not reappear, Maxie went looking for her, checking the library to see if, perhaps, Sarah had sought a more private room. "She's gone, Maxine," Cora Leib informed her, sadly. "I saw her go out the side door. I'm so very sorry." Maxie started for the door, but was held back by Cora, who put her hands on Maxie's shoulders, turning her around. "Let her go, Maxine. I couldn't stop her, and neither will you."

"Should I call the police? Where did she go? Did she say anything to you?" Maxie babbled frantically.

"No, not exactly. Listen, however upsetting the circumstances are right now, you must not lose your courage, my dear. Your mother has done an abominable thing, but you must go back inside to the party. Your family needs you." Cora let her hands drop by her side, feeling the tension relax in Maxie's shoulders. She took Maxie by the arm and led her into the auditorium, applying gentle pressure at the elbow. "Smile, Maxine. Your guests will take their cues from you."

Maxie fought back tears and forced herself to smile. The cocktail hour was in full swing. Waitresses in black-and-white uniforms were passing trays of beef teriyaki, knishes, potato latkes with applesauce, and stuffed mushrooms. On a long, skirted table there were chopped liver, herring, gefilte fish, vegetable crudites, and salads. At the makeshift bar stood Arthur with Susan and Don. Spotting Maxie, he excused himself from the conversation. The band played a selection of lively European klezmer music, warming up for the next hour of anticipated circle dances. Arthur came up behind his wife, offering her a glass of wine. "You look like you can use this," he said. "What's going on?"

"She's gone, Arthur. Mrs. Leib saw her running out of the building." Maxie took a long swallow of the wine as Cora and Arthur exchanged looks of concern. Intent on not being sucked further into the epicenter of Sarah's storm, Cora thought it best to slip away for a few moments. "You two may want to discuss your thoughts in private," she said. "Please excuse me while I see where my husband is. But I'll be back to check on you," she added.

"I'll be all-right—I think. All of a sudden I'm feeling almost *glad* that she's left!" Maxie confessed. Turning to Arthur, she said, "Come on, let's do what we came here to do."

Maxie's friends told the caterers to quickly and discreetly rearrange the head table. They suggested that the staff remove the place settings for those who would not be present and to plan on packaging the extra meals for the family to take home after the party. Arthur advised the bandleader that Ashley and Rachel would still wheel in the Bar Mitzvah cake, but that their grandparents would not be included in the candlelighting ceremony.

"Do you want to ask someone else to light their candle?" the bandleader asked, innocently.

Arthur thought about asking the Leibs, then decided not to put them on the spot. "No," he answered. "Just play a lot of upbeat stuff, guys, please."

By two o'clock, the storm ended, the sun broke through the clouds, the ice and snow began to melt away. Maxie and Arthur survived the afternoon intact, grateful to their friends and relatives for keeping the spirit of the day alive. At times, Maxie almost forgot how miserable she was. She danced and raised her glass of wine in dozens of toasts. She drank to everyone's kindness, and she drank not to feel. "Be careful, Maxine," Cora Leib warned. "You may regret how much you're drinking." Regret, however, was not what Maxie worried about.

***

As Maxie dreamed, a lone stranger appeared, stood in the starlight of a summer's night. Stars winked and nodded as the luminous, spectral figure spoke to them of elusive truth and of the realities it may sometimes have to hide. The stars nodded their assent as the stranger spoke. "Intentionally, beneficently, time alters and often distorts what we remember as the truth. The longer we are removed from the actual events, the less accurate are our recollections of detail and complexity—less likely are we to be unequivocal in their recounting. In so doing, time softens the razor-sharp edges of certain moments, blunting our memories and modifying our perceptions of their totality." The stars kept on nodding.

The stranger shook his shrouded head; a tear spilled from his hooded eyes. "However," he continued, "the pain inflicted by those thrusts and assaults on our psyches rarely surrenders itself to expediency. Although often camouflaged, pain endures in its original, immutable state. Deep and intractable, pain resides in the soul. It is relentless in its mission to forever bind us to those truths, with no intentions of freeing us from their bondage. As irrefutable evidence that it has been there, pain leaves an indelible ring of residue around our hearts."

Maxie could not recognize the stranger in her dream, but she did understand that later she would meet him in some form, some guise, and he would make her confront those truths—however faulty, however imperfect their reconstruction. Were those truths her real demons? If so, were they so threatening because she could not bear the opening of the casket of her now-dead dreams? How could the cold ashes of her failed attempts to make Sarah love her still singe her so cruelly?

Maxie did not feel at all well and slept past six o'clock, when the ringing of the phone beside her bed rattled her awake.

"Hello."

"Hon, where have you been? Did I wake you? What took you so long to answer?" It was Arthur, disconcerted.

"I'm sorry. I must have been in a very deep sleep. What time is it?" Maxie asked, still groggy.

"It's a little past six. Do you want to go out for something to eat?"

"No, thanks, Arthur. I'll cook you something. I'm not hungry enough to go out."

"Aren't you feeling well, Maxie?"

"I'll be fine. I guess my session with Dr. Weissman shook me up a bit. I'll tell you about it when you get home."

"Sure. I'll be leaving here in about ten minutes. See you soon."

"'Bye, hon." Maxie hung up. Leaning back on the pillows, she wondered if she would have the strength to see this thing through, despite her promise to Dr. Weissman. Again the phone rang; it was Susan.

"Hi, Maxie. How'd it go today?"

"Oh, it was all-right. I think I'm going to have a shitload of work ahead of me."

"Did you show him the letter?" Susan asked.

"No. I never got to it. Maybe next time."

"Listen, Maxie," Susan probed, "did you tell him about your father's funeral?"

"No, I guess that's where we'll pick up next time. Frankly, I'm so wiped it was probably a good thing that the time did run out."

"I'm really glad you decided to go today. I was hoping you would for a long time. You know, Mrs. Leib saved your life once, many years ago, but now you need to take care of it."

"Sue, you're right. I know what I have to do. Can you meet me at Joe's for coffee tomorrow morning? I have a few errands to do, but I also need a little hand-holding." Sue was the best hand-holding friend in the business. Over the twenty years of their friendship, Sue had been there to see Maxie through the worst of times with Sarah. She had been Maxie's surrogate sister when her own memory of Toby had receded to a blurry outline in her imagination. To Maxie and Arthur's children, Sue and her husband Don were family—a bridge that carried them to the other side, to the safer banks of a river perpetually swollen with turbulence.

"Meet me at 9:30 at Joe's," said Susan, "and, Maxie, please don't drink a lot tonight. I know you've been trying to numb your feelings, but you really haven't been looking so great."

"Thanks for the compliment, friend. See you at 9:30. Love to Don."

Maxie went downstairs and poured herself a glass of wine. She knew she was trying hard not to feel. As she began to prepare a frittata for Arthur, she thought about all the wasted years she'd spent obsessing over her mother's inexplicable behavior. *She's so bitter. She must be—what else can explain all the hurtful things she does to me? I can understand her loathing for Philip—well, maybe not. Arthur has a good point when he says that Philip was the way he was because of Sarah. Sadness must have eaten away the same large holes in his soul—maybe he felt as shabby as I do . . . like a street urchin begging pennies from her—charity from the great withholder.* Maxie diced an onion, peeled and sliced two potatoes, and chopped a green pepper. *Susan does her best to help. She means well, but the stranger in my dream was right: pain does reside in the soul—it does leave a ring of residue around the heart. And like Blanche Du Bois, I seem to "always rely on the kindness of strangers."*

With the back side of a knife, Maxie scraped the vegetables into a frying pan and added some olive oil. She placed the pan over a low flame on the gas cooktop.

When the potatoes and onions were tender, she added some chopped broccoli. Four beaten eggs, grated Parmesan cheese, Italian seasonings, and a few tablespoons of water completed the recipe. She covered the pan, adjusted the flame, and sat down at the center island. Braced by another glass of wine, she would get through the ordeal of telling Arthur what had transpired at her therapy session. A good listener and a supportive ally, he would want to know everything about her visit. *I'll be careful not to get dramatic,* she warned herself. *Arthur detests Sarah's theatricality—he deals best with the facts.*

***

Arthur arrived home as Maxie was setting his place at the table. Walking through the mudroom door into the kitchen, he smiled. Putting his attaché case down, he walked over to Maxie and embraced her. Over her shoulder, he spied the half-empty wine bottle, but said nothing.

"Something smells wonderful. A fritata?"

"Uh-huh. I just need to melt some cheese over the top. Want some wine?" Maxie withdrew from their embrace and busied herself at the stove. Inexplicably, she could not look directly into Arthur's eyes. Through Maxie's frequent bouts of depression, Arthur managed to keep her focused and grounded in reality. Only once did he insist that she ignore her instincts. Feeling that it was "right" for her to attend Philip's funeral, he had told her, "Maxie, he was, after all, your father. I wouldn't want you to regret your absence—it's not something you can undo." However well-intentioned and reasonable, Arthur's advice had been a mistake. He could not have estimated the depths of Sarah's callousness; he could not have predicted the viciousness that Sarah unleashed on Maxie's already battered psyche. Sitting down at the table, Arthur unfolded his napkin and placed it on his lap. He readied himself to listen and to be wary of any palliatives that may creep into his response. Maxie, he knew, could not be mollified by platitudes that insulted her intelligence.

"Dinner looks great, Maxie. But you know, we could've gone out. You look done in. Come sit down and tell me what happened today." Seeing no dish at Maxie's place, he asked, "Aren't you joining me?"

"No, I'm not hungry. Maybe later," she sighed, dropping into her chair like a weighted sack. Taking Arthur's hand in hers, she kissed it and held it up to her burning cheeks. Maxie loved the feel of his large, strong hands; holding them, she felt safe, protected—they infused her with strength she did not have. Not unexpectedly, tears began to fall, released from a faucet clogged by years of detritus. As the valve to her restraint opened, a steady stream flowed down to her chin, over Arthur's fingers. Accustomed to this way

Maxie had of holding on, Arthur sat quietly, immobile, waiting for the tide of tears to recede. He would wait for the moment when words again could be spoken. Their twenty-five years together had taught him that her holding his hand was sufficient—that later, she would need all of him. Exhausted, she would then sleep deeply, profoundly. But, he knew, also, that in the morning, she would reawait the demons that stood as guardians at the chasm of her grief.

•16•

Tuesday morning Maxie arose unusually early with a sense of urgency and nervous expectancy. Although looking forward to her coffee date with Susan, she felt herself drawn to the park bench by the lake. She showered after Arthur left, lingering as the steaming spray worked like massaging fingers on her stiff, aching muscles. Eventually, tension gave way to the pleasure of the gentle pulsations loosening the tightness in her neck, shoulders, and chest. Toweling off quickly, she dressed in a light, neutral cotton shirt and shorts, having heard a blistering day forecast. After straightening up the bedroom and giving the kitchen a cursory once-over, she was out the door.

This morning, the beach was magnificently white. Brilliant prisms, like dancing diamonds, frenetically skipped along the water's surface. Alone at this peaceful hour, severed from all the peripheral people, yet worried about meeting herself in every little corner of her past, Maxie wondered if she was making too much of remembering. She was doubtful that she would ever make sense of her own feelings of betrayal. *I'm just all worked up about the girls' going off to college—maybe I'm worried that they won't be happy. I've got to do this separation thing right—not the way Sarah did it.*

Shifting her weight, trying to find a more comfortable position on the bench, Maxie watched the sparkling diamonds and their faceted interpretations. The beauty of this random display momentarily distracted Maxie from her ponderous ruminations and spoke to her, instead, of opening oneself up to the possibilities of the unpredictable. *This must be pleasure, she thought. It can exist.* To make order out of chaos was her greatest desire; to know the unknowable was her greatest challenge. Maxie wished she could know with the same depth with which she felt. The facts, she thought, would unlock the secrets of her past; they would free her to move forward. Knowing, however, meant uncovering new pain. It meant that she would have to slum around in the barrio of her repressed memories, in the poverty of her lost dreams. She had been a prostitute to Sarah's insatiable demands, sacrificing her soul on the altar of her mother's perfidy. Life had not been reciprocal in its love; it had been jealous and covetous. More than anything, Maxie wished for a sense of integrity and worth. Arthur had said that she needed to "reclaim her self"—that she must be determined if she hoped to persevere. *Would determination include a means by which I could learn to love myself too? Can a child learn to love herself when her mother does not love her first? I want Ashley and Rachel to know that it's all right to be happy—they mustn't feel guilty for that. I want them to* feel *my love.*

Saturated with her own questions and doubts, Maxie left the bench and went to meet Susan. Today, she needed her friend's constancy, her unwavering trust, and all-abiding tolerance. To Maxie, Susan was a sister. Toby had aligned herself with Sarah many years ago, fulfilling Anna's legacy of divide and conquer. Maxie decided to cast her bad mood out over the water and head for Joe's.

Susan was waiting, writing notes into her pocket calendar. Seeing Maxie, she smiled and put her things back into her purse.

"Hi, Sue," Maxie said spiritedly. "Hope you haven't been waiting long." Susan's blue eyes searched Maxie's face.

"No, I haven't, but, you look absorbed. What's up?"

"I'm not sure I know. Last night I had another crisis of spirit. I could feel my will draining. This morning, at the lake, as I remembered all the times that my mother conspired to make me disappear, or worse, to make my self disappear, I got angry—really angry. On the way over here, I decided that no matter where this venture with Dr. Weissman takes me, if I survive intact, it'll be a price worth paying," Maxie answered.

"Maxie, the price you've paid in the twenty years *I've* known you has been huge. Why don't you consider this an investment?"

"You know, I've never added up the cost, but you're right—it's too much. I've been a damned fool to let them do . . . what they do."

"You've said that before, Maxie," Sue reminded her sadly.

"I know, but I'm trusting you and Don to keep me honest. Don't you remember way back when you literally snatched me out of their salivating jaws?"

"Sorry to say, I remember it all too well," Susan replied, shifting in her seat. "Sarah left you high and dry with two newborns and a three-year-old."

"Yeah, but you forced me, despite the panic attacks, to get out of the house and back into the business of living." Maxie gave a perfunctory wave across the aisle to her neighbor who sat with her husband. A waitress approached to take their order.

"Just a toasted sesame bagel with slices of tomato," said Maxie.

"Same for me," added Susan. At Joe's, no one ever had to ask for coffee—it flowed freely, like the gossip. Other "regulars" were beginning to file in, and Maxie had to fight the urge to bolt. It was not that the others were unpleasant—she merely did not wish to indulge in the inanities. She was impatient with having to exchange meaningless amenities. Susan, reading her with precision, distracted her from the crowd. "Maxie," she pressed, "that was twenty years ago. Why can't you get past all that?"

"Because, had you not come to my house and adamantly refused to leave until I got dressed, I might still be in my bathrobe!" Maxie was not trying to be facetious.

"Maxie, for heaven's sake, it was your birthday! With Arthur at work, you were home with three little ones, and there was no one to make your day special!" Susan, though small-framed and unimposing, could, by her sheer genius of persuasion, convince the most cynical of something she truly believed in. Acknowledging birthdays was one of those things she held most dear.

"Yeah, but you insisted. You said you wouldn't leave until I hired a sitter for the kids and went out for a while with you."

"You, my friend, needed to get out of that house. For four months, all you did was take care of the kids and Arthur, cook, clean, wash, iron. Before that, you'd been bound to that awful recliner. After that, you couldn't walk. I had to get you out of that house, panic attacks and all." Susan was flushed with the emotion of reliving an unpleasant experience, unaware of her repeated motion of rearranging her long blond hair, brushing aside strands that had strayed only in her imagination. Always impeccably attired and self-controlled, Susan was now exhibiting that side of her she reserved for only those she allowed into her guarded, private nature.

"If you hadn't been your old persistent self," Maxie said, quietly and calmly, "I probably would not have made it then . . . or now."

"Listen, I'm not a saint, as you well know, but I love you, and I love your family. If there's anything I can do to help keep you sane, I'll do it. You and Arthur are much too dear to us. We'll never let you or your kids down." Fortunately for Susan, now sensing the tears welling, the bagels arrived and the coffee replenished.

Taking a large gulp of the hot brew, Maxie was able to push down her own tears. She decided to turn the conversation around to Susan. "I'm changing the subject, which is obvious," she said. "Tell me what's been happening with Don and the girls."

"I know when you no longer want to discuss something, Maxie.

I'll change the subject, but promise you'll talk to Dr. Weissman about the funeral. Please!"

"It's a deal," agreed Maxie, recoiling from the thought of having to make yet another promise. "Now tell me what Dr. Gold said. Are you going to start taking estrogen?" Maxie added some milk to her cup.

"I guess so. Not being able to sleep makes me so irritable It's really the pits! Dr. Gold says his own wife has started the therapy. I hope it works. So does Don!" she added with a smile.

"Me, too," Maxie said, although she had her own misgivings about taking the hormone. "Remember when my father called me the night of my hysterectomy?" *Now, what made me bring that up?* she asked herself.

"How can I forget? After going two years without speaking to you, he called you in the hospital, right?" Susan was still angry at Philip.

"Right. He called to wish me 'good luck.' Ha! He was calling to assuage his guilt. Maybe he was making one of his famous deals with God." Suffering from advanced emphysema, Philip held to the superstitious belief that wishing Maxie well would save his own soul—that such an act of contrition would endear him to the Avenging Angel.

"Are you worried about the estrogen affecting your migraines?" Maxie asked, fingering the remains of her bagel, playing absentmindedly with the sesame seeds that had fallen onto her plate.

"Yes, I am worried, but at this point, I'll try just about anything for relief." Changing the subject herself now, Susan asked how Maxie was progressing with getting the twins ready for college. For the first time, the girls would be separated by a long distance; they were going to have to learn to function independently. Ashley was itching to go as far away as Arthur and Maxie would allow. She chose a large Midwest university. Rachel, more unsure of her ability to govern herself and to trust her basic instincts for survival, chose a small liberal arts college in New York State. Each daughter caused Maxie no small measure of worry.

"I have to be so careful, Sue. Their leaving isn't abandonment—the way Sarah saw my going away to school."

"They're not you, Maxie," Sue scolded, "and you're not Sarah. What does it take to get you to see that?" Maxie concentrated on Joe who was behind the deli counter, slicing corned beef. "Apples *can* fall far from the tree if its branches are wide enough. Listen, do you need me to take the girls shopping? You know I'd love to." Susan was offering to do what Maxie enjoyed least—shopping.

"I just want things to be different for them, that's all," Maxie sighed. "As for the shopping, thanks, but no thanks. They're both pretty much set. They just have to get a few things. Ashley wants lots of coffee. I guess she figures on some late-night studying." Susan smiled. They both knew what the coffee was for. "Rachel wants to wait until the very last minute to get her things. She says she can always get whatever she forgets once she's settled in. I think she just doesn't want to make any of it real."

"You're right," Susan agreed. "She does seem reluctant." Susan had two daughters who were going back to college. They had chosen to stay within an hour's drive of Shafton, and would come home often. Susan did not have to deal with not seeing her daughters for extended periods of time. Remembering how Alden had benefited from having to stay at school for months at a time, Maxie could only sigh and resign herself to missing them, and to paying enormous phone bills.

"We'll all survive, I guess," was all she could say.

"Don't worry about them so much," Susan cautioned. "They're old enough to look after themselves, and they'll be just fine. It's *you* that you need to worry about—*you* need to be fine. When do you see Dr. Weissman again?"

"Next Monday. Actually, I'm looking forward to it, in a funny sort of way."

"Good. I know you're going to be happier in the end, even though you'll be digging up all the unpleasantness. I hope it goes quickly—those dark bags under your eyes are big enough to pack."

"Thanks a heap. Only you can get away with saying that," Maxie smiled.

"It's only because I care about you, Maxie. Come on, let's get out of here. I have some returns to make at Saks. Wanna come?" Susan was an inveterate shopper; Maxie avoided shopping as if it were a plague.

"No, thanks. I have some errands to do at the cleaners, the bank, food shopping. Call me later and we'll firm up plans for the weekend."

"Sure. Talk to you later. How about a little smile?"

Outside in the parking lot, Maxie forced a smile to please her well-meaning friend. Susan gave her a warm, affectionate hug in return. "Thanks, I needed that," said Maxie.

"We all do," said Susan. "See ya."

•17•

Ashley and Rachel were sunbathing by the pool when Maxie returned home. After putting four bags of groceries on the counter, she walked over to the glass doors which gave her a full view of what she called her "oasis." At home in the garden, at peace with earth on his hands, Arthur created an exceptionally beautiful and fascinating refuge for all of them. The many different kinds of shrubs and perennial plantings guaranteed brilliant color from early spring to late autumn. He loved working in and among the trees, planting huge beds of annuals that punctuated the greens with luscious pinks, purples, reds, and whites. The girls did not notice her standing by the doors, observing their relaxed, unself-conscious repose. The yard, fully encircled by imposing oaks and maple trees, offered sublime privacy. The outdoor speakers boomed with pop music as the girls lounged, quite oblivious to everything—except, of course, the phone which rang constantly. It was ringing now, and, as Ashley jumped up to answer it, she spotted her mother. Smiling broadly, she raised her index finger to indicate "one minute," and ran for the phone in the cabana. Rachel, now also aware of her presence, waved and smiled. Maxie opened the door and went down to talk to her daughters.

"Hi, Mom. What's up?" Rachel asked drowsily. She was sunburned, having disregarded Maxie's warnings about ozone-layer depletion and the importance of protecting her very fair skin. Her jet-black hair was pulled back in a ponytail, setting off emerald-green eyes that could look joyful and sad at the same moment.

"Hi, honey. Nothing's up. How ya doing, besides getting too much sun?"

"Am I getting a tan?" Rachel queried.

"How about putting on some of that sun block?" Maxie could not help sounding annoyed.

"I was just about to go in and shower anyway," Rachel finessed, with a touch of her own annoyance. "Do we have any salad or tunafish in the refrigerator?"

"I just came back from the market. You can make whatever you want." Maxie answered, intentionally not volunteering her services. *If I want her to start being responsible, I have to stop doing everything for her.*

"Maybe I'll eat later. I'm not that hungry anyway," Rachel countered, picking up her towel and throwing it over her shoulder—wincing only slightly at the pain she felt from the sunburn.

"I'll be in shortly, Rachel. Just want to say 'hi' to your sister."

"Just don't go in my room, Mom. It's a mess. I need to get my stuff organized—haven't gotten to it yet."

"You've got a lot to do, Rachel. You can't keep putting it off until the last minute." Maxie broke the promise to herself about keeping her own counsel.

"You've already told me a hundred times. Don't worry, I'll get it done!" Rachel was not disrespectful, but her defensive tone did nothing to hide her anger.

"I won't mention it again." Maxie wanted to be conciliatory toward Rachel, but her own impatience with Rachel's foot-dragging and her reluctance to pack up her things for college departure were beginning to appear slightly manipulative. Rachel had not said so, but acted as if she believed her mother was anxious for her to leave.

Can't she see how hard I'm trying? No, that wasn't fair of me. On the day that Maxie left for Boston, Sarah wept like a castigated child. Her mordant tears said, in effect, "You're wounding me." What she did say was, "You're so lucky to be getting out of this house, Max. Wish it were me instead. But you go—I'll be all-right." It was never all-right; nothing Maxie accomplished that first year at Selby could vitiate Sarah's contempt.

"We'll see each other often, Mom. I'll come home a lot," Maxie had promised, trying to comfort Sarah.

"No, you won't. You'll be having too much of a good time. Never mind, I'll survive. Don't worry about me."

As Rachel walked slowly, slumping back to the house, Maxie considered asking her daughter what was really troubling her. *Maybe I'll talk to her later when we have some quiet time alone.*

Ashley, in high gear, interrupted Maxie's thoughts. "Hi, Mom. What's cookin'? Say 'hi' to Ted." Obliging, Maxie took the phone that Ashley was holding out to her and exchanged a minute or two of bantering with Ted. She sensed that Ted was of enormous importance in Ashley's life, at least for the time being. Handing the phone back to her daughter, she sat down on a lounge chair to wait. Ashley finished her conversation, emerged from the cabana with the flush of excitement, and hurried over to Maxie, giving her one of her special bear hugs and one of those mmmmmm kisses they always joked about. Her olive complexion had turned to a golden brown. Rachel, who could not acquire a tan, would add this to her long list of inequities.

"How are you, honey?" Maxie asked.

"Great. Ted asked me out for dinner tonight. Will that spoil your plans? If you want me to, I'll stay home and eat with you guys."

What a turnabout this is, Maxie thought. *I have actually lived to hear this!* "No, you go. Dad and I are going out for a quick bite tonight."

"What time do you want me home?" Ashley asked.

Maxie could not believe her ears. In the past, it had always been a battle of the curfew. Now, Ashley was asking! "No later than one o'clock—and please tell Ted not to drink and drive."

"Ted's past that stage, Mom. He's twenty-one and responsible. Don't worry."

Asking Maxie not to worry was like asking her not to breathe. "Just make sure you're equally responsible." A few years ago, such a comment would have ignited the short wick of Ashley's explosive temper; now she wanted to demonstrate a more mature understanding of her mother's obsessions, her overprotectiveness. The contentious years of adolescence had past, and Ashley knew that she would soon be leaving what she could now recognize as more of a haven than a "prison." She allowed herself the freedom to admit that she had loved the *idea* of adventure.

"You look wiped," Ashley observed.

"I'm fine, but I think I'll go put the groceries away and lie down for a while. What time is it now?" asked Maxie, yawning and stretching.

"It's six. Are you still going to go out with Dad?"

"Yes, but tomorrow is Wednesday—his day off. Let's have a barbecue and enjoy the day together. I'll make that vegetable dish you love."

"Sounds good to me," Ashley said, retrieving her towel and lotion. "I think I'll go watch some TV."

Maxie returned to the kitchen to discover that Rachel had done the job for her—the groceries were stored and the brown paper bags were put into a drawer, neatly folded. Rachel's very complex nature made it a challenge to anticipate her next move. Her loving and sensitive heart wanted so much to please, to be loved, and regarded highly. This helpful gesture was her way of demonstrating her remorse for being short with Maxie.

"What do we have to do to convince her that she doesn't have to earn our love?" Maxie often asked of Arthur.

"We just keep loving her," Arthur answered, "and eventually she'll come to believe in herself." He hoped he was right.

Upstairs on her bed, Maxie stretched out, closed her eyes and tried to relax. It was only moments later that thoughts of Sarah disturbed her rest. She was, no doubt, winding up her yearly six-week summer visit to Toby's in Rhode Island, where she would wield power like a Titan. At Toby's, she would have a captive, assenting audience to whom she would spew and sputter about her "uncaring daughter in Boston," disparaging Maxie.

"Your sister thinks she's so high and mighty," Maxie imagined Sarah saying.

"She thinks she's better than the rest of us—big-shot Boston college graduate." Toby rued the day she flunked out of junior college.

"Don't you think she should call *me? I'm the mother*, not her."

"She won't call here, Mom. She's afraid Stu might answer." *Toby was afraid Stuart might answer.* Maxie envisioned Toby snuffing out a cigarette, twisting the butt in the ashtray.

"Too goddam proud, always was. Well, when she can see her left ear is when she'll have *me* crawling to *her!* Sarah Kahn crawls to nobody!" Sarah would, no doubt, arrogantly jut her chin forward, turn her nose upward, thrust her bosom forward.

"So, she's the one without her family, not us. She couldn't care less, I'm sure. Maybe she's happy with her Mrs. Leib and doesn't need us. Forget about her, Mom," Toby said, needing to believe that wishing could make things so.

"Yeah, your sister the intellectual hasn't got a brain in her head. Can't see why Mrs. Leib would want to bother with her either." The more Sarah would spew, the better Toby seemed to enjoy it. Sarah's hostility toward Maxie always made her own task of placating Sarah much easier. And during those six to eight weeks that Sarah spent with Toby each year, just an hour from Maxie's door, Sarah would make no attempt to communicate with her daughter in Shafton. She would, instead, return to Florida, wait a few days, then call.

"Max," Sarah would whine, "I would have called you, but you know the hell Stu would have raised if I used his phone to call *you.*" *Double bubble, toil and trouble.* It was how Sarah did business, how she stirred the cauldron.

Maxie tolerated Sarah's summer visitations to Toby for several years until later, worn out by her own cowardice, Maxie decided to confront Sarah. "Mother, what you do is hurtful. Don't you know that?"

Lying on her bed, Maxie could still feel the tightening around her heart. *Why did you make your lying so transparent, Mother? You wanted me to know that you didn't care enough to act convincingly. Why?*

"Oh, Max," Sarah had said, time and time again, "there you go again, trying to start something, trying to make something out of nothing. If you say I hurt you, then I'm sorry. I won't do it again. I don't know why you see it that way though."

"You do, and you'll continue to do it—that much I know."

"Geez, Max, you always make such a big deal about everything. I just don't know what it is you want from me."

You, Mother, Maxie was still thinking. *I want you. Is that asking too much?*

•18•

The week preceding her next appointment with Dr. Weissman provided Maxie with some sorely needed distraction. Wednesday evening's family barbecue was a success. In the absence of petty bickering between the twins—with no sarcasm, no ragged edges of tension to dilute the easy pleasure of being together as a family—Maxie could allow herself to be hopeful. She did not permit one negative thought to ruin the camaraderie, the closeness they all felt toward each other. *It can be this way,* Maxie assured herself, *I just have to let things happen—naturally. I don't know what makes me think I can control everything that goes on around here.*

On Sunday, Maxie and Arthur basked in the bright sunshine, they cooled off with an occasional dip in the crystal-clear pool that Arthur worked diligently to maintain. She watched with pleasure as he swam rhythmically, back and forth, slicing through the water with strong, controlled strokes. As Arthur swam, Maxie leaned her head back against the cushioned lounge, closed her eyes. Much to Arthur's surprise, she fell asleep. Keeping an eye on his wife as he swam, Arthur continued doing easy, seemingly effortless repetitions of the backstroke and the crawl. Maxie was deeply into another dream, strapped to the back of a renegade silver stallion, streaking through the night like a silver bullet into a wall of darkness ahead. Clutching the long, silky mane, she tried to slow the animal, to stop it before hurling them both into a dark void. Despite the recklessness, the speed of the charging animal, Maxie found something beautifully dangerous, scintillating about the ride. She awoke both startled and excited, just as the stallion prepared to leap over the wall.

"Maxie, wake up, honey. You're dreaming again." Arthur was standing over her, dripping cool water onto her bare legs. "I saw you thrashing about and figured I'd better wake you."

Maxie awoke a little disoriented. "Arthur, I just went on this unbelievably fantastic ride. It was so weird . . . frightening and fun at the same time. I can't explain it. I'm really thirsty and hot. How about you?"

"Let's have something to eat—maybe some cheese and fruit—and you can tell me about it," Arthur offered.

"I'll tell you what I remember." Maxie stood up, gave Arthur a hug, and went inside to get some snacks. *I must recall the details for Dr. Weissman,* she decided. *I want him to know what just happened. But what did happen?*

Arthur sat down on the end of a lounge, wrapped a beach towel around his shoulders, and ran his fingers through his wet hair. As he sat, staring blankly down at his feet, little streams of pool water dripped from his bathing suit onto the concrete deck, forming small puddles under the chair. His gaze was diverted by the frenetic activity of some worker ants. He watched with studied amazement as thousands of tiny insects scurried in and out of a huge ant hill, all with the singular purpose of satisfying the queen ant inside. These small creatures, their roles so clearly defined, went about their business unencumbered by dreams of destiny. *Even in her dreams she suffers,* Arthur thought. *Will she ever get over this . . . obsession? Sarah, the queen, has her subjects going off in every direction, everyone bound by some crazy sense of duty to please her. But, she won't allow it. She doesn't want to be pleased—she wants to be empowered. Maxie must see that—she must. And this dream she just had—sounds to me like she's driving herself mad.*

Arthur's concentration was interrupted by the sound of tinkling glasses. Maxie was making her way from the kitchen porch down to the pool, carrying a tray of fresh fruit, wine, and crackers. Arthur met her half-way down the hill and took the tray. "Oh, good, our private little picnic," he smiled, forcing himself to be cheerful. "Who needs a country club when we've got our own?" He arranged the snacks on the round table adjacent to the pool deck, sat down, and uncorked the bottle of wine. Maxie spread some cherry gourmandise on a cracker and handed it to Arthur. He stuffed it into his mouth whole.

"What were you thinking so intently about a few minutes ago?" Maxie asked. "I was watching you from the kitchen window."

"Oh, I was just watching the busy little ants scurrying about—fascinating creatures, doing their jobs so diligently. Don't the male ants sprout wings after mating, then die? Mother Nature sure is unfair," Arthur opined.

"What about *human* nature?" Maxie brushed crumbs off the table with her napkin.

"I like to think humans have choices—options to change whatever seems unfair," Arthur ventured, plucking some red grapes off their stems and popping them into his mouth, one by one.

"If they can," Maxie qualified.

"If they must," Arthur countered.

"I'm trying, Arthur, really I am. Don't you believe me?"

"Of course I do," Arthur said, reaching for her hand. "I just want so much for you to be happy. This thing you have with Sarah makes you so sad, so defeated." *And I don't want you to die.* Thinking this, Arthur almost choked on a cherry pit.

"I know, I know," Maxie said, softly. "But it's going to happen, Arthur, I can feel it. Let me tell you about my dream—maybe you'll see it as a positive sign."

Arthur listened with concern to Maxie's description of her frenzied ride on the runaway stallion. When she finished, she seemed radiant, enervated.

"It must mean that I'm moving toward something powerful, Arthur—that I'm going to make real progress. I feel . . . driven." She munched on some cantaloupe and appeared convinced.

Arthur thought differently: *Or maybe it means you're on a collision course with disaster.* As the evening sun made its way west over the feathered tips of the tall pines behind them, Arthur thought he saw the darkly familiar profile of Sarah Kahn as it cast a long shadow of uncertainty over his heart.

•19•

Good morning, Maxie," said Dr. Weissman beaming, looking especially dapper in what appeared to be a new gray pinstriped suit with a coordinated paisley tie and a crisp, white shirt. His shoes were tasseled loafers that squeaked from newness. The extra poundage around his middle made him a softer, more approachable figure. *He seems fallible and capable of making imperfect choices—just like the rest of us,* Maxie mused.

"Hi, Doctor. It's good to see you looking so well." Giving compliments to a psychiatrist was an unspoken taboo. "Well" was obtuse enough to allow for the acknowledgment of his spiffy appearance.

"Oh, thank you for noticing, Maxie," he said, frankly unconcerned, not concealing his pleasure in having been so appraised. "I have a rather important business engagement this afternoon. Appearances often do influence the decision-making process, you know, especially when it comes to requests for funds." Maxie had a suspicion that Dr. Weissman had a lunch date with an attractive young woman.

"So, where shall we begin?" he asked. "How was your week, and how are you feeling?"

"Dr. Weissman, it's been a most remarkable week—not for what I've been able to understand—but for the way things have . . . well, *appeared* to me in dreams and in moments of disconnection. I check out every now and then. I know this habit is disconcerting to those around me—still, I find myself *visited* by strange emissaries, so to speak." Maxie was not liking the way she described her experiences; she made it sound as if she were hallucinating.

"Tell me about it, Maxie. Take your time. I notice that you have a sense of urgency about you today. If we run over, we run over. Not to worry."

What Maxie most vividly remembered about Dr. Weissman was that once to the quick, the ensuing probe would be surgical. She proceeded to relate the dream regarding the out-of-control stallion. Hoping for some elucidation, she sat back in her chair and waited. Dr. Weissman, however, had another approach in mind. "Let's leave this dream and whatever we may deduce from it. Instead, can we return to the second-most distressing event that you expressed much interest in relating last week? According to my notes, what brought you back to therapy was the great emotional stress you incurred at your father's funeral. My guess is we'll be able to tell more about your dream after hearing about this event."

Although disappointed, Maxie relented and launched into her narrative. She began the tale of Sarah's final act of revenge and malice.

"All right," she sighed. "It's a long, difficult story, but here goes. As you know, Sarah and Philip spent their summers with Toby and Stuart. My parents had moved to Florida ten years ago, and it was their custom to spend those weeks with my sister while Philip was still able to travel. Never once in all the years of those vacations did they try to see us—there was never a single call to inquire about the grandchildren. The hostility and jealousy that Sarah had so painstakingly inculcated in both of us was her key to keeping us apart. She told each of us stories about the other, all laden with lies. I caught onto this perversity years ago and tried to share my thoughts with Toby. In return, Toby related what I had said to Sarah."

"Go on," Dr. Weissman coaxed. "What happened after the summer?"

"Well, Sarah and Philip would return to Florida and call me. In the last few years before Philip's death, she would say that they had to return because of his worsening condition, and that he wouldn't be making any further trips. She added that because he was deteriorating so quickly, we'd better go down there to see him for what may be the last time. She also said that she had been a prisoner in Toby's house, forbidden to use the phone."

"Did you try to tell her how she made you feel?" queried Dr. Weissman.

"A few years ago, I did—but, initially, I bit my tongue. There was no doubt in my mind that she knew exactly how I felt. That was the whole point. She would just blow me off and go on about how she had purchased new glasses, and that she had some new outfits to wear—that Toby had *made* her get them."

"What does *made her get them* mean?"

"It means that Toby paid for them. What was *I* going to do in kind?"

"You've told me before that you'd paid a considerable amount of money for their move to Florida, as well as for many of their furnishings. Didn't you pay for new clothes, medical bills, legal expenses, and various gifts?"

"Yes, and so much more, but none of that mattered. For Sarah, I could never do enough—enough was never good enough. Anyway, this pattern of visits continued for years. Each time they returned to Florida, I would go into a tailspin and stop calling for weeks. Weeks would turn into months. The last time it happened, Sarah had been visiting in Rhode Island, as she apparently had been doing quite regularly. Philip was gravely ill, but she had left him with a caretaker. One night, after seven months of not seeing or speaking to each other, Philip called me."

"What did he say?"

"He told me that Sarah was up in Rhode Island 'in cahoots with Toby,' as he put it, talking to lawyers in an attempt to wrest what was left of his money from his bank accounts. He warned me that if anything should happen to him, I must call his lawyer at such and such a number, and to say that he was still of sound mind, if not of body—to know that they were trying to 'do him in.' I reminded him that he had legally signed over the power of attorney to his son-in-law years before, and that now it was too late to ask me for help. I also wanted to know why he thought he could call me for *anything* when, in truth, he had never given me the chance to be his daughter. I asked why he'd refused to consult with me before selling their home before their move to Florida, or on the purchase of their new condominium. 'What can you expect me to do for you now, Dad?' I wanted to say. 'Why didn't you show up at Alden's Bar Mitzvah or the girls' B'Not Mitzvah? You wouldn't recognize your grandchildren if you stumbled over them.' I was calmer than I dreamed possible. I wanted to ask him what he thought I owed him."

"I'm assuming that you did not say that," Dr. Weissman interjected, "that you continued to bite your tongue."

"No, it was too late for that. Besides, he only cared about what was happening to his money, not to me," Maxie explained. Her breathing was labored as she remembered the conversation. "In any case, about a week later, we received a phone call at suppertime from Sarah. In a chilling, matter-of-fact tone, Sarah said, 'I'm calling to tell you that your father is dead. It happened just a few minutes ago.' She told me that she didn't know anything else—that the hospice nurse was there, and they were waiting for the ambulance to come. Taken so off guard, not knowing how to react, I told her I'd call her back. She said that that would be fine. The lack of emotion in her voice didn't surprise me. I remembered how many times she'd told me that she'd have trouble deciding which dance to do on his grave when the time came. I remember that I called Alden and assured him that it was not necessary for him to leave in the middle of his exam period at college to attend the funeral of a man he hardly knew. He asked if I would let him know about 'all the gory details.' I marvel at his prescience, and the absence of mine. We were still sitting at the supper table, all of us privately trying to sift through our feelings, when the phone rang again. Arthur rose to answer it, and I heard him say, '*What?* He's *not* dead? What kind of cruel trick is this, Mom?' His color was scarlet. Watching him pace in confusion, I couldn't believe what I heard him say next: 'Maxie is *not* coming to the phone right now. How could you've made such a mistake? No, Sarah, but the next time you call to say he's died, you'd better be sure of your facts.'"

"You mean he *hadn't died*?" asked Dr. Weissman, eyebrows arched incredulously.

"No, he had a bad choking spell, hyperventilated, and passed out," explained Maxie. "The hospice nurse just assumed he was dead. I guess she didn't check his vital signs. Maybe she hoped not to find any! Sarah is most adept at poisoning other people's minds."

"Please, continue," prodded Dr. Weissman.

"After recovering my equilibrium," Maxie continued, "I called my aunt Belle. Appalled, she talked to me for quite a while, trying to settle me down. In her inimitable way, she made me smile, saying that this news was probably nothing more than premature rumor, maybe wishful thinking by Sarah. But she cautioned me to expect another call in the not-too-distant future. 'I suspect Sarah has already written the obituary for the newspaper,' Belle told me. She wanted to know what I'd do when the inevitable call did come. I told her that I wouldn't go to the funeral.

" 'Think twice, Maxie dear. He is, after all, your father,' she had said.

"I tried to argue that Philip would never know the difference, but Belle told me that *I would,* that these things always come back to haunt you. She warned me to avoid being sorry that I didn't do the right thing. 'Don't worry,' she said to me. 'I'll be there for you. I won't let them hurt you. They'll have to get through me first.'

"Though still not totally convinced, I agreed. Sarah had hurt Belle time and time again. How could she protect *me*? I told Belle that I loved her very much.

" 'Sweetheart,' she said, 'I love you too. You're the child I never had, but I think of you as mine. Your mother, my sister, is a lot of things. One, of course, is blind—another, stupid-selfish. But I don't think she'll treat you unkindly when so many people will be there to bear witness.'

"I figured she knew better than I did about Sarah's obsession with image and pretense, so I said I'd go. Arthur and the girls were still reeling from Sarah's call. I related my conversation with Belle to him and he agreed that, with all of us there, nothing could, or would, happen. He was wrong."

"What did happen?" asked the doctor.

"Well, two weeks later, on May 1, a Sunday morning, I received a call from a Jamaican woman identifying herself as my father's nurse. She said, 'I am calling to advise you that Mr. Philip Kahn expired this morning at 7:21. Mrs. Kahn is not available to come to the phone.'

"I asked her where my mother was. The woman told me that she'd sent Sarah next door to be with a neighbor until the medical examiner and the ambulance left with the body. Although not convinced, I politely asked her to tell my mother to call me back. Barely veiling her feelings toward me, she coolly assented and hung up. I was quite sure that Sarah had filled her with woeful tales of lament about me. Several hours later, Sarah did call, exhausted from her 'ordeal,' as she called it, and apprised me of only sketchy details concerning the funeral. She promised to let me know more on Monday."

As Maxie sat back in the armchair, she paused, took a deep breath, and folded her arms over her chest—her feet were planted squarely, uncrossed, on the carpet. "Did your mother call on Monday?" Dr. Weissman asked, wondering if this was, indeed, the end of the story.

"Oh, yes, she called. She informed me that Stuart would be taking care of all the arrangements. I told Sarah that I didn't remember the location of the cemetery, that Arthur would need directions. Sarah said she'd call back the next day with the details. It struck me that she'd not mentioned one word about where she would be observing the mourning period. She told me how terrible the past few months had been for her, that she was on the verge of a collapse. Admitting that she'd gone to Rhode Island a few weeks before, she explained that it was 'to get away from him'—that if she hadn't, the strain would've killed her too. Then she cried about how she'd lost twenty pounds and couldn't seem to get control of her nerves. 'You probably won't recognize me when you see me,' she said."

"How did you feel at that moment, Maxie?" asked the doctor.

"Well, thinking back on it, I can't say that I was feeling guilty, even though that's what Sarah intended. I felt frustrated and apprehensive. My children wanted to know why I wasn't crying. Arthur tried to explain that I couldn't. I just didn't want them to know how angry I felt. My anger surrounds and protects me. It keeps me from falling apart—at the moment anyway—the deeper and more profound my anger is, the better I can continue to function." Hearing herself talk, Maxie was becoming more aware of how inappropriately she had used her anger, how cowardly she had been, hiding behind its destructive power.

Looking at his wristwatch, Dr. Weissman encouraged Maxie to continue. "Go on, please. I know we're going to run overtime, but I do want you to finish the story."

"Well, the next day Sarah called to inform us that the service would be held at graveside at 11 A.M. on Wednesday, the fourth of May. She then read the directions to the cemetery which Stuart had given to her. The conversation was brief, as she said that she had a lot to do. She had to cancel the oxygen supplies, call the hospital-bed rental office, and ask some friends to care for her car while she was away. She also said that she was having Philip's room 'fumigated'—the smell of death permeated the apartment. Stuart was flying down to 'take her home.' She would see me at the funeral on Wednesday. After I hung up from Sarah, I notified her sisters. Belle reiterated her promise to be my shield.

"On Wednesday morning, we all rose with the sun, somehow knowing that we were about to be players in a serious drama. With Stuart's directions in hand, we set out on our two-and-one-half-hour drive. Everyone was working out his or her individual feelings about Philip, wanting to feel something, even pity. We were all trying to find something—some fond memory of some distant moment when Philip was kind, gentle, or caring. No one wanted to seem uncharitable, but Philip had not been any of those things.

"We arrived at the cemetery at 10:30. Not only was it deserted, but the gate was clearly marked 'CLOSED! NO TRESPASSING.' After rechecking Stuart's directions and the designated time, Arthur drove around the perimeter of the grounds, looking for signs of life. At 10:50, Arthur drove to a nearby pharmacy and called the temple offices. When he returned, ashen, his jaw was set in that way that always indicated trouble. Getting into the car and throwing the gearshift into drive, he hit the accelerator with a vengeance.

"I tried to calm Arthur down. I couldn't imagine why he was so upset. He told me through clenched teeth that Stuart had sent us to the wrong cemetery, seeing to it that we'd miss the whole thing and look really bad to everyone. With the new directions that he had been given on the phone, Arthur sped across town, muttering that Stuart would live to regret this move—that we might be late, but we'd be there. Arthur was fuming.

"When we finally pulled into the dirt road leading up to the burial grounds, one of my cousins was waiting, chain-smoking and very distraught. She had been sent down the hill by Belle to scout for us. She told us that Stuart wanted to start without us, but Belle told the rabbi she knew we were on our way. I told my cousin that that son-of-a-bitch sent us to the wrong cemetery. I ran up the path to receive the black ribbon of mourning from the rabbi, which he then cut with a knife. My mother and sister refused to look at me directly. They didn't even try to conceal their disappointment in our arrival. As the rabbi signaled the mourners to advance down the slope toward graveside, he held me back, instructing me to *follow*, not join, the rest of the family. I looked frantically for Belle. She caught my eye, put a finger to her lips, and pressed her eyes closed. Like this," Maxie demonstrated. "It was her entreaty not to protest—to proceed quietly and respectfully down the hill. As we approached the grave, I noticed that Philip's casket had already been lowered into the ground. The rabbi, whom no one there knew, whom they had recruited from somewhere still unknown to me, gathered Sarah, Toby, Stuart, and their children around the grave. Forming a tight semicircle, they turned their backs on us. They did not acknowledge our presence and created a barrier that precluded our drawing near. But I got a glimpse of the shiny bronze coffin, gleaming inside the dark hole. The large, gold Star of David on top of the casket reflected the midday sun, making it almost beautiful, if you didn't have to think about who was in it."

"What were you thinking about when you actually saw your father's coffin, Maxie?"

"To be honest, I was thinking about how much Philip reminded me of King Lear, another poor bastard who should've done better.

He shouldn't have been old till he had been wise. Once, Toby glared over her shoulder, as if to dare me to approach. The malice in her cold eyes spoke volumes. The rabbi, having no idea who my father had been, could find nothing more to offer than a few, sterile, irrelevant remarks. Sarah, supported by Toby's son and daughter-in-law, didn't look at me. My heart was pounding so loudly I could hear it. I wanted to bolt, but my feet seemed cast in concrete. My poor children were dumbfounded and frightened by their ruthlessness—and my stomach churned as that old serpent uncoiled in my gut."

"Which serpent do you mean?" Dr. Weissman had counted quite a few.

"This one was shame. I was certain that I wouldn't recover from this humiliation. I could feel my insides twisting. I wanted to crawl into the dark hole where my father lay, cold and unassailable. I wanted to be in that coffin, Dr. Weissman! In my grief, I searched for Belle. She stood there with tears streaming down her cheeks. Her bottom lip was quivering, and she looked at me with such pity, hurting because she hadn't been able to keep her promise. As Belle watched Sarah and her consorts file past me and my disbelieving family, without so much as making eye contact, her lovely face contorted and I could see her put her hands up to her face—a vain attempt to conceal her anguish from me." Maxie covered her eyes with trembling hands; her lower lip quivered, remembering.

"You can stop now if this is getting too upsetting, Maxie. We can continue next time if you think you need a break." Dr. Weissman had correctly assessed Maxie's agitation, but she kept thinking of that ride on the stallion.

"No, I'll hang on. I've got to get it all out." Maxie took another deep breath and continued. "Sarah made her way back up the slope to the waiting limousine and disappeared inside it. Some cousins and a handful of friends expressed their sympathies to her from outside the vehicle while Toby stood guard. Someone took hold of my arm and pushed me forward, telling me that I must go to my mother. With bold defiance, I approached the car, and, much to my amazement, Toby retreated. I stuck my head into the limo and saw two fiery eyes glaring at me. All she said to me was that they were going back to Toby's, but she didn't suspect I'd want to be there. Doctor, my mother's voice sounded more like a hissing! I told her that we'd be leaving for home. As I backed out of the darkness, Toby and her family brushed me aside and got into the car. Sarah instructed the driver to leave the grounds, and, within a few seconds, they were gone."

Dr. Weissman got up from his desk chair and padded quietly over to the water cooler. He served himself some water in a paper cup and lifted his arm to Maxie, offering some. She shook her head "no."

"Go on, Maxie," the doctor instructed, resuming his place at the desk.

"Belle found me in a state of numbness—I found Belle in a state of shock. She begged me to go to her house for awhile, but I declined, wanting only to be far away from all this madness. My legs could barely carry me as Arthur supported me under my arm. He was determined that I walk away upright, with a semblance of salvaged dignity. On our way to the parking lot, I felt a hand on my shoulder. It was Connie, Philip's personal secretary for dozens of years. In her late sixties, Connie was still a beautiful, seductive woman. She always reminded me of Miss Kitty on that television series *Gunsmoke*—you know, tough but sensitive too. For as long as I can remember, Sarah harbored suspicions of Connie that she couldn't prove. She just accused Philip of having some kind of 'thing' going on with 'that blonde.' Taking my hand in hers, she told me faltering somewhat, that she and Philip had been 'good friends'—that she was especially sorry for what Sarah had just done to me. Then, Doctor, she said to me—and I remember her words exactly: 'Philip always wished he could tell you that he didn't mean to hurt you—he just didn't know how not to.'"

"Were you angry at Connie too?" Dr. Weissman asked, scratching his head.

"My reaction was, 'Well, Philip had actually been clever at something!' I released her hand and nodded my appreciation for her telling me, even though I didn't fully understand how I felt about it. I had no voice—no words in me. As Arthur led me to the car, he looked back and saw Connie crouched down next to my father's grave; her hand rested on the pile of dirt as she threw a rose on the coffin. I think she was very sad that my family didn't have the decency to cover Philip's coffin with earth. Arthur said, 'So now we know it's true.' But my head felt too light to know anything. Doctor, does not knowing how not to hurt me excuse him?"

"That depends, Maxie. He may have hurt you *because* he loved you. Perhaps he was ashamed of his weakness, angry more at his own impotence than at you."

"I really don't understand," Maxie sighed.

"Did you ever love him, Maxie?"

After a very long pause, Maxie said, almost whispering, "Yes, the day I saw his coffin in the ground. The thrashing . . . over for him . . . the hook removed . . . a dull, dead eye." Dr. Weissman listened carefully as Maxie lost herself in her thoughts. A tear slipped out the corner of one eye, staining her face with a new sadness. "If Belle hadn't died just a few weeks after Philip's funeral," she continued, reentering the present, "I might've found some comfort in Connie's confession. Sarah, hiding out at Toby's, didn't attend Belle's funeral. I hate her for that." Maxie, for the first time, felt the wonderful rush of release that only truth can elicit. Flushed, she looked away from the doctor, concentrating on a flaming red cardinal perched in an immense oak tree just outside the office window.

"Whew," said Dr. Weissman, "that was quite an ordeal, wasn't it? I can see that the retelling has been painful for you, Maxie. Let's stop here for today."

"Doctor, are you familiar with the writings of Virginia Woolf?" asked Maxie.

A little bewildered, Dr. Weissman replied, "Yes, fairly so."

"She wrote about filling up the bowl of one's life with memories—memories which become the base of one's life."

"Yes, I am familiar with that concept. With what have you filled your bowl?"

"Anger, Doctor, seething anger. It's the glue that has kept me from coming apart, from breaking up into a thousand tiny shards. I'm so afraid not to be angry."

"You're certainly entitled to your anger, Maxie, and I want to know more about it. What I'd like you to do for the next time is to try and go back in your mind to when you first began to feel depressed or angry or confused. Go back to that first year at Selby when your friend Mrs. Leib changed you or, perhaps, saved you. Go back and ask questions, Maxie, because there's truth to be found in the seeking. Take care of yourself. We'll talk more about this next Monday," he said, rising to open the door for her. She passed through it as if sleepwalking.

Maxie took the elevator down to the parking-garage level and made her way to her car. Once inside, she sat for awhile until she felt steady and focused. She marveled that, although agitated by the recall, she did not have morbid thoughts. She actually felt lighter, buoyed by an unfamiliar sense of hopefulness that had eluded her since . . . since she first began to understand that Sarah did not love her. Dr. Weissman had said that she was "entitled" to her anger, that now she must start asking why. He had intimated that Mrs. Leib might be able to help. Maxie made a mental note to reread the letter she had received from Sarah four months after the funeral. Stuffed away deep within her desk drawer, this letter needed to be read again. This time she no longer would be afraid of its sting. As she pulled out of the garage, she decided to call her friend Barbara. A trusted friend for many years, Barbara had tried to encourage Maxie to return to therapy and would be pleased to see her efforts realized. Like Dawn, she did not take Maxie's hibernation personally. It had been months since they last spoke. Maxie tentatively dialed Barbara's number on her car phone.

Barbara answered on the second ring. "Hello?"

"Barb, it's me. I'm in my car, not too far from Chestnut Hill. Want to meet me for lunch?"

"Well, hello, stranger! It's so good to hear from you. Let's see . . . I have to be back for Ellen at 2:30, but I can meet you for a little while, at least."

Maxie was relieved that there was no hesitation in Barbara's voice. "Great," she said. "It's only 12:30. I can meet you at the café inside the mall. Is that all right?"

"Sure. I'll leave in five minutes. See you soon."

It was so like Barbara not to ask questions; she just seized the moment for its singular importance. A woman of keen intelligence and uncompromising standards, her insight was always clear and grounded in the facts that she cared enough to remember and to store. She had no patience for stupidity; practicality was her touchstone. Maxie was feeling truly regretful for having distanced herself for so long.

***

Parking at the mall during lunchtime was always a challenge, but after several trips through the parking garage, Maxie found a spot being vacated by an older, elegant matron of this well-heeled area. The woman deftly maneuvered her black Mercedes sedan out of its space; gave Maxie a practiced, polite smile; and drove off. Maxie pulled her own car in with far less ease and emerged from it with less grace, forgetting her handbag on the front seat, having to open the locks to retrieve it.

The café was alive with chatty shoppers, scurrying waiters, and the commingling aromas of freshly prepared salads, pastas, rolls, pastries, and ground coffees. Maxie asked for a nonsmoking booth in the back room, remembering that Barbara was particularly sensitive to noise and bright light. The waiter escorted Maxie to a booth where she waited for her friend.

"Coffee, Madame?" a waiter asked.

"Yes, please, with milk. I'm waiting for someone, and she'll want tea with lemon when she arrives."

The waiter brought the steaming black coffee, and Maxie sipped it appreciatively. The warm, dark brew felt comforting and satisfying, and she was happy to be taking delight in something so ordinary, so routine. She spotted Barbara across the room and waved. Barbara, of medium height but regal stateliness, approached with a warm and embracing smile. She was not comfortable with hugs or kisses, especially in public places. Sliding into the booth, she quickly appraised Maxie's calm, relaxed demeanor and grinned. Her short, dark hair was cut in the new asymmetrical style which set off the lovely angles of her cheeks and jaw; her blue eyes sparkled with the pleasure of seeing her friend.

"Hi, there. It's great to see you again. What news doth to Caesar?"

"It's good to see you again too. Thanks for making the time," Maxie said.

"Nonsense. Now tell me what's been happening—if you want to. Are you well? Is that a smile I see, perchance?"

"Yes, it's there, and your tea will be coming along shortly, I hope. First, let me say that things have been rough for me all summer, and I finally decided to return to therapy."

"Oh, Maxie," beamed Barbara, "I rejoice. You have at last heeded the words!" Her smile was irrepressible.

"What words?" Maxie asked.

"Illegitimati non carborundum est."

Maxie laughed aloud at Barbara's touching precisely on the heart of the matter. "Yes, those bastards have ground me down for much too long."

"Did you go back to Dr. Weissman?"

"Yes, and though it's still pretty new and a bit unsettling, he does give me what to think about. I've just come from a session, and Barb, I went through the whole scene from my father's funeral without losing it!" Maxie said proudly.

"Don't worry about 'losing it,' Maxie. It's important to cry if you need to. Tears are not a sign of weakness nor vulnerability—in fact, they're good for you."

"Well, right now I feel as though I'm on a mission. I've got a task to perform, a focus on a new goal that I want to pursue, no matter the outcome." Maxie was leaning forward in great earnest, wide-eyed with determination.

"Take small steps, Maxie," Barbara cautioned. "Remember to breathe in and exhale while you're moving forward. It's a long, hard trek you've set ahead of yourself, and you may get pretty winded on the uphill, especially since you're out of shape. By the way, did you show him the letter?"

"I appreciate your analogies. I know they come from your own experiences, Barb. I'll try to go slowly and expect some backsliding. No, I haven't shown him the letter. It was on my mind as I was driving over here though."

The waiter brought Barbara her tea. After dunking the bag into the hot water, she wrapped the string around the teaspoon and squeezed out the residual liquid. Dropping a wedge of lemon into the teacup, she asked gently, "How long has it been since you've seen or spoken to your mother, Maxie?"

"It was six years, this past Mother's Day." Maxie remembered the day well. Observing Barbara's movements, she thought, *Damn! What she's doing with the teabag . . . reminds me of her!*

"Do you think you'll ever see her again?" Barbara probed.

"I hope not," Maxie sighed.

"Maxie, what's it like not speaking to your mother for so long? I mean, knowing that she's down in Florida, making trips to Toby's and all? It's just so hard for me to understand her—or you."

"What's it like? It's like living with her ghost, but knowing she's alive. Every morning when I wake up, the first thing that goes through my mind is that I do, and yet I don't, have a mother. Then I ask, 'Why?' I can only guess that she doesn't want me. And then, after I've convinced myself for the zillionth time that I haven't done anything to deserve not being wanted, I feel an ache in my heart that just never goes away." Maxie swallowed hard.

"Have you thought about calling, for your own sake?"

"Yes, many times, and I have. But it's hard for me to rationalize calling someone who keeps rejecting me."

"Do you know for sure that she'll reject you? Maybe she's being stubborn. Maybe she really wants to hear from you, but since so much time has gone by, it's awkward for her."

"Barb, if you love your own child, awkwardness is not a legitimate excuse for cruelty."

"All right, so maybe it's a pride thing. You've told me that Sarah is a very proud woman."

"As I see it, pride has two sides. When I do something positive, or when something turns out well because of my efforts, I'm proud of myself and of what I've accomplished. Sarah's is a false pride. She hides behind a self-serving insistence that she's been an admirable mother—that *she's* the one who is wronged, despite her countless efforts to be a good mother."

"If she *believes* that, then it's true for her. It *is* pride that's keeping her distant."

"Sarah believes whatever will make her feel better, less guilty. Sarah believes in a world she's created and falsified. She functions in that world by virtue of utter denial and total conviction that things are the way she sees them. She has no responsibility to the truth."

"Whose truth, Maxie?"

"Mine, I suppose. Or the truth I'm after."

"Can't you just see the bigger picture—see it for what it is and go on from there?"

"That's the problem. I don't know what it is. When I try to see a total picture, I see shadows, reflections that aren't clear. Without the details that have shaped my life, I can't trust perceptions—what you call the 'big picture.'"

"Maxie, I love you, but frankly, I'm still not sure that I agree with your logic. You're a mother too. Don't you sometimes act in ways that make your kids question your devotion or wonder about your sincerity?"

"I've never intentionally hurt them, never planned their punishment. My children never doubt that I love them, even when I'm angry. They know that it's what they might have *done* that causes the anger. I haven't *done* anything, Barb, that could be so bad that Sarah would want to lock me out of her heart."

"I give up. I've been playing devil's advocate, but I can see that I'm not any closer to understanding than I was before. Well, at least I tried."

They each ordered a sliced turkey sandwich on sourdough and asked for refills of their drinks. Barbara knew that when Maxie changed the subject, it had not been a reproach, but the words of someone who already felt very weary and overwhelmed by a journey just begun. They talked about their families, about Maxie's twins' preparations for college, and they made a date to go out as a foursome with their husbands.

"When will you be driving Rachel up to New York?" Barbara asked.

"Arthur's going to take a long weekend at the end of August. I guess that's Labor Day weekend. What I'd like to do is to continue on to Montreal after we leave her at school. If the Leibs are free, we could visit with them. Perhaps I'll start asking some hard questions."

"Sounds like a good plan. It'll be good for both of you to spend some time getting used to the idea of the empty nest. I'm sure Mrs. Leib will be delighted to see you too." The sandwiches arrived, and they each ate in silence for a few minutes. Dabbing a green linen napkin to her lips, Barbara asked, rhetorically, "Isn't it funny how life keeps falling back on itself? Will the Leibs be planning a visit to you this year?"

"Yes. I hope they'll come sometime later in October. Barb, I'm glad that you could meet me here today. As always, you've helped."

"You've got to learn to take care of yourself, my friend. And, please, try not to be afraid of what you may find out in your sessions with Dr. Weissman," she said uncharacteristically placing her hand on Maxie's.

"I've been a coward until now, running for cover every time Sarah drew her bow and aimed at me with her hateful lies. No truth could ever hurt me so deeply. I'm going into battle with a courage I never thought I had."

Barbara thought otherwise. She saw it as premature and untested optimism in which she held no real confidence. Rather than stay and make the mistake of saying too much too soon, she decided to come down on the side of caution. Looking at her watch, leaving half of her sandwich uneaten, she slid out from her side of the booth, prepared to leave. "Sorry to take off so soon, Maxie, but I've gotta run. Jack asked me to pick up his suit at the cleaners before I go home. Speak to you soon. Love to Arthur and the family," she chirped.

As Maxie watched Barbara disappear into the crowd, she was struck by her friend's hasty retreat, as well as by Barbara's reluctance to validate her statement of courage. *What was Barbara's big rush? She looked more like she was escaping!* Maxie thought. *I can deal with insouciance but not with evasion. She must not believe me! Well, I'll prove her wrong—she'll see.* Maxie had a sense of ill-boding. *Perhaps, though, I was being too critical, reading too much into the leave-taking. Maybe I sounded too lofty, too sanguine. Yes, that must be what it looked like to Barbara,* she thought—*a beginner's naiveté or a fool's delusion. I must remember not to sound so expansive, to temper my enthusiasm so that Arthur does not detect fanaticism in my new-found mission.*

Arriving home at 3:30, Maxie went directly upstairs to change into some lighter, more comfortable clothes. She eyed the bed with longing for a nap, but vetoed the idea as soon as she heard footsteps on the stairs. Ashley found Maxie pulling on some navy shorts and a white cotton T-shirt.

"Hi! What's up?" Ashley asked, with her characteristic perkiness.

"Hi, toots! Not much. How about with you?" Maxie was not a good liar.

"I've spent the entire day getting all my stuff ready to ship out tomorrow. Dad said he'd help me weigh the boxes tonight so UPS can tell me what it's going to cost." Ashley was flushed from the mix of the day's organizing and the anticipation that was building in her with just one week left before taking off for the Midwest.

"Honey, I guess I never told you this before, but I'm very proud of you. In a way, I envy your courage to seek a new adventure. We'll miss having you home, but there's so much out there for you to see and experience. Go for it all, and don't be satisfied with less than what you think you deserve. Of course, I hope you'll remember the three B's."

"I know, Mom: Be Good, Be Careful, and Be Smart. You've said it so many times, I hear it in my sleep. Don't worry—I'll remember."

"Just one more B, sweetheart: Be all that you can, whatever path you choose. We love you, and we'll do all that *we* can. You need to embrace every possibility that will enhance your life with self-confidence and respect." Maxie knew she had leapt into a sermon; it was as much for herself as it was for Ashley.

"Mom, lighten up. Let's go make supper and, well, thanks. I'm really going to miss you guys." Giving Maxie a quick hug, she left and disappeared down the steps into her bedroom, where she would set her stereo to its highest volume and lose herself in the pounding rhythms of a heavy-metal band.

Maxie was left to ponder her own revealing choice of words; she had counseled Ashley to embrace possibility. *Had I done so, myself, I might know more about what I was saying.*

***

"So, how are you going to be?" Arthur asked, spooning up the last strands of pasta with his knife and fork, not looking directly at Maxie. He seemed to be asking the question more of himself.

"What do you mean—how am I *supposed* to be?" Maxie asked in return. She knew she was being quarrelsome, but she needed to be quarrelsome, even grating, if she was going to get through this last week of summer, this last week with her daughters. Already she could feel the prickly sensation at the back of her neck—the anxiety of separation and loss that was so familiar to her, so painful.

"Listen, we haven't been alone, I mean just you and I, for over twenty years. You've invested all those years in the kids, choosing to stay home, being here for them. What're you going to do now that there won't be anyone needing you to be home at the end of each day, except for me?" Arthur explained, as tactfully as he could.

Dinner had been so pleasant. Everyone had enjoyed the meal, and there had been unexpected dialogue on current international events, local politics, the value of a liberal arts education in today's technological world. The exchange of ideas had been lively, surprisingly cogent, and the girls had tried so hard to sound more grown-up, avoiding the expressions "like" and "he goes" or "she went" instead of "says" or "said." Their effort was a musical gift to Maxie's ears. Why, Maxie wondered, was Arthur dampening the moment with his insatiable need to be practical? It had all gone too smoothly. Maybe it was himself he was worried about, she considered.

"Arthur, let's first see them off with smiles and wishes for good luck. Of course, it's going to be hard for both of us. We went through similar pains when Alden left. We'll get used to this as well." Her choice of "we" was intentional.

"That's not what I mean, Maxie. I still have my work to go to each day. What will you do to fill in, to keep your mind off their not being here?" Arthur was still not looking at her.

"I'll survive. I'll look for another teaching job, or I'll tutor in the afternoons. Don't worry. I won't spend my days pining for the need to be needed." She had not convinced herself; surely Arthur would remain skeptical.

"Just think about it. By the way, after we drop Rachel off, are we going to continue on to Montreal to see the Leibs? Why don't you call tonight, get it all arranged?"

"Yes, I need to talk to her again anyway. Dr. Weissman wants me to ask her help in reconstructing those early years when I first left home. I know they'll be visiting with us next month, but it does seem like a good time to go," Maxie agreed.

"Hon, our girls are the same age you were when you left home. Dr. Weissman is right. Now is a good time to evaluate what happened to you and how you're going to handle the girls' 'leaving' you. I know you're trying hard to keep the two periods separate and unequal in your mind, but your feelings are probably confused, jumbled up, like the pasta in that pot." Arthur drained the last of the wine from his glass and looked solemnly at his empty plate.

"I'll call tonight," Maxie assured him. "My life began on the day I met Mrs. Leib. There was nothing more extraordinary than the day she touched my life with hers. In every respect, that was the moment when I was truly born." *And I've tried with all that is in me to give my children a feeling of that essence, that feeling of knowing they matter. I've nurtured their desires to be content with their oneness, their uniqueness. I can only hope that I've succeeded. Please, God, give me the strength to change, to grow with them. Let it never be said that I was selfish, that I expected too much, that I didn't learn from my own anemic adolescence how to fail with grace, to achieve with humility.* It was a silent prayer, offered in the solitary confines of her heart and mind. Arthur, too, seemed to be offering his own silent prayer; his was for Maxie.

"Help me clean up, please," Maxie whispered. "When I'm finished here, I'll call Mrs. Leib."

"Shall we stay at the Towers again?"

"Yeah. If it ain't broke, don't fix it, as they say."

Arthur wrapped his arms around Maxie and gave her a bear hug. Silently, he wondered what was going to break.

***

Maxie dialed Cora Leib with her usual mix of excitement and reserve. The Leibs were her dearest friends for thirty years, scholars and intellects who called themselves "humanists"; theirs was a world of international acclaim which preempted, or so it seemed to Maxie, uninitiated first-name familiarity. It was no exaggeration, simply a fact, that the Leibs were part of a culture to which Maxie and Arthur could only aspire. Dr. Leib's longtime association with Harvard provided some common ground with Arthur, but Maxie often felt inadequate and provincial, obliged to relate on a personal, emotional level. That she adored the Leibs was no secret—that they figured so eminently in her life was no accident. Not wanting to overstep the boundaries of the friendship they had painstakingly constructed, Maxie sometimes felt constrained. What she wanted most was to break down the imaginary dividing line that kept her from a confessional. Mrs. Leib was the mother she so desperately needed, but Maxie was not her child. The threshold of propriety was sacrosanct. Maxie would never consider crossing over; she took whatever she was given and was sustained by it. She was made to feel whole and was enriched by the love the Leibs bestowed on all of them. Of necessity, an objective distance kept the imaginary boundary in place. Paradoxically, they were able to sustain the relationship with informal formality, with partial impartiality.

"Hello?" Mrs. Leib answered on the third ring.

"Hello, Mrs. Leib, it's Maxie."

"Oh, Maxine, how good to hear from you again. How are you, dear?"

"Everyone is just fine, thank you. How are you and Dr. Leib feeling?"

"We're just great. Just got back from Chile and Peru. We had a marvelous time there. My husband was the principal speaker at several symposia and, of course, he was inundated with requests for more. So, what are you up to?"

"We were hoping you'd be free over the Labor Day weekend. We're taking a somewhat reluctant Rachel off to college in New York and thought that we might continue on to Montreal after she's settled in."

"How lovely! Of course you must come. We're delighted. Deposit your daughter and then come here for some cheer. We'll be expecting you with open arms." Mrs. Leib was effusive in her invitations; her sincerity, never doubtful.

"We'll call you on Friday afternoon from the Towers. We're happy that you have the time to spend with us," said Maxie, already feeling the warm rush of anticipation.

"Call us as soon as you get in. We'll be waiting, expecting you for dinner. No arguments, please. Tell Rachel and Ashley that we send our love and best wishes for much success in their endeavors."

"Thank you, I will. Just one more thing, though. I must ask you for some help." Maxie was being intentionally evasive.

"What kind of help, my dear? Is something wrong?"

"Well, I need you to help me reconstruct who or what or where I was thirty years ago when you first knew me as a student at Selby. Will you do that for me?"

After a brief pause, Mrs. Leib said, "Maxine, my dear, sweet girl, I will do anything you ask of me, if you say it will help you. There are limitations, however, to my own memory. It's been quite a long time, you know. So, we'll talk, as we always do, and I'll do my best to honor your request. Until we meet, we send our love and kisses to all of you. We look forward to your visit."

"Thank you, Mrs. Leib. Arthur joins me in sending love to both of you. See you soon."

Arthur had walked into the bedroom as the conversation closed.

"All's set. They're looking forward to our visit."

"Then what's the frown for?" Arthur asked.

"I don't think she was being totally, well, forthcoming, Arthur. Not exactly dishonest or anything like that—just, well, mysterious, edgy." She was sitting on her bed, looking beyond her confused husband, through him, really, into the waning hours of light and destiny outside her window. There were but a few moments of lightness before the night would be upon them.

Maxie weighed the significance of the upcoming weekend in terms of all that it promised, for all that it might alter in her understanding of place and time. She was already drifting aimlessly in space, with no precise trajectory, colliding with the unknown. She shivered and wrapped herself in her own arms. "I'm cold, Arthur," she complained.

"No, hon, you're scared," he offered, and held her until the chills subsided.

•20•

Seeing the girls off to their respective destinations was accomplished with great effort at efficiency and organization. Ashley had sent her essentials ahead and kept herself busy by scouring her bathroom, emptying dresser drawers, and fastidiously ordering her closet. She was trying to divest herself of her high-school collectibles, reminders of what had been pieces of her life—sometimes frivolous, sometimes disappointing. A ragged teddy bear, a diary, prom flowers pressed between the pages of an old photo album constituted her sense of who she had been and where she had come from. Her new life would, she knew, challenge her need to feel safe, to run home to the concrete memories that validated her existence. "Change is never safe, Ashley," Maxie had counseled her. "It asks us to be brave way beyond our years. But it's change that allows us to break away from the things that don't seem to fit into our real worlds anymore. Try not to be afraid. Just hold onto yourself in the process. Don't let go of yourself." It had been another one of her sermons, but it served to comfort both mother and child, to make some sense of the separating. Still, she wondered how her children suffered these philosophical indulgences.

On Wednesday of that last week, Maxie drove Ashley and Arthur to Logan Airport. Arthur had offered to accompany Ashley and to assist in her moving in, to help her set up her dorm room.

Except for the obligatory stop for Ashley's favorite coffee, the ride was quiet, yet charged. All three valiantly guarded their emotions, trying to act as if this rite of passage were natural—nature's way of processing a new generation. Maxie guided the car up to the curbside check-in, released the trunk latch, and waited for Arthur to collect the luggage. He was traveling very lightly—a tote bag with essential toiletries and work clothes. Ashley's bags were bulging. Maxie stepped out of the car to embrace her daughter. It was a long, powerful embrace in which they rocked side to side and buried their faces in each other's hair. At last they disentwined and said their good-byes.

"Mom, I'm going to be fine. Don't worry. Just ten weeks till Thanksgiving. I love you!" Ashley did not wait to hear a reply. She knew it was stuck in Maxie's throat; she did not want to provoke tears. Arthur stepped in to give Maxie a hug and a kiss. He squeezed her hand and told her, "I'll call you tonight, hon. When you come to pick me up on Friday, we'll go to Michael's for a nice dinner."

"Have a good flight, Arthur. I'll wait for your call. Yes, dinner sounds like a great idea. Ashley is inside. Go to her. I'll calm down in a little while."

Arthur disappeared into the terminal as Maxie got back behind the wheel. She looked once more to see if she could catch a glimpse of Ashley, but her intrepid daughter had moved on with the crowd. What Maxie did see were countless other mothers and fathers going through the same ritual. Some wiped tears from their eyes; others solemnly shook hands and patted each other's shoulders. As Maxie pulled away from the terminal and merged with the traffic, she thought about the older woman she had overheard in the park, and what she had said about how like birds parents are. They teach their young to fly, then send them from the nest, reluctantly, so that they will. She wondered if the elder birds worried that their young might forget how to fly every now and then. She needed the forty-minute ride back to Shafton to collect herself. She had to present a calm, perfectly-in-control demeanor to Rachel, who took her cues from any nuance of weakness, real or imagined. With her twin sister gone, Rachel could not help feeling lonely and insecure. She had dreaded this week more than she had the junior prom, as she now had to admit that however much the two sisters had fought and harangued at one another, however much they differed in style and substance, however much it was her very own shadow that had consistently eclipsed Ashley, she missed that one person whose judgment she most often sought, whose trust she most valued. And she truly regretted her perfunctory 'good-bye' to her sister. She could not bear having Ashley see how torn apart she already felt.

On her arrival home, Maxie found Rachel in her bed, under the covers, listening to Barbra Streisand. Rachel had declined the invitation to accompany them to the airport, bemoaning the fact that so much needed to be done. None of it had been, of course. Everything was as much in disarray as before—a reflection of her unsorted thoughts and feelings.

"Hi, sweetie. How ya' doing?" Maxie tried to sound cheerful as she sat down on Ashley's neatly made, empty bed. "Ashley said she'd call you very soon, and to tell you that she's really going to miss you."

Rachel rolled over, pretending to rub sleep from her eyes. "Yeah, sure she did. She couldn't wait to get out of here!" Rachel was trying to provoke, in an attempt to conceal the raw circle that her sadness had left around her heart. It was easier to quarrel than to admit that she was genuinely distraught over her sister's leaving. *She* was supposed to be the strong one, the one who could tough it out. Wasn't it *she* who had won all those awards for her athletic skills and scholastic achievements? Hadn't *she* been the one to capture the attention and admiration all these years? What was she going to do now that her sister was not in the stands to cheer her every maneuver on the basketball court? She wanted so much for those high-school spotlights to shine on forever. She did not want to have to prove herself elsewhere over again, to make new friends, to be tested at the risk of failure, to face uncertainty.

"Honey, I know you're not ready to make any of this real to you, but there are just a few days remaining. You do need to get your things together." Maxie was trying to be firm, yet gently prodding. Rachel's volatile temper would most certainly erupt, raging and roaring about all the indignities heaped upon her. Maxie held her breath and waited for an answer; none came. Rachel rolled over, pulled the covers back over her head, her not-too-subtle message that she wanted to be left alone. Maxie left the room and closed the door behind her; she didn't want to hear the wails and the sobs, nor the pounding of fists on the back wall. When Rachel was through the worst of her anguish, she would slam the bathroom door—the signal that the storm, at least temporarily, was over. She would reappear, eyes swollen and bloodshot, to contritely apologize. Maxie went upstairs to read, to settle her nerves. What ran through her mind now was that old Double Mint chewing-gum commercial jingle: "Double your pleasure, Double your fun. . . ." At times like these, motherhood seemed more like dubious pleasure, dubious fun.

Once upstairs in the seclusion of her own room, Maxie decided to reread a letter that Sarah had written to her four months after Philip's funeral. She went to her desk and fished it out from a bulging file of similar cards and notes. Settling into the rocking chair beside the picture window, Maxie opened the letter and began reading. When she had finished, she let the letter drop onto her lap, where she fingered it nervously. *This is preposterous and grotesque. Reading this is like being at a macabre masquerade ball, replete with Transylvanian overtures. A poseur's how-not-to-do-it. What an agent of the devil my mother has been.* Maxie closed her eyes and fell asleep.

***

Arthur returned on Friday. As planned, Maxie picked him up at the airport and drove to Michael's for dinner. On the way, animated and cheerful, Arthur reported how he and Ashley had managed to gain early access to the dorm room, for a small fee, of course, and had been able to get Ashley all set up in her eleventh-floor room. He was impressed, he said, with the cleanliness, orderliness, and apparent efficiency of the staff, but especially with the openness and congeniality of the Midwesterners he had met. He assured Maxie that Ashley was doing just fine—that even before he left her, she had already made two or three friends. Their two days together had been a strong bonding experience. He was moved to what Maxie thought were tears.

"Sure am going to miss her, Maxie," he confessed.

"I know, hon, I know."

Pushing down the lump in his throat, Arthur tactfully changed the subject. "What shall we order?" he asked, pretending to care what was on the menu. They decided on the special salmon en croutte with steamed vegetables, eschewing the Parisian potatoes. Neither tasted a thing. The warm, homemade five-grain loaf of bread with molasses lay untouched, cooling in the linen-lined bread-basket. Tonight, food neither soothed nor assuaged their hungry souls.

"Rachel gave me a pretty hard time Wednesday evening, as I might have expected," Maxie confided, still sipping her wine. For some reason, the alcohol was not doing its fancy footwork. "I should have realized that Ashley's leaving was a shot of reality for her. She's coping with loss and her own fears of failure and of disappointing us. I tried to talk to her, but she sent me packing. After the maelstrom, she came upstairs and apologized, the way she always does."

Many minutes passed in silence as Maxie mindlessly stirred and restirred her coffee. Arthur studied her with a mix of curiosity and concern.

"Maxie, where are you? Where do you go when you leave the moment?" he asked, annoyed.

Shaken from her reverie, Maxie replied, "When the system goes on overload, I have to pull the plug, Arthur. Otherwise, I'll short-circuit. I go someplace safe and quiet in my head. I'm sorry if this upsets you. It must be hard to understand."

"It's just that your eyes become so vacant, your whole effect is, well, flat. You look as if you're in some kind of trance." Arthur was trying to be tactful, yet he was conscious of his own escalating anxiety.

"I just check out for a few minutes. I do come back, you know. Let's just call it my sensory safety valve."

"OK. We're both exhausted. Let's go home. Just do me one favor, please. Tell Dr. Weissman about the frequency of these 'overloads.'"

•21•

Her appointment was scheduled for 11:30 the following Monday. Rising early and agitated, Maxie decided to go to the lake to . . . what?—to think, to bolster her resolve to read Sarah's letter without revealing her contempt and revulsion? Susan had called early to ask if Maxie needed company today. She appreciated the implications of Maxie's reading of Sarah's letter. She knew that Maxie would appear calm and casual, that she would arrive for her appointment looking fully in control, in pursuit of the rational, the factual, the tangible. Susan knew that Maxie would do what she deemed necessary to conceal the anguish—Susan wished Maxie wouldn't.

"Let me go with you today," Susan had cajoled.

"No," Maxie had replied. "I'm a big girl; I can handle it."

"You're a grown woman, Maxie, not a big girl. Remember that when you read the letter to him," Susan chided, understanding that Maxie was not acting out of conviction. She had something to prove about perseverance.

Worried that Maxie was not going to handle the truth this time any better than she had before, Susan asked, "Will you meet me for coffee afterward?"

"No, Sue. I need to do this day strictly by the seat of my pants. I'll call you later."

Minutes later, she was taking her accustomed position on the bench at the lake. Maxie wondered how she would be able to explain to the doctor her feelings of rebirth. Sarah had conceived her and given her life, only to take it away, selfishly and premeditatively. Mrs. Leib had resuscitated an emotional corpse and given it new life, sustenance, and possibility. Could what she had experienced with Sarah be called love, or was it exploitation? Did Sarah actually *punish* her with a false love, giving and denying simultaneously?

It was not a particularly splendid early morning. The sun was withholding; the clouds were darkening as they hung low and heavily over the deserted beach; storm clouds were gathering. Maxie, unaware of the ambiance, both literal and figurative, sensed she had entered a new phase of her psychic journey. Alone with her thoughts, she envisioned a discovery that would reveal why Sarah had cast her out, why Sarah could not and would not love her. *Could it be that Mrs. Leib knows something I don't? I don't understand why she didn't sound eager to talk about Selby. She's usually so enthusiastic.* Maxie knew she was getting closer to the truth—how much it would hurt her rested on her resolve and on Mrs. Leib's willingness to be a part of the journey back in time. Stories abounded in the daily news of mothers who went to jail, who risked life and limb for their children—who would do the unthinkable, the unpredictable, the most unfathomable, and improbable acts to safeguard the security and well-being of those children. As a mother herself, Maxie could not think of a sacrifice too great that would ensure her children's happiness. Sarah, for whatever her reasons, had made Maxie *her* sacrifice; she had appeased vengeful gods with psychic blood. Isaac had fared far better. *Some of us are born more than once,* Maxie thought, *often in different ways. I am who I am today, not because Sarah bore me, but, really, because I lived—in spite of her. I had to die once. Too bad. Should I mourn for me? I don't know. Maybe I should just bury that me and think of who I am as someone new, different. But who?*

A raw and restless wind was blowing in toward shore, reminding Maxie that she had sat longer than planned. On her way to her car, she passed a young, distraught mother who was desperately trying to persuade her small daughter to leave the beach area. The child rejected all appeals; she threw herself down on the damp sand and began kicking and flailing. The onslaught of tears worked up to a feverish pitch as the child squealed, "I hate you! I hate you! You never let me have fun! Go away! I wish you were dead!"

Maxie felt the dread of this horrible scene and the embarrassment of the hapless mother. Their eyes met and locked; both were held hostage and rendered immobile by the sheer cruelty of the child's words. Maxie tried to think of something useful or encouraging to say, but nothing came to mind. What she did poignantly remember was that moment, frozen in time, when she had cried to Sarah, "I bet you wish *I* were dead. You wish you didn't have to think about me at all, don't you!" Maxie and Sarah had just returned from their weekly food shopping. Sarah would arrive at the highschool and patiently wait for the dismissal bell. When she sighted Maxie, she would slide over to the passenger side of her car to allow Maxie the privilege of driving her to the market. All Maxie's friends were jealous of this apparent luxury of her driving Sarah's car instead of having to sit on the crowded, noisy school bus smelling of teenage sweat and adolescent adrenal activity. Maxie would get behind the wheel, depositing her weekend workload on the back seat, and pretend that the next few hours of female bonding were what she had looked forward to all day. Sarah was delighted to have some company. Her friends had long since abandoned her for the country club and for the company of other women whose husbands could engage in civilized conversation. These outings were, in fact, the highlights of Sarah's week.

Looking back on it now, Maxie was struck by the realization

that Sarah could have done this chore any other day of the week, at any other time of the day. She chose, instead, to make this Maxie's job. Sometimes, as a token of her appreciation for Maxie's carrying in and storing all the items in the cupboard or refrigerator, Sarah would buy a half-dozen 45rpm popular recordings. It was the Sixties, and Maxie was as much enamored of Johnny Mathis and Elvis as were her contemporaries. After Maxie finished unloading the groceries, Sarah would entreat her to demonstrate how to dance to these new recordings; after all, Sarah would assert, the steps kept changing to each new rock-and-roll hit. Upstairs, where there was a fairly capable hi-fi record player, Maxie, a graceful and energetic dancer, would take Sarah by the hand and lead her, instruct her in all the new fashionable steps and gyrations. Sarah learned quickly and seemed to whirl, spin, strut, and gesture as if *she* were the schoolgirl, losing herself in the jerky, awkward movements of the dance. Closing her eyes, she would imagine herself a young woman happily twirling, unself-consciously floating on the upbeat rhythms of lifelike sensations. Thinking about it now, leaving the lake, Maxie could see that she had been used, taken. *She suckered me again. But it felt so real, as if we were doing something . . . together.*

On one of those Friday afternoons, in expectation of a weekend visit from Toby and her odious husband, Sarah had shopped to excess. For hours she complained, criticized, spewed invective over Toby's sorry choice of a husband, yet she bought far more than was necessary. She wanted to send the newlywed couple home to their cockroach-infested apartment in Philadelphia laden with food and supplies. Having heard quite enough of her mother's chronic complaints, Maxie asked, in irritation, why it was that Sarah felt it necessary to provide this scoundrel Stuart with good food and home-cooked meals. Sarah's reply had stung her. "Why are you so jealous of your sister, Max? Why do you have to start up all the time?" Without waiting for an answer, Sarah disappeared into the bathroom, calling out from behind closed doors, "Please cut up the salami and scramble up some eggs for your dear father. While you're at it, you can add a little arsenic."

Maxie called into the bathroom, "Wouldn't it be better if *I* were dead? Don't you wish *I* would just disappear?" No answer.

***

Maxie left the screaming child and the distraught mother, feeling so much kinship to that little girl. The child, she knew, would get over her temporary unhappiness quickly, probably with the promise of an ice-cream cone from the dairy or a longer bedtime story.

Maxie, however, was still embattled, still kicking and screaming over past injustices. She understood, then, that although silent and camouflaged, her tantrums had become a form of mental illness—that her flailings were not only unproductive, but also potentially lethal. Until now, Maxie had never experienced the real, naked desire to inflict pain on anyone—she had never known the irrefutable desire to kill. Her life, as she was now beginning to see it, was a gift box, gaily wrapped, complete with ribbon and bow. But life's secrets can be explosive when exposed to fresh air and daylight. Say thank-you, Max, but don't open it. In her contempt, Maxie felt the grief of having been denied the contents of this box. Opening it now might be a mistake, yet she was bound to find out what had been kept so assiduously under the wrapping.

***

Dr. Weissman did not keep her waiting. Spared having to mindlessly thumb the pages of *The New Yorker* that lay in her lap, she rose. Dr. Weissman extended her his hand in a warm, cautious greeting. The magazine fell onto the carpet.

"Come on in, Maxie. How've you been since we last met?" he said.

"Doctor, I'm about to implode!" Maxie answered.

"Implode or explode," he queried, "and why?"

"I'm not explosive by nature, Doctor. But if I set a single emotional spark to all the combustible material in my brain today, I'll self-destruct!" Maxie's breathing was labored, audible.

"What would constitute an 'emotional spark,' Maxie?"

"One more lie, one more goddamn trick!" she seethed.

"There are no tricks here, no lies. You're safe here. Please try to calm yourself for a minute. I can wait until you're ready. You may begin wherever it's comfortable for you. Would you like a glass of water?"

"No, I want to keep my momentum going—I want to be angry. Look, I brought along this letter, and I'm determined to read it to you." Reaching into her bag for the envelope, she could feel herself tighten, then loosen. Extracting the letter, she looked at it in disgust. Inexplicably, she was calmer now, as steady as a hunter with a bead on his prey. Maxie looked up to Dr. Weissman, who nodded for her to begin. She read:

"Dear Max and Arthur:

"As long as I can't reach you by phone, I thought I would try to explain to both of you by letter. Please read this letter before you tear it up.

"I really don't understand what happened to our wonderful relationship. I just want you to know that I love you with all my heart. I don't want to hurt you or your family, even though that is what I seem to do. I do love you all.

"Please understand the pressure I was under. Back in December, I spoke to you and told you I was on the verge of a breakdown. My doctor insisted I go away for two weeks. He referred your father to hospice care, and through them I got a Jamaican woman to take care of him. I was waiting for an invitation from you, but when you told me you were having problems of your own, I didn't want to be a burden to you—because I was *bad!* The hospice nurse called Toby and explained to her what was happening to me. She told her I must get away. I only went to Toby's because you didn't ask me—not because I love her more.

"It wasn't easy for me to see your father wasting away to nothing. He weighed eighty pounds when he died. Cancer had spread everywhere in his body. I finally had to get a nurse's aide to live in and care for him—he wouldn't go into the hospital or a nursing home. He wouldn't sign the necessary papers. Therefore, I couldn't take him in by force. I paid the woman $350.00 a week. I kept her for four-and-a-half months. I tried to cope, but my nerves gave way. I had graveside services because I thought it would be better for all of us. I went back to Toby's, and she didn't think I was ready to go back to Florida in my condition. I lost a lot of weight. My pressure went way up, and she tried to get me out of the deep depression I'm in. While there, I also got a bladder infection.

"About my not going to my sister's funeral—I guess I just couldn't make it. I don't want to believe that she's gone.

"I hope we can again have a relationship as we did in the past. Please remember—whatever happens to me, I want you to know that I love you all very much.

Mother"

Dr. Weissman waited for a few moments. In the silence, he thought he detected an almost imperceptible smile forming at the corners of Maxie's mouth, which was now relaxed and missing the tight lines.

"Maxie, on the surface, that letter sounds convincing and heartfelt. Your mother seemed to be making an effort to communicate her feelings. Why the smile?"

"Because, Doctor, none of it is true. First of all, Philip did *not* have cancer. Secondly, it was *I* who offered to pay for a live-in nurse way back in May when Ashley and I went down there to help. *I* pleaded with Sarah to contact hospice care, *not* Toby. My sister had begged off with a lame excuse, but I knew it was because she didn't want to diminish her inheritance. When Sarah went to visit Toby, I knew nothing. Philip called me late at night to say that, through his lawyers, he had found out that Sarah, Toby, and Stuart were trying to find legal means of declaring him incompetent. They were conspiring, he insisted, to take over whatever money and assets he had left. He begged me to call his lawyer and to try to stop the thievery. Sarah was not having a breakdown—she was colluding to strip him of whatever assets remained. Did you notice how she referred to my father as 'him'? She was relentless to the point of depriving Philip of his own name. As for her sister's funeral, she was too ashamed to show her face. She knew that Belle saw what she had done to me and my family at Philip's funeral. Many months later, I found out from Toby's daughter that it was Sarah who orchestrated the scenario at that funeral. She explicitly instructed each of them to turn his or her back to us, to ignore us, to keep us away from the gravesite."

"What about these problems that she said you used to dissuade her from coming to visit with you? What about her loving you, as she says?"

"I called her a few weeks after receiving this letter. She'd been at Toby's for nine weeks, never once trying to reach us. When we spoke, I told her, trembling, that I was willing to put aside everything that had gone wrong between us in the past. When she asked me to 'forgive her for hurting' us, I told her that it was God's business to forgive, not mine, but that if she ever hurt me again, it would be for the last time!"

"And was it?" Dr. Weissman asked.

"No, certainly not. It was then that she asked me for nine-hundred dollars to help pay for Philip's headstone, and then insisted that

I make peace with Toby as well."

"What happened?"

"I said 'no' to both. I didn't hear from her for two months after that conversation, but she did send us a Jewish New Year's card wishing us health and happiness."

"Did you send her one?" the doctor probed.

"Yes, but I signed it as impersonally and succinctly as she did."

"Then what happened? How did Sarah's behavior affect you?"

"I became very depressed, withdrawn, and generally incapacitated by a weird mix of anger, grief, and confusion. The facts had always been so twisted and distorted, I couldn't fathom what was real about me and what I had imagined. I began to doubt my own sanity. I began to wonder whether I could continue to function in a real world. I began to sense that I was falling apart, piece by piece—descending into a hell I had never known before."

"How were these feelings manifested, Maxie?" Dr. Weissman prodded.

"I developed a ten-month-long siege of hives. I looked freakish and didn't want to be seen in public. I didn't look like a human, so I didn't feel like one either. There were too many prescriptions and tests. The bottom line was that I was rendered inchoate by the drugs."

"What do you mean by *inchoate*? Didn't you have an understanding of yourself or of your disease?"

"There wasn't a medical specialist anywhere who could help me. To me, the implication was that I was about to go insane."

"If you don't mind my saying so, Maxie, that sounds like the stuff of Italian operatic tragedy. Why were you thinking retribution? What price did you think was being extracted and why?"

"Doctor Weissman, I wanted to believe that I was the good daughter I had always tried to be. I wanted to believe that mothers love their daughters even if they don't fit the preferred roles assigned to them. My mind was being savaged by a ruthless liar, and what was happening to my body was a symbolic protest—a physiological show-and-tell of what turmoil was going on in my mind. It wasn't until I made the conscious decision to get well that I recovered." Maxie realized that she had, at last, confessed.

"Maxie, you have a keen intellect that doesn't allow for circumlocution. You're much too insightful for what I would, ordinarily, delay for many weeks." Pulling his chair up next to Maxie's, looking at her with great sincerity, he said, "Let me ask you this: Are you ready and willing to choose life?"

"Are you thinking that I may choose to die, Doctor? Sometimes the thought is very appealing—very tempting. Sometimes I say to myself, 'Maxie, you're not any good to anybody like this, least of all yourself.' I've had periods of self-doubt that have nothing to do with reality, when all I've wanted was to erase 'me.' Problem is, I don't know who that 'me' is. I need answers, Doctor. Can you understand why that's so important to me?"

"Maxie, you mustn't let your search for truth become a destructive obsession. Take your time as you peel back the many layers of this pungent onion." Dr. Weissman was uneasy with Maxie's haste to unravel forty-eight years of layers.

"Peeling onions does bring tears to my eyes," Maxie countered, "but I'm willing to endure."

"Very well, Maxie. I'll do my best to steer you through these very troubled waters. Let your mother's letter be a catalyst. Let it be the price of passage on a new ship, a new course. You must promise me, however, that when the seas get rough, you'll let me navigate."

"Doctor, I won't do anything to compromise your position, nor mine."

"Thank you for saying that. I'm your friend and ally, Maxine. Please don't hesitate to call me if you think you're sailing off course.

You're not crazy—despite what others may have you believe. I intend to do my best to keep you safe while you prove that to yourself."

"I guess I didn't implode, did I?" Maxie said, sheepishly. "Thanks."

"In this business, we learn to thank ourselves," the doctor corrected.

With these last words of confirmation, Maxie left Dr. Weissman's office. She was in control, totally focused on her purpose. On the way out of the building, she held the door open for an elderly woman bent over her cane. And smiled.

•22•

With every inch of the trunk and half of the back seat packed with Rachel's past, present, and future needs, the Lanes set out at daybreak for the three-hour drive to Albany. Check-in time was 9:30 A.M. Crunched up in the right corner of the back seat, her head resting on her favorite bed pillow, Rachel did not want to speak, did not want to be spoken to. She was angry and frightened; she wanted to stay home where it was safe and familiar. All her friends had gone off to their respective colleges with great hopes and enthusiasm; Rachel remained sullen and withdrawn.

"Would you like to stop for breakfast?" Arthur asked.

"Is that like having my last meal before they throw the switch?" Rachel asked defiantly.

Arthur did not reply. His aim was to get through the day with the least amount of turmoil as possible.

"Dad," Rachel moaned, "can you kill the sound? I've got a real 'thumper.'" Rachel's migraine headaches began when she went off to nursery school; her "thumpers" were invariably precipitated by anxiety.

"Sure, no problem." Arthur turned off the radio. "Did you remember to take along your medication?"

"It's packed away somewhere," Rachel groaned.

"How about some aspirin?" Maxie offered, reaching into her

handbag.

"No, I'll just bury my head in the pillow," Rachel answered, turning over on her side, punching a hollow spot into her pillow.

When at long last they pulled into the rear parking area of Rachel's designated dormitory, Arthur announced, "Well, here we are! Let's find out how we go about getting all of this stuff to your room, Rachel. Why don't you come with me, and we'll find someone to help us."

"Oh, goody," was all Rachel replied, as she unfolded herself and got out of the car, stretching and yawning in a transparent attempt to appear like a nonchalant cat. Father and daughter went off to investigate as Maxie stayed behind to observe the other new arrivals. Everywhere there was excited, purposeful activity; everywhere, amid the smiles and handshakes and embraces, there was palpable anxiety. Whose was greater, Maxie wondered—the students' or their parents'?

They found Rachel's assigned room at the end of a long, gloomy corridor; a single overhead light fixture, filled with the shadowy remains of mosquitoes, flies, and moths, cast a dim light on already sickly yellow walls. The unmistakable smells of old, wet sneakers, cold pizza, and smoked grass lingered in the hallways, assaulting Maxie's senses. Still, neither she nor Arthur could help being reminded of their own desultory "homes away from home," as the memories of those malodorous dormitories came rushing back in a wave of nostalgic nausea. Pinned to every door was a huge paper star on which was written: "Welcome to Lawrence Hall!" The name of each entering student was spelled out in glitter on it. On corkboards scattered throughout the charmless barracks were announcements for this or that action committee meeting, posters whimsically designed to inform newcomers of special floor meetings and, of course, the ubiquitous lists of floor rules. High-pitched, nervous voices seeped out of adjacent rooms as the new arrivals introduced themselves to their roommates, each scrutinizing the other stranger with curiosity, hoping that the "match" was going to work out well.

The Lanes did their best to hide their disappointment, and began hauling boxes and crates up and down the stairs, bringing all Rachel's belongings to the small, dark room. A cushioned window seat lent the only homey touch to an otherwise sterile cubicle. Rachel's roommate Ginny had written in August to tell Rachel, rather self-importantly, that she had been selected to play on the soccer team and would be arriving two weeks earlier. She made no mention of waiting to discuss who got which bed, which side of the room. In fact, she had already clearly demarcated her side of the room with her answering machine, lined bookshelves, and countless rows of cosmetics and medications. The plastic prescription bottle of birth-control pills did not escape Rachel's eye; obviously, it was not meant to. Maxie saw it, but decided not to mention it. Ginny, of course, had usurped the window end of the room, guaranteeing herself easy access to the seat. Rachel was relieved that soccer practice was now in progress. "Oh, my!" was her only comment.

Maxie was trying to help Rachel set up her drawers and closet, but was totally baffled by the randomness with which the clothes had been packed. Standing in a heap of clothes, personal articles, and hangers, Maxie was not making progress. Finally, overwhelmed, Rachel plunked herself down on the pile of clothing strewn on her bed, becoming one with it. With as much tact as she could summon, she said, "Mom, Dad, why don't you just let me work through all this by myself? I'll find places for everything later. Just please hook up the fridge for me, and then maybe you can get back on the road to Montreal."

Arthur and Maxie had gone through the difficult ritual of parting with Alden four years before. He had not been so tactful when he summarily dismissed them with a graceless, "Why don't you leave now?"—a remark that had stung them. This time they were more prepared for the dismissal, having more appreciation for the child who was so anxious and filled with misgivings.

"Are you sure you wouldn't like to have some lunch first?" Maxie coaxed. She, too, was aching to retreat to the safety and privacy of the car—to shed tears she could not allow Rachel to see.

"Yes, I'm sure. Go on ahead, I'll be fine. Call me from your hotel room and please give my love to the Leibs."

They hugged, kissed, exchanged thank-yous and good lucks, then departed. Rachel looked so dejected, so pitifully sad. Dread was cutting deeply into Maxie's heart.

"Guilt? For what, Maxie?" Arthur asked as they worked their way out of the campus and onto the main road. There was exasperation in his voice, a look of incredulity on his face.

"I feel as if I'm sending her into the lion's den," Maxie sighed.

"That's exactly how she feels. Let's be honest. My guess is that after everyone else is settled in, she'll start to make some friends and calm down. You have to give her some time. She's never been away from us—except for those four fateful weeks at summer camp—and she needs to prove to herself that she can do this. We'll call her tonight, if that makes you feel any better." Arthur did his best to placate both of them.

"Arthur, I wish I could be so linear, so uncomplicated. You're just pretending that you don't have the same concerns as I do," Maxie said, adjusting, "but I know you better than that. Now, shall we put on the new CDs?"

Arthur took her hand in his and kissed it. He loved his wife and was looking forward to their being alone. Silently, he wondered how alone they truly would be if Maxie continued to dwell on Rachel's ability or inability to handle new challenges. For now, however, he had his wife beside him, promising in her own quiet way that she was as much looking forward to "their room" at the Towers as he was. There would be wine, some special cheese with crackers, and, he hoped, laughter. How dearly he yearned to hear Maxie's laughter again—lusty, vibrant, and seductive. How differently she responded to his touch when they were away. As the speedometer hit 90mph, Maxie scolded him. "Slow down, hon. We've got the whole weekend." Playfully, she pinched his thigh and winked.

Gazing out the window, Maxie was entranced by the early brilliance of red, orange, and yellow splashed on the canvas of the White Mountains, punctuated by the deep green hues of majestic pines and the dabbles of white from ageless birch. Lost in the wonder of this visual feast, she almost forgot about the wrenching that she had just experienced in New York—almost forgot the apprehension over what she might learn in Canada. Questioning the wisdom of her impetuous request of Mrs. Leib, Maxie now felt discomfited. Maxie wondered if she had imagined Mrs. Leib's uncharacteristically tentative, ambivalent response to her former student's request for help. She seemed almost reticent to reconstruct those first two years at Selby, to relive the events that had created a permanent union of their souls. This time, there was something off-key in this woman's voice. *I must have sounded too serious—maybe I rushed into it without giving her a chance to think.* Maxie's thoughts were racing now. *I should have waited until we got to Montreal. What if Mrs. Leib really doesn't want to remember? I'm going to test the waters slowly. If it's a choice between finding out about something that happened thirty years ago and upsetting Mrs. Leib, I'll just back off. It's not worth it to me to make her uncomfortable—I can't run the risk of hurting her.* Maxie thought about ways to initiate the inquiry while, at the same time, protecting the integrity and well-being of the woman she loved so profoundly. Barbara's counsel to moderate the zeal, to tone down the crusade, was beginning to make more sense.

***

Traffic and construction on the Champlain Bridge delayed their arrival for what seemed like hours. Finally, they pulled up to the entry of the Sheraton Centre Towers and exchanged their usual pleasantries with the affable Jacques. Everything was the same, and yet, it wasn't. Maxie felt different, inexplicably unhappy. The excitement that she had always felt running through her veins just wasn't there. In its place was a heavy foreboding. *What's the matter with me? Why do I feel so nervous and weepy?* With tremendous effort, she tried to dispel the bad mood. Entering the airy, immaculate corner room that had always been a source of pleasure, spotting a fresh rosebud in a crystal vase, recently delivered fruit, and wine glasses, Maxie had to force a smile.

Noting the lateness of the hour, Arthur put all other considerations on hold and said, "Why don't you call the Leibs while I unpack. Would you like me to uncork some wine?"

"Yes, that would be great. It's been a rough day, and that construction did not do wonders for the nerves." Sitting down on a king-size bed, Maxie dialed. Her eyes wandered to the lovely Laurentian Mountains, falling into the shadows of what had been beautiful autumnal sunshine. From another window she could see Lake Champlain and Old Montreal, recalling memories of fun-filled, crisp afternoons with her family.

"Hello? Is that you, Maxine?" asked Mrs. Leib.

"Yes, it is I. Forgive the delay in our call. We were quite tied up in traffic. How are you?"

"Oh, we're so glad you arrived in good order. I know about that dastardly traffic on the bridge, but as long as you're here, we can relax and enjoy a bit of dinner and food for the soul. We're anticipating some conviviality and pleasure in time shared together. Come soon, won't you—as soon as you're settled in?"

"Yes, we're anxious to see you too. I hope all is well."

"My dear, all is never completely well with anyone. We have our distractions and disappointments as much as anyone else. We've just learned to concentrate more on the positives—wherever and whenever we can find them. Now, since you and Arthur are two of those positives, tell me when to expect you."

"Is 7:30 too late?" asked Maxie, hoping to sit, unwind, and share a glass of wine with Arthur.

"Can you possibly make it 6:30? I know you're tired, but this way we can end our first evening at a reasonable hour, and you can return to the hotel for some much-needed rest."

"I see your point," Maxie conceded. "We'll come at 6:30. See you then."

"*Hasta entonces*," replied Mrs. Leib, "*cuando nos abracemos.*"

"*Hasta entonces*," responded Maxie as she returned the phone to its cradle, warmed by the words that told her she was wanted, that they were awaited with joyful anticipation.

"Here," Arthur said as he handed her a glass of their favorite wine. Lifting his high, he said, "To us. And to a great weekend together."

As they clinked glasses to Arthur's toast, Maxie suddenly remembered that they had promised Rachel a call to assure her of their safe arrival. "Arthur," she said, "why don't you let Rachel know we're here and where she can reach us? I'll go freshen up before we leave." Reading Arthur's questioning eyes, she added, "Maybe it's better if I don't speak to her so soon. Tell her I'm showering or something, and that I'll speak to her in a few days."

"If you say so," Arthur replied. He dialed Rachel's dorm room while Maxie busied herself in the bathroom, changing her clothes for dinner. When she emerged, Arthur was sitting on the bed, perplexed.

"Did you reach her?" Maxie asked.

"I got her answering machine. She's out for the evening." Arthur sighed.

"Did you leave her a message?"

"Yes. I told her we'd arrived and left the number where she can reach us."

"Maybe it's a good sign. Maybe she's made some friends to go to supper with. Who knows, maybe she even likes her roommate." Maxie was overshooting her reach for optimism.

"Well, we'll know soon enough, won't we?" Arthur said, resigned, emptying his glass with one exaggerated movement. He gave Maxie a strained smile—what Maxie had called his "linear, uncomplicated" way of seeing things was being tested. "Come here, I need a hug," he said, adding, "badly."

Shortly, they were in the lobby of the condominium building, pressing the code numbers which connected them to the Leibs's phone.

"Is it you?" Dr. Leib asked, jovial.

"It is I," said Maxie, "with a close relation."

Arthur tickled Maxie's ribs and whispered, "A *very close* relation."

"Well, do hurry up," Dr. Leib said, as he released the security-door lock that allowed access to the inner lobby and elevators. "We're on the third floor."

"Yes, we remember," said Maxie, as she took Arthur's hand and walked to the elevators. Inside the lift, Arthur pressed Number 3, and they were on their way to a greeting that would befit visiting dignitaries.

***

The Leibs stood in the marble-pillared hallway—he, having donned jacket and tie to signify the importance of this visit; she, in an elegant, multicolored wrap from South America, radiated joy as her eyes sought out Maxie's.

"Welcome, welcome, dearest friends. Please come in and make yourselves comfortable," Dr. Leib effused. Into Maxie's ear he whispered, "How are you, my little daughter?"

"I'm just fine, thank you," replied Maxie, warmed by the very personal greeting. She knew she was home, where she belonged.

"Arthur, dear boy, come in, and please say you're hungry," Dr. Leib intoned.

"I'm always hungry, you know that," answered Arthur. Maxie could see the muscles of his body relaxing, responding to the sheer pleasure of feeling special. As Arthur entered the apartment, Mrs. Leib guiding him by the elbow, he hoped that whatever it was that Maxie would learn this weekend would not result in chaos. He was not convinced that stirring up the tempest-pot of her past would bring her much peace of mind.

Dr. Leib put his arm around Maxie's shoulder and led her into the warm, familiar living room, decorated with the unique stamp of their individualism. Although not bound to a particular style nor design, nor to any trendy "look," the room was alive with its colorful collection of memorabilia and *recuerdos* from the Mediterranean Ocean to the Baltic Sea, from wherever their travels took them. A darkly lacquered, Oriental bench upholstered in deep crimson velvet, Guatemalan wall hangings, a brass samovar tucked into one of many niches in a hand-carved curio cabinet, and an intricately woven rug depicting an Aztec god that lay beneath an Italian kidney-shaped coffee table all seemed to be comfortable together in a room where nothing was circumscribed by convention. This room was an expression of unbound freedom, unlimited in its potential to please, to amuse, to mystify. And, at the center of it all stood a baby grand, a Steinway, dominant and proud, ready to fill the rooms of seeming randomness with sweet, comforting harmony.

"Please, sit down and make yourselves at home, as this is for you, always. Thank you for the most welcome of visits to which we must make a toast. Could I interest you in some sherry?" Dr. Leib was fussing over them, genuinely pleased that Maxie and Arthur had come.

"Thank you, we'll join you with some sherry," Arthur replied. Mrs. Leib came out of the kitchen bearing a variety of canapés and some dip for the chips already on the cocktail table. After everyone had partaken of the aperitif, Dr. Leib raised his glass once again to his guests and said, prophetically, "To our guests, dear friends, who, we hope, will continually find wonder and discovery along the path they walk together. Today the path leads to us. Therefore, here's to our sharing of affection and good times."

Arthur, accustomed to the ritual, raised his glass again and said, "To you, our dear and cherished friends who take us into your hearts as well as into your home with a graciousness we truly appreciate."

"That calls for some more sherry," quipped Dr. Leib, clearing his throat as he rose to refill the glasses.

"So tell us, Arthur," Mrs. Leib asked, "what has everyone been up to? How did it go with Rachel in Albany?"

"Oh, about as well as we expected," Arthur answered, glancing to his right to assess Maxie's demeanor.

"Well, don't worry so much. She'll adjust, I'm sure of it. Transitions are always difficult in the beginning, regardless of one's age." Suddenly, she was on her feet. "What do you think of our new acquisition, this splendid piece of sculpture? Look, it's a young couple embracing, but it comes apart. The pieces can be separated, then rejoined. Isn't it rather unusual?"

"It's very beautiful," Maxie said, with less enthusiasm than she intended.

"The artist, our friend Lilah, gave this to us during her last visit here. Her work has gained her international recognition, you know. She's a most talented young woman."

"Yes, I've heard of her," Arthur said, glancing again at his wife.

"Can you imagine, though, that when she comes here, she informs us that our place is too . . . too . . . what was the word she used, darling?"

"'Cluttered,' " Dr. Leib reminded his wife.

"Yes, she said there was just too much to take in at one time—that there was no space. Lilah gets distracted by our mementos."

"I can't see how anyone can have too many distractions," Maxie blurted, wishing immediately that she hadn't.

"I suppose we could be a bit more selective, but then again, why not see the whole spectrum of experience, all the lovely memories attached to each one?"

Maxie felt restless, uncomfortable with the turn of this conversation; she wondered if it were just coincidental that they were discussing memories.

"We don't see your home as 'cluttered'—not at all," Maxie said. "It has its own unique voice, and it speaks to all that you've seen, and done, and enjoyed—together. That's worth remembering."

Straightening his posture, adjusting his bowtie, Dr. Leib said, "Thank you, my dear, that was a sensitive remark, and we appreciate your understanding. Also, you must keep in mind that at our age, forgetfulness is not unusual. Now let's see; where were we? Oh yes, Arthur, you were telling us about your trip to Albany."

Maxie could not stand the tight knot in her stomach. Unconsciously, she began to fold down the corners of her cocktail napkin, refolding each one, methodically turning it over in her lap until it was small enough to roll between her thumb and forefinger. Spying the glass French doors behind Dr. Leib's chair, she let her consciousness drift up, like a weightless leaf tossed by a gentle autumn breeze. Her thoughts yearned for flight, for escape through the open doors. From somewhere distant, out of context, she heard her name as an echo, caroming off the walls of her inner sanctuary.

"Maxine," Mrs. Leib was saying, shaking Maxie's shoulder, "come into the kitchen and help me with the last preparations for dinner. The two of you must be starved."

Maxie saw the hardness in her friend's eyes, the firmness of her jaw. Now Maxie's regret was undeniable. She was sorry for being so damn self-indulgent, for making such an absurd request. Mentally slapping herself into the present, she arose and sheepishly followed Mrs. Leib into the narrow back kitchen. *Uh-oh; I'm gonna catch hell, I know it,* she thought.

What she caught was sympathy. "I know that look, Maxine, when you leave—when you go somewhere else in your mind," Cora Leib said gently. "Please, dear, don't be afraid that something is wrong. Tonight we'll have a quiet, joyful evening. Tomorrow I have planned for us to take a picnic to this lovely little town of Chambly, just south of here. There's a national historic park with an interesting old fort on the banks of the Richelieu River. We can sit and watch the rapids emptying into the basin . . . and, we can talk. How does that sound to you?" she asked, gently touching Maxie's cheek, stroking it in a rare physical display of affection.

"I'm sorry for the brooding. I promise to behave. A picnic does sound like fun. Arthur will take pictures, I'm sure. But to be honest, your own sad expression gives me pause. Are you not feeling well? Is there something you're not telling me?" Maxie had not considered these possibilities until this very moment.

"Everything is, and everything will be, all right, Maxine. You must not allow for self-reproach. You must not be the maker of your own undoing. All is fluid and transitory—there's only one thing that is immutable. Please keep this idea in your mind for tomorrow. Tonight, we shall laugh, make merry, and embrace each other in friendship."

It had been a carefully worded preface for what was to come. Maxie understood that whatever it was she would hear the next day, she would be expected to fit it into a context of fluidity, transitoriness, and blamelessness. She was being given the night to come to grips with what all of that meant.

"Now," Mrs. Leib asserted, "you may call the men to the table. Will you be having some of this baked chicken or are you going to be stubborn, as usual?" It was not a rebuke; Cora Leib was smiling as she opened the oven door.

Maxie tried her best to eat. The savory aroma of tarragon and basil pleased her senses, but she had no desire to actually chew and swallow the chicken set before her. Mindlessly, she played with a spear of broccoli, pushing it around her plate, rearranging the tiny, red bliss potatoes that had been served to her. As Arthur and Dr. Leib ate and discussed world events, Mrs. Leib sat pensively, her heart aching with apprehension. She buttered a small slice of baguette and handed it to Maxie. "Here, at least, have this," she said softly. Maxie accepted the bread and forced it down her throat with what remained of her wine. "Thanks," she whispered.

At midnight, Dr. Leib looked at his watch and decided that he should allow his guests to depart. "Maxine," he said solicitously, "you're looking a little drawn from your travels, and, I might add, from the lateness of the hour. Although we'd do nothing to hasten the conclusion of such a fine evening, I suggest that you and Arthur dispatch to your hotel for some rest. We have a lovely day planned for tomorrow, and we should all retire at a reasonable hour so as to be fit to enjoy this beautiful spot. What do you say?"

Dr. Leib's words were the cues she had been hoping to hear without blatantly eliciting them. "Yes, we are tired, however much we hate to conclude such a delightful evening. Both of you have been so gracious, but it's late and we really must be going." Maxie was already out of her seat and gathering up her jacket and purse as she made this declaration. Arthur rose slowly, almost reluctantly. Walking them to the doorway, Cora whispered in Maxie's ear, "Maxine, do not let your anxieties interfere with the opportunity for intimacy tonight. Remember Viola—be 'like Patience on a monument smiling at grief.'" There was a plaintive quality to her remark, and Maxie squeezed the hand that held hers as a sign that she understood.

"Good-night, sweet dreams," Mrs. Leib chirped. "Call us in the morning to arrange a meeting time."

"Drive carefully, old chap," called Dr. Leib.

"Good-night, and thank you for everything." Maxie and Arthur made their way to the elevator.

In the car, Arthur took Maxie's hand and kissed it, drawing her nearer to him. Her hands were cold, despite the unseasonably warm and humid night air. With the exception of a young man and his German shepherd standing beneath the yellow haze of a lamppost, the streets were quiet, sleepy. A vigilant policeman sat in his cruiser at the corner of St. Catherine and Avenue Reneé Lévesque, sipping hot coffee from a plastic cup. He eyed Arthur and Maxie as they stopped for a red light.

"Whew, what a great evening. Did you enjoy, Maxie?"

"Of course, but I felt funny—I don't know—picking up on vibrations, I guess."

"Vibrations? I picked up on a few from you too."

"What do you mean?" Maxie asked, wrapping her arms around herself, feeling queasy.

"You were quiet and constrained after dinner, Maxie. You had that faraway look about you, even when you were pretending to participate. What's the matter?" Arthur had been blunt. His own good time had been compromised by her behavior.

"I didn't think you'd noticed. I'm sorry. I did try not to ruin it for everyone," Maxie said in what was almost a whisper, close to tears.

"You're not going to tell me what you two were talking about in the kitchen?" asked Arthur.

"No, because nothing definitive happened—all was innuendo and the way Mrs. Leib seemed to me. She told me we'll talk tomorrow."

"Well, that's good. Hopefully you'll learn more."

When they entered their hotel room, the maid had already turned down the cool, crisp bed sheets; had set the radio to romantic listening music; and placed wrapped chocolates on each of the pillows. These they saved for Dr. Leib, whose sweet tooth was legendary. As Arthur approached her and drew her body close to his, Maxie's eye caught the red blinking of the message button on the phone. In the semidarkness, it pulsated with urgency. "Arthur, wait—we have a message. Please call down to the desk," she implored. Arthur called down, connected with the front desk operator, and Maxie heard him mumble, "Uh-hum, uh-hum. Well, thank you. *Oui, merci.*"

"What is it?" Maxie was holding her breath.

"The message was from Rachel. She said if we got in before midnight to call her. She's very unhappy. But," he added, "we're not going to call her now. We'll wait until morning. Maybe she'll settle down."

Maxie sat on the side of the bed, studying her long, slender fingers as she often did when she was too preoccupied or distressed to think. The involuntary twitching of a muscle just above Arthur's jaw revealed his own concern. His brow was deeply furrowed—his eyes sad.

"Please, just hold me," begged Maxie.

As Arthur tenderly wrapped his great, strong arms around his wife, she seemed to be shrinking, becoming smaller and more fragile by the moment. He held her, afraid that she might, indeed, disappear. Maxie lay her cheek against Arthur's chest. She could feel the pounding of his heart.

***

Maxie awoke to lambent sunshine that bathed the entire room with a golden peacefulness. For but a few moments that hung dreamily suspended in time, Maxie immersed, body and soul, in the tranquillity. Musing that this sedation required no physician's prescription, of which she had had too many, she reached for Arthur; but he was not there. Of course, she reasoned, he had gone down to the fitness room to work out his angst, his disappointment, his frustration. Collecting her thoughts, she remembered that they had fallen asleep fully clothed; neither had had enough energy nor the inclination to perform bedtime rituals. They had drifted out onto the cold, dark waters of sleep until some early morning hour when Arthur must have thrown off his own clothing and gently removed hers. *Poor Arthur,* she thought, *still nurturing and loving despite his own discomforts. His own solid store of patience must be waning. Even a stalwart with his intestinal fortitude had to have his limits.* Arthur was centered in his universe, grounded in his family's love.

She, however, lived hopelessly on the fringe of context, imbued with the sense of not belonging to or being part of a greater whole. She clung to the cusp of an orbit that was spinning out of control, being sucked into a dark hole. What she wanted was to matter other than cosmically. She needed to matter—to feel anchored to a good feeling, to being alive. *I wonder what it feels like to smile inside,* she pondered.

The sun slipped behind darkening clouds as her brooding dimmed the brightness and cooled the room. She speculated that Arthur had turned the air conditioner to maximum. His internal combustion invariably raised his body temperature and propelled him into action—any action that would alleviate the heat of anxiety. Pulling the covers to her chin, she tried to restore her equilibrium. A day of tremendous portent lay ahead of her, and she needed to regenerate some usable energy.

The jangling of the phone rattled her taut nerves. Resisting the impulse to ignore it, she reached for the receiver. "Hello?" she answered tentatively.

"Good morning, my dear. Did you sleep well? You appeared to be so tired last night, we felt guilty for keeping you." Mrs. Leib's voice was once again hale and hearty.

"Yes, we slept—adequately," she said, groping conspicuously for the right choice of words.

"Is something the matter, Maxine? Didn't you get enough rest?"

"Yes, yes, of course. Arthur went down to the health club and should be returning momentarily," Maxie improvised. She had no idea what time it was nor how long Arthur had been working out.

"Well, then, what time shall we expect you? We've already had our morning walk, and it's truly a splendid day for a picnic. Are you still up to it?" The question was loaded with innuendo and subtlety.

"I await the unfolding of this day with unbridled curiosity and expectation. How's that for enthusiasm?"

"Maxine, if nothing else, you're never obtuse. Come soon and come hungry. We shall have a surfeit of delights on which to satiate the most voracious of appetites. You, who eat so little, will receive a different sampling of sustenance."

"Now you've countered the obtuse with the oblique—touché. We shall be at your door at 12:00 noon. I must have at least one cup of sobering French coffee for my fortification. See you then."

"Oh, Maxine," Mrs. Leib interjected, "have you heard from Rachel?"

"Oh, my goodness, I almost forgot! Rachel is awaiting a call from us. She left a message here last night that she was really unhappy and to please call her!" Maxie, caught off balance by the repartee, heard her voice rising.

"Well, I'll let you do that now. Please try to rein in your sympathies though. Be understanding but firm. Try to encourage her to give it time, for these uprootings are always disturbing to one's sense of security and self-confidence. And, oh, yes, please send her our love. Tell her to write to me; perhaps she'd like that."

"Yes, I'll do my best to convince her," sighed Maxie, totally unsure of her footing on such slippery terrain.

Maxie heard Arthur's key in the door and was relieved to see him enter the room looking refreshed and more relaxed.

"You look rejuvenated," she said.

"I had enough energy for two more hours worth, but I figured you'd be waiting for me. You're still in bed though. Feeling all right?"

"I've been on the phone with Mrs. Leib. They expect us at noon." Glancing at the clock, she saw to her relief that it was only 10 A.M. Feeling cowardly, she asked, "Arthur, would you please return Rachel's call? I don't have the patience nor the will right now to do it. Please?"

"Sure, all right. But first I need a hug—a big one," he teased.

"A big hug is all you get, for now."

"Go ahead, Maxie, start getting ready. I'll call Rachel and try to put out the fires."

Relieved, Maxie jumped out of bed and made haste for the bathroom. She knew Arthur would say the right things; she didn't need to coach him. As he dialed, she disappeared into the safety of fragrant soaps, body lotions, and plush towels, taking more time than she needed; it was time she really wanted. Finally emerging from the steamy bathroom, wrapped in a thick, white terry cloth robe, skin shining and pink, she found Arthur sitting by the window, reading a chapter in *The Dental Clinics of North America*, a traveling staple.

"Well?" Maxie asked, hesitantly.

"Well, she's miserable and wants to go home. I made a deal with her," said Arthur, irritated, barely looking up at Maxie. "I agreed to leave here early on Monday and visit with her on our way home."

"And what is *her* end of the deal?" Maxie interrupted, impatiently.

"She's to do her best to meet some girls and to try to find some positives. I also told her that since her classes wouldn't start till Tuesday, she should hold off on impetuous first impressions or judgments."

"You said the right things. Now let's hope she keeps her part of the bargain." Maxie was not optimistic. She folded her doubt like a dollar bill and stuffed it into her mental wallet.

"Finish dressing and let's get going with the day. I'm hungry for some of those tasty treats in the breakfast room." Arthur was signaling his wish to end the conversation.

Maxie, however, asked ruefully, "Did she ask where I was?"

"I told her you were showering and would speak to her tomorrow."

"That's fine. Tomorrow it will be my turn," she said, worried about the appearance of her not caring.

•23•

There is something symbolic—spiritual, perhaps—in the vertical alignment of the hands on a clock as they designate noon and midnight. Maxie perceived the union of time's hands in a heavenly projection as a way to lend a sense of order and exactitude to each day—a day that otherwise might be random and chaotic. People did things either before noon or after, before midnight or after, structuring their days with the assurance of at least two constants in mind.

Maxie had arbitrarily chosen noon as their meeting time and wanted to be punctual. The bells of Notre Dame Cathedral pealed in the distance as Arthur pulled up to the curb fronting the Leibs's condominium. Emerging from behind glass doors, smiling broadly, the Leibs appeared eager for the planned festivities. Dressed in a red floral skirt and white cotton blouse with a jewel-neck collar, Cora Leib looked youthful, expectant. Her dangling silver earrings swayed merrily with each hurried step toward the car. A straw tote bag of picnic "goodies" hung from straps looped over her forearm. Bowing deeply, with exaggerated chivalry, Dr. Leib opened the rear car door and helped his wife into the back seat.

"Good day to both of you!" Dr. Leib proclaimed, taking his seat behind Arthur. "We've missed you since last night!"

"Good day to you, Professor. We've really been looking forward to today," said Arthur, reaching around to exchange hearty handshakes with his friend. "Judging from the size of that bag you're holding, I'd say we're going to be eating all afternoon!"

"How do you know you'll like what I made?" Cora teased.

"Because you never disappoint me," Arthur countered, checking for traffic in the rearview mirror before pulling away from the curb.

"Did you have a good night's sleep, Maxine?" Dr. Leib asked.

"Yes, despite the noisy guests in the room next to ours. They were quarreling over something for quite a while."

"You should have called the front desk to complain," Cora said testily, "what with the exorbitant rates they charge!" There was an uncharacteristic tenseness in her voice, a barely perceptible half-beat out of step that quickened Maxie's breathing. "Anyway, the weather has decided in our favor. I thought earlier that it might rain. So, Arthur, onward ho!"

This is not like her, Maxie thought. *Earlier, she said it was a "splendid day." Now, she's pessimistic.*

"Do you know the way, my boy?" Dr. Leib asked, leaning forward, patting Arthur on the shoulder. "I believe you need to go south on the *autoroute*, your next right, if I'm not mistaken."

"Yes, I checked a map before leaving the hotel. You're right," Arthur assured them.

"Well then, I'll just sit back and enjoy the view. By the way, I was thinking more about our discussion last night concerning the sorry state of affairs we call our educational system," Dr. Leib commented.

"Yes, so was I," Arthur said.

"You know, there is a lack of real thought by this new generation of college students. They seem to think that body language is the true conveyance of concrete ideas."

"Maxie and I were discussing that very point after dinner with the girls—just the other night," Arthur said. "A bit disingenuous, don't you think?"

"Indeed. And it's not just the younger generation," Dr. Leib continued. "Public discourse among adults reflects no real understanding of the historical, cultural, or political contexts from which certain events are spawned." Warming to his subject, annoyance crept into his voice. "Everyone has an opinion, regardless of his or her capacity to comprehend what the press, those information bartenders, mix up for the evening newscasts."

"First they distill information so it can be swallowed in one gulp. They get you drunk on your delusions of being knowledgeable," Cora chimed in. "Don't you agree, Maxine?"

Disengaged, Maxie groped for a reply. "I'm sorry. I was still thinking about that couple arguing last night," she feigned.

Cora reached forward to playfully tug at a lock of hair on the back of Maxie's head. *Stop worrying, I know—but I just can't,* Maxie fretted, turning around to look behind her. Cora winked conspiratorially, fingering her silver pendant necklace, wrapping it around her forefinger. *She can't fool me. I can tell when she's nervous.*

Dr. Leib and Arthur continued their discussion without further input from the women. Maxie and Cora remained captive to their private fears.

"We're here," Arthur announced triumphantly, parking in a vacant spot. "Everybody out!"

Alighting from the car, Maxie, Arthur, and the Leibs heard the low, pulsating hum of the rapids muffling all other sounds of raucous humanity. Unlike the dramatic exhibition of Niagara Falls, where nature roared and thundered its power, the cool, pristine waters of Chambly tumbled gracefully in a peaceful, soothing rhythm. Maxie stood motionless, unable to break the spell that quieted the constant hammering in her ears. Cora was the first to speak. "These waters are said to have ameliorative, healing powers for suffering souls. The falls have a legendary effect on the psyche. Some would go so far as to liken the sounds and sensations to being in a womb. Whatever the validity of those claims, I, for one, already feel more relaxed. Come, fellow journeymen, let's make our way to the picnic tables and some shade."

Cora spied an unoccupied table in the shade of an ancient oak tree. "This spot is ideal. Let's stay right here," she suggested, sitting down on the wooden bench attached to a picnic table. Dr. Leib deposited their straw bag on the table and stuck his hand inside it, pulling out turkey breast sandwiches on crusty rye bread, each tucked in a plastic baggie. "Wait till I distribute the paper plates, sweetheart," Cora scolded gently. "Oh, I forgot bowls for the gazpacho!" she wailed.

"I remembered," Maxie told her, producing the bowls she had packed in the cooler.

"Bless you, dear. Now, let's see. We have potato salad, coleslaw, carrot sticks. For you, Maxine, a few little tortilla chips too." As she spoke, Cora extracted plastic containers from the bag, lifted the lids, and pointed out what each contained. Dr. Leib handed out forks, spoons, and knives.

"What would you like to drink?" Arthur asked, placing a variety of beverages on the table. "Everything stayed cold, Maxie. I'm surprised."

Maxie sat down to unwrap her sandwich, determined to get at least half of it down. Cora watched her out of the corner of her eye, silently vowing not to make a big deal over Maxie's eating habits.

After taking a mouthful of his sandwich, Arthur turned to Maxie. "Where did you put the camera? This calls for a picture."

"It's right beside me—off the ground and out of the sun—what you always tell me."

"Good. Can you hand it to me?"

"Shall we lift our cups and make a toast while you snap those pictures?" Dr. Leib had his cup already raised.

"Great idea. Now wait just a minute while I get the right focus. There—all set—OK—everybody smile at the camera." Arthur clicked away as three plastic cups came together, raised high over the center of the table.

"To life, *lechayim!*" Dr. Leib toasted.

"*Lechayim,* to life!" Arthur responded.

"So, when do we get dessert?" Dr. Leib joked, an impish grin on his face.

Maxie could not help laughing. She was so full of love for the Leibs, so grateful to them for every kindness, every word of reassurance. *How I wish these moments would last forever,* she thought, absently turning a soda can around in circles.

Munching on his sandwich, Arthur asked, "Do you know anything about that old stone fort over there?" He was pointing Dr. Leib's attention to a structure in the distance, down by the river basin.

"No, but I have a feeling you'd like to investigate."

"Sure would. It looks interesting."

"What a splendid idea," Cora said, pleased that her husband was quick to seize upon an excuse for separating.

When they finished their meals, Dr. Leib rose from the table and took Arthur by the elbow. "My boy, there are times when we men must seek some diversion, some adventure. Come, let's you and I explore. You can snap some good pictures, and I'll pose for posterity!"

"Have fun," Maxie said, pleased that she would have time alone with Cora. She watched the men slowly descending the knoll that sloped toward the footpath below. Arthur turned to wave, then put his arm around Dr. Leib's shoulders. Their outlines faded into the crowd and disappeared. "Arthur seemed excited, like a little boy," Maxie remarked. But Cora, uninterested in small talk, did not answer; she did not look up. Maxie hung back, unnerved by the eerie feeling she was experiencing, wondering about Cora's disengagement. Finally, aggrieved by what she was about to do, Cora sat down on the bench, laying both palms of her hands downward in front of her, as if holding on for balance. She stared at a mustard stain on the wooden table and tried to rub it out with her finger.

"What is it, Mrs. Leib?" Maxie asked, instinctively reaching for her throat. Her voice was raspy, strained.

"Maxine, what do you want to talk to me about? You mentioned that you wanted to ask me questions about your college years—years I should think you would want to forget."

"I need to know why I felt so hollow, so lost when I arrived at Selby. I kept falling, stumbling around in the dark, constantly depressed. I suffered every day, not knowing what was fueling my desperation." Maxie stopped to catch her breath, anxious to spill it all out of her roiling gut—vomiting the poison that made her sick. "Then you were there—and I could only feel better when you were. You made me feel—alive. I used to watch you leave the campus in your little gray car. I'd wave to you from my dorm room, knowing that you could not see me. I missed you as soon as you were gone."

"And then I did go away—for quite a long while, didn't I? Is that why you wrote those letters to me in the hospital?"

"I know this sounds crazy, but I felt abandoned, scared to death that you wouldn't come back. Did I imagine that?" Maxie felt so ashamed, so vulnerable again.

"I didn't fully appreciate the depth of your feelings, Maxine. How could I? I saw your sadness all the time, in your eyes, in the way you searched mine, looking for something to connect to. And then I began to feel it."

"Why didn't you walk away from me—from my torment? Everyone else did. I mean, how much of my despair could you possible stomach?" *There I said it—what I've been so afraid of all these years—that she would, at some point, get sick of me and leave.*

Cora Leib, having prepared herself for this moment, did not flinch from Maxie's outburst. In fact, Cora was calmer now than during the tension-filled ride to Chambly. She waded deeper into Maxie's troubled waters. "Maxine, I have never seen you *this* distraught in all the years that I've known you." Leaning forward, taking Maxie's hands into her own—a trembling passed like electric current between them—she began: "You're a grown woman with a child's heart, my dear. And I'm very much like an army courier bound to deliver a wartime telegram to the parents of some hapless young man blown up in the trenches. I'll be that much responsible for the intense emotion you'll undoubtedly feel when I'm finished. So, I must appeal to that part of you that is now a woman. Only you have the power to nurse and comfort the child within you." As she spoke, Cora released Maxie's hands and reached into her handbag, producing an envelope clearly yellowed by age. "This, Maxine, is a letter written to me almost thirty years ago by your mother."

Stupefied, Maxie gasped, "You received a letter from *my mother?* Sarah wrote to *you?"*

"Yes, my dear. And having wrestled all these years with the opposing forces contained within, I now have decided to let you read it. I'm not at all sure I am doing the right thing. I appeal to your sense of balance, your need to see perspective. It's an execrable letter, but perhaps it will help you to break the chains of your emotional enslavement—and get on with your life." There were thin, luminous tracks of wetness on Cora's timeless face. "Here. Perhaps you may want some privacy as you read. I'll be over there by the promenade alongside the water. Come join me when you're able." Mrs. Leib rose slowly, lips pressed tightly together. She retreated silently.

Maxie took the saw-toothed letter from its plain envelope. Recognizing Sarah's tight, self-conscious script—almost identical to her own—she flushed with embarrassment. Sarah had written to her . . . to *her* dearest friend. *How could she do this to me?* she fumed, as she began to read the letter.

March 8, 1963

"Dear Mrs. Leib:

"Although we have never met, I feel that I know you very well. You are all Max seems to talk about these days. She has told me about your car accident and hospitalization. For many weeks she has been so worried about you. I'm glad to hear that you're back to your teaching duties at Selby, and I hope your recovery has been complete. Max has been wretched since your departure, and will, I hope, recover along with you.

"I'm writing this letter as one woman seeking the understanding and wisdom of another. The fact is, I need your help. To be more specific, I need your solemn oath that nobody will ever know about this letter, especially Max. It is a commitment that I am pleading for, as I'm sure that over the years we will meet, be together at future family affairs. You are family to Max and no celebrated event in her life will be complete without you. So, I'm asking you to pledge secrecy and help that only you can give.

"My adult life has been as bitter and disappointing as my childhood. There have been losses I have never been able to accept. My marriage, in particular, has been a curse. After the first insufferable six years of marriage to a cold-hearted, ignorant man, I decided to go to him to beg for a divorce. As you know, in those days divorce was not a socially acceptable alternative, and I was risking all financial security, as well as my reputation. My own mother had told me that I had to 'sleep in the bed I had made,' that she wouldn't take me and my daughter Toby back into her house. I did not take into account the full depth or range of Philip's violent temper. He gave me his answer in the form of a brutal beating and tongue-lashing, calling me a whore and telling me that he would show *me* who wore the pants in his house. After ripping the phone off the wall and severing the wires, he raped me. Maxine was the product of that terrible night, one which left me with no options, with nowhere to go. Having one child and pregnant with another, I was forced to live with my 'answer.'

"And now comes the hardest part to admit. Please find it in your heart to understand. I made various attempts to abort this child I was carrying. Even before she was born, I knew that I could never learn to love her. Abortion, at that time, was as shameful as suicide. I could not consider the latter because I had another child.

"Mrs. Leib, Maxie was born 'defective' as my husband put it because, I'm convinced, of some of those efforts to abort. Caring for a helpless child requires time and patience. It is heartbreaking when you love that child. But every time I looked down at my daughter, I relived that tragic night and all of the evil that created her. Taking care of her was further punishment to me.

"I have not been kind to Maxie. She has tried tirelessly to make me love her. There was nothing this child did not do to try to win my approval. It just was not there to be had. I have caused her untold pain, I know that. I guess I just cannot help hurting her. That is why I'm asking for your help. Will you, whom she adores, take my place in her heart? Will you please tend to the needs which I have never made the effort to care about? Will you love her as I have not, as I cannot? My guilt and shame must disgust you. Please, do this for Max. She is about to crack from the strain, from what she correctly sees as a life of lies. I have bared my soul and most intimate feelings to you. You are the only person who knows. And this is the only truth I have told for twenty years. Please help us both.

Sincerely,
Sarah M. Kahn"

Maxie crumpled the letter in her fist, then threw it down in anguish. Dizzy from the shock of Sarah's confession, she put her head down, burying it in the crook of her left elbow. Involuntarily, she began to shake. *Oh, my God—Oh, dear God in Heaven. No—*

Yes! So it's true, after all—I'm falling, falling—can't breathe, can't hold on—Please, let me die!

Suddenly, she felt the warmth of another body envelop her in an embrace so strong, so penetrating. With trembling fingers, Cora stroked Maxie's face, caressed her wanting spirit.

"It's all right, my child. You will endure this startling revelation. I have known death on many levels. I am well-acquainted with loss. I say to you that you *will* have lightness in your heart again. Do not permit the tentacles of devastation to enter your soul. Be strong, my dear. Have courage." Holding Maxie close, Cora rocked her gently, as if she were a child. Wrapped in this maternal embrace, Maxie could feel the fire that burned her throat, scalded her eyes. Giving herself up to the flames, she lowered her exhausted self down onto Cora's lap, buried her head in the folds of Cora's exotic print skirt, and emptied the sealed vessel of her emotions. Cora waited out the storm with relief; this wrenching and heaving was what she had expected. She continued to gently stroke Maxie's hair, gentle strokes that Maxie felt far below the surface of her scalp. When Maxie was fully drained of her despair, she lifted her head. Her eyes were swollen; her face blotched, etched with grief.

"What now, Mrs. Leib? What do I do now?" Maxie whispered.

"Let us start with your calling me Cora. That is my name, you know."

"No, I can't do that. Don't you see that would just spoil everything," Maxie argued, groping in her pocket for a tissue.

"No, Maxine, you're wrong," Cora said, lifting Maxie's chin with her finger, skewering her to the moment with smoldering intensity. This was the Cora of years ago, at Selby, burning into Maxie's very being. "Would you have me hide behind some pretense, a conceit?"

"I don't understand."

"You didn't know it at the time, Maxine—there's so much I've kept from you. But those poignant, hopeful letters you wrote gave *me* something to hang onto. You cared more than—most." Taking a deep breath, letting it out slowly, she added, "I didn't need to be *told* by Sarah to love you—I already did. I am, after all, a mother too."

Maxie's tongue seemed wrapped in gauze—cheap words, trapped in cotton.

"I never wanted you to think of me as Sarah's substitute, a surrogate mother," Cora Leib confessed. "I wanted to love you more perfectly than she could—or would. And what I wanted was for you to need me with the open honesty of a child. Does that make sense to you?"

"I can need you because you *want* to be needed?"

"Exactly. We're all *somebody's* child, and we all have childish needs, even when we're grown. There's no shame in needing."

"So, I was right—my mother did hate me. No wonder she refused to tell me that she loved me," Maxie said, a huge lump forming in her throat.

"Neither have I—till now."

"You never had to."

"And you were afraid that your feelings toward me wouldn't be returned, yes?"

Maxie nodded, embarrassed.

"Rejection truly is the cruelest punishment I know, Maxine. It's a slow death of the soul." Cora looked away then, far across the Chambly basin to another, distant shore. Her words, like the cascading falls, washed over both of them, absorbing, while being absorbed.

Maxie straightened, took a deep breath, ran her hands over her damp face. "I didn't think I was worthy of you," she said, staring down at Sarah's letter which lay crumpled on the ground.

Facing Maxie once again, her brow pleated with pity, Cora continued. "Imagine that one day, you're in a museum, standing before and marveling at, say, Picasso's *Guernica*, when suddenly a madman comes rushing in and slashes it with a razor blade. How do you think you'd feel?"

"The thought of it makes me cringe."

"That's why it hangs encased in glass, shielded from such depravity."

"But what are you saying about us?" Maxie asked, confused.

"I'm saying that our priceless friendship has had to be protected—we knew that instinctively, the day our hearts came together. So, we erected a shield around us to keep ourselves safe."

"You mean from Sarah?"

"Yes. From Sarah."

Maxie smiled as she felt her anger cooling, her sadness receding. Hoarsely, she said, "I'm feeling so tired. Can we go back now?"

"Of course, dear Maxine, but first you must straighten your hair, pull yourself together. Do you have sunglasses? You may want to put them on. The men are on their way back, and I'm certain that Arthur will be frightened if he discerns the depth of your upset. Tell him later, when you're alone. For now, modestly entice him to return to the hotel."

"Yes, I understand," Maxie complied, gathering herself and her things about her. "Later. Thank you, Mrs.—I mean—" She could not make herself say the name. Not yet. Maybe some other endearment, but not "Cora." And then, like a bolt of lightning, it hit her. "You've kept your promise, haven't you?" she asked.

"To one of you, at least," Cora Leib replied, philosophically adding, "Have I waited too long, dear Maxine? Have I not done the most curative thing?"

"You've always known. All these years—why didn't you tell me?"

Cora rose, smoothed the front of her damp, wrinkled skirt, and sighed. "I thought that as you matured, you would make a new life—that you would look to Arthur and your children for pleasure. I hoped that the role you had ascribed to your mother as the key to your happiness would diminish, never suspecting that my own role would become so critical." Unexpectedly, she sat down again. With hands now clasped tightly in her lap, her head bowed, she added, "Perhaps I didn't want to believe that I was, somehow, *responsible* for your happiness. No one is, you know."

Trying to digest Cora's words, Maxie replied, "It seems to me that truth stays the same no matter how it changes anyone who discovers it. Look how many lives have been altered by one random, senseless act!" She was remembering the tearful stranger and the nodding stars in her dream.

"Yes, my dear. But it's from our greatest pain that we fashion beauty."

"What will I do when you're no longer here to love me?" Maxie asked, unabashedly.

"Hopefully, by then, you will have learned to love yourself," Cora answered, rising again to greet her husband and Arthur with effortless poise and composure. "Darling," she said to her husband, "we're about ready to leave now. If it's all right with you and Arthur, we'd like to head back."

Dr. Leib, rocking back and forth on heels and toes, raising his shoulders and then relaxing them fully, said, "No objections from the defense, Your Honor. Proceed at will." With quiet ceremony, the Leibs collected their belongings and started back to the car.

Though perplexed, Arthur lifted the cooler and hung his camera around his neck. On the way to the car, Arthur put his arm around Maxie's waist, slowing her pace, wanting to drop back a few paces behind the Leibs. "Maxie, why the big rush? Geez, you should've seen the inside of that old fort. It's a mini-museum with artifacts and old maps, and a neat little movie about the French resisters. You ought to. . . ."

"Maybe next time, Arthur," Maxie cut him off.

"Hon, what's going on?"

"We'll talk back at the room."

"You're not mad at me for going off to the fort, are you?"

"No, I'm not mad—just totally exhausted."

They caught up to the Leibs waiting patiently by the car. "We're ready to roll whenever you are, Arthur," Dr. Leib said. As Cora settled into the back seat behind Maxie, Dr. Leib helped load the trunk. He then took his seat beside his wife, looking deeply into her darkened eyes. Cora's discreet nod confirmed what he wanted to know. Maxie rested her head against the front passenger window and closed her eyes, wishing that Arthur would get into the car more quickly. To her chagrin, Arthur was setting up his tripod, preparing to take a picture of the falls. Prickled with impatience, Maxie called out to him, "Arthur, we're all anxious to leave. Can you take just one?" Knowing nothing of the day's unraveling, Arthur called back over his shoulder, "The lighting is just perfect for scenic pictures, hon. Just hold on a sec." Maxie groaned and repositioned her head against the window. When, at last, Arthur took to the wheel, he found Maxie asleep. With a puzzled look, he turned around to the Leibs in the back seat.

"It's been a tiring day, Arthur," Cora Leib informed him. "Maxine will tell you about it when you two are alone."

Arthur turned back to the wheel, started the engine, and slowly backed the car out of the parking area. As he maneuvered onto the highway, cautiously merging with oncoming traffic, he could not figure out what had happened. "I thought it was a beautiful day."

"It was, Arthur," Cora assured him, "but beauty has its price."

"I'm feeling very left out," Arthur complained, dissatisfied. As they drove home in heavy silence, Arthur tried to catch glimpses of the Leibs in the rearview mirror; he did not recognize what he saw on their strained faces—sphinx-like visages, inscrutable keepers of a mystery he could not fathom. "You can't do this to me," he wanted to shout, but didn't. Cora, appreciating Arthur's dilemma, leaned forward and whispered, "Sometimes things have to worsen before they can improve, Arthur. Some of us, at times, must be instruments of the former. You'll have the chance to make things better for Maxine, I promise you. Please don't feel rejected."

"She's found something out, hasn't she? It's what we were both afraid of."

"Don't be afraid," Cora said, settling back in her seat. "Don't be afraid."

***

After returning the Leibs to their condo, Arthur promised to call them concerning dinner arrangements—if indeed there were to be a dinner—then drove Maxie back to the hotel. Tossing his keys to Jacques, he said, "Don't bring it down to the lot, all right? We'll be going out again in a few hours."

"No problem, Dr. Lane. I'll keep my eye on it." Jacques opened the car door for Maxie to assist her in getting out. She smiled at the doorman, very grateful for his steady hand. "Is there anything you need sent to your room, Madame? Some fresh fruit, maybe?" Jacques asked.

"No, we'll be going for dinner soon, but thanks," Arthur replied, amazed at how quickly Maxie had entered the lobby. She was already heading toward the elevators when he caught up to her. "Hey, wait for me," he called.

On their way up to the thirty-second floor, Maxie rested her head on Arthur's shoulder. "I really am tired. I need to lie down, unwind, sort things out."

"What things?" Arthur asked, stepping out of the elevator,

reaching in his pocket for the door key.

"Arthur, Mrs. Leib gave me a letter to read today. It was written thirty years ago."

"So?" Arthur asked, opening the door, flicking on the light switch.

"Sarah wrote the letter."

"Sarah? To Mrs. Leib? Why did she do that?"

Maxie flipped off her shoes and sprawled out on top of the bed, not bothering to fold down the top quilt. "She felt some perverse need to tell Mrs. Leib why she cannot love me."

"WHAT?" Arthur could not believe what he was hearing. "What did she say?"

"Her big secret, Arthur—that Philip raped her, got her pregnant. You're looking at the result. Mrs. Leib has known all along, and I never suspected."

Arthur, taken more aback by Maxie's succinct manner than with the disclosure itself, paused. "Yes, I think you did. Be honest," Arthur urged. "I think you always guessed there was some deep, dark secret that made Sarah treat you so cruelly. It's just so weird that she would tell Mrs. Leib. Geez, the whole damn thing is weird," he said, sitting on the bed Indian-style, elbows on his knees, his head supported by two fists under his chin.

"In a way, things are less weird, now that I know. The only thing I don't get is why she took it out on *me.* Wouldn't it make more sense to hate Philip?" Maxie turned over on her side to face Arthur.

"She did hate Philip, remember? Maxie, your mother's mind is in total chaos—she's never been able to think things out rationally. Sarah's a fatuous, selfish liar, but also a very sick woman. I know she's your mother, but if I ever see her again, I'll. . . ."

"You'll what? Slap her? Kick her face in? Maybe kill her?" Maxie felt the futility of retribution. There was nothing to be gained from wanting to settle the score. "There's no shred of maternal instinct left in that woman you call 'my mother'—if there ever was any. I've got to learn to accept that—somehow." Maxie rolled back over onto her back and stared at the ceiling.

"You can start by disassociating her actions from who you are or, for that matter, who you're going to be from now on. You have to stop wringing your hands like some Lady Macbeth—and soon." Arthur turned to his wife, reached out to her; but Maxie had begun to recede into the darkness of that other place where she sought reprieve, refuge. "I love you, Maxie," he whispered. "Please don't go away in your head again. Please stay here with me."

"Love me now, Arthur," Maxie begged, resurfacing.

In the afterglow of a luminous sunset, incipient shadows crept along the banks of the Richelieu. Like an afterthought, Sarah's letter fluttered in a gusty, aberrant wind, then tumbled across the picnic area, past an old man dozing upright—his worn, floppy fisherman's cap pulled down low over his brow, hands folded on his chest. Weightless, unnoticed, the crumpled paper floated to the cataract. Rippled fingers snatched the indictment, sucked it downstream, and silenced its message in a churning current.

***

Cora Leib sat at her piano and played nonstop for an hour, but the Chopin and Brahms eased her spirits only slightly. While this was normally her most efficient release of energy and fear, she was, nonetheless, burdened. She continued to question her decision to confront Maxie with that revolting letter. Yet, she had felt obliged to help her guileless friend capture a crumb of peace. They were all getting older; she could no longer hide her role as unindicted co-conspirator. Cora truly believed that she had withheld the letter from Maxie all these years to protect, to shield. Turning the pages of her music, playing with an unusual heaviness of hand, she pondered what to do next. What could she possibly say to this little bird she, in fact, had wounded herself. Her husband, reading on the sofa, listening to the intensity of sound emanating from the piano, watched in silence as his wife of fifty years struggled with her conscience, with yet another dilemma. Peering over his half-glasses, Dr. Leib studied her lean frame bent in close to the keyboard, illuminated by the glow of a floor lamp that teetered from the vibrations. With a practiced hand, Cora kneaded the keys, coaxing the dulcet tones that, like old friends, gave her strength, cheered her. High color rose in her cheeks; perspiration clung to the nape of her dark, silky hair. Dr. Leib wished he could tenderly run his fingers over the deep tracks of worry on his wife's brow, but knew to leave her alone; she would come to him when she was spent. Finally, reaching to her right, Cora turned off the small brass piano lamp, closed the book, and rose from the bench.

"Come sit beside me," Dr. Leib said quietly, patting the cream sofa cushion next to him.

Cora complied, curling up like a kitten, soft and vulnerable. Slipping her arm around his, she sighed, "I hope she'll be all-right. I cannot bear the thought of another tragedy."

"She doesn't have to know, my love. Maxine will endure. I'm positive of it. She needs time to face the devils head-on, in the lair. I have a feeling she'll be looking at herself differently now. Truth is, and always will be, preferable to perverse deception for our Maxine. She appealed poignantly to your sense of fairness and honesty. She must feel, in the end, indebted to your courage to tell her." Dr. Leib patted his wife's hand affectionately. He continued to hold it in silence until both drifted off into suspended quiescence, each feeling the nibbling of uneasiness, the niggling of uncertainty.

***

The shrill ring of the phone rattled the stillness in the air. Arthur awoke from a deep sleep with a start, disoriented. Reaching for the phone, he accidentally knocked it off the cradle. Clumsily, he retrieved it and answered, catching sight of the radio clock.

"Hello?"

"Dad? This is Rachel."

"Oh, hi, honey. Mom and I just dozed off for a bit. All that country-fresh air made us sleepy, I guess," Arthur fibbed, quite sure that Rachel was not about to believe his excuse for being in bed at 6 P.M. "How are you doing?"

"Well, I called to tell you that you *don't* have to come down here tomorrow on your way home. I decided to try and work things out myself as best I can. I still don't like it here—I still feel very uncomfortable. My roommate's hardly ever around. She spends all-nighters with boys she's just met."

"I think you're doing the right thing, honey. It just takes a little time. Please be patient."

"Can I speak to Mom?" Rachel asked.

"She's right here. Hold on," Arthur said, handing the phone to Maxie who was already awake and listening intently.

"Hi, sweetie," Maxie said brightly, shaking off the previous day's guilt.

"I just told Dad that you don't need to come down here for me tomorrow. He'll fill you in on the other stuff. How are you enjoying your weekend? How are the Leibs?" Rachel changed the subject so that she would not change her mind.

"We're all enjoying our time together, as usual. Today we had a delightful picnic with the Leibs at this charming park and fort in Chambly. I guess we all tired ourselves out and needed to take naps."

"Mom, Dad doesn't take naps," Rachel replied, with some mischief in her voice.

"Well, my love, he's on vacation, you know," Maxie countered with good-natured banter. "We'll call you during the week, after you've had a chance to meet your professors and size up your classes. Good luck, and honey . . ."

"Yes, Mom?"

"I love you very much. And I'm so very proud of you."

"I love you, too, Mom. Talk to you soon. Best regards to the Leibs."

Maxie handed the phone back to Arthur, who returned it to the cradle. "Did she tell you she wants to try and see it through—at least temporarily—by herself?" he asked.

"No, but I got the gist of that from your end of the conversation. Let's hope she's adequately equipped to do it," Maxie sighed.

"You just *gave* her what she needs," Arthur said. "Now, we'd better call the Leibs. Do you want to get together for dinner? I'd like to take them out, if you're up to it."

"Sure," Maxie said, cheered and strengthened by Arthur's sensitive remark. I'll call and set it up. You can start getting ready."

"Tell them I won't take 'no' for an answer, to be ready at 7:30." Arthur was already in the bathroom.

Maxie waited for what seemed like an eternity before Mrs. Leib answered in a soft whisper. "Hello?"

"Hello, Mrs. Leib. This is Maxie. Did I wake you?"

"My goodness, I guess we inadvertently dozed off, or rather fell deeply asleep. What time is it now? Have we ruined our plans for dinner?"

"No, no, on the contrary. We just spoke with Rachel. She seems to be making more of an effort to adjust. We, too, dozed off for a while. Would you like to be our guests for dinner tonight? Arthur says he'll be offended if you refuse."

"Well, are you up to it, Maxine? Are you coming to terms with what transpired this afternoon?" Mrs. Leib tactfully inquired.

"I'm just fine, and I'll be finer having dinner with you tonight. Can you be ready at 7:30? We can go to Gibby's for old times' sake."

"It sounds much too tempting to resist," Mrs. Leib answered, the lilt coming back into her voice. "We'll be downstairs at 7:30 with bells on toes, and buttons and bows," she sang, revitalized and obviously relieved.

"Before you hang up," Maxie interjected, "I want to thank you for—well, for having had the courage to show me that letter. It had to be a difficult day for you too."

"Maxine," Cora Leib said, her voice cracking with emotion, "you are dearer to me than you can imagine. Sometimes we must endure the deepest, most exquisite moments of pain in order to emerge with transcendent joys and untold pleasures. Adversity can lead us to a renaissance of the spirit, provided that we don't lose our hope. I detect a nuance of that hope in your voice right now, and that reassures me. Good-bye until 7:30."

Arthur emerged from the shower to find Maxie smiling and weeping simultaneously. Confused, he asked, "What's wrong, Maxie?"

"Nothing is wrong. I have just learned the meaning of agony and ecstasy." Maxie smiled warmly, happily at her husband. He dried her tears with kisses.

"Time to get dressed, hon. That shower is going to make you feel terrific. Are we on for 7:30?"

"Yes, but, do we have any bells?"

"Bells?"

"Never mind—bows will do." With that, Maxie disappeared into the shower.

•24•

For Maxie, leaving Montreal was much like leaving home for the first time—at least, how she imagined it should have been. As Arthur drove onto the Champlain Bridge, Maxie turned to look out the back window. As she watched the Montreal skyline shrink, recede, and finally disappear, she could feel her heart pulling her back, pleading to stay. Her mind became a theater in which a newly composed overture had just begun, filling the empty spaces of her being with rich, resonant harmonies. Turning back in her seat, Maxie wished only to listen to the music of her memories.

With his right hand on the steering wheel, his left elbow resting on the door, Arthur massaged his forehead. He, too, was lost in thought, remembering, as a little smile crept into the corners of his mouth and tickled his lips.

For over an hour they drove in consensual silence—both savoring the memory of their evening with the Leibs at Gibby's. The sweet smell of anemones had wafted through the open courtyard on a pillow of gentle breezes, tantalizing their senses with a provocative caress. Maxie had felt the texture of the fine, white linen that draped their table, and had caught the reflection of the candles' flickering flames in Cora Leib's eyes. Arthur had made a toast.

"Maxie and I want to thank you for being in our lives, for caring as much as you do," Arthur began, raising his glass high. "I'm especially grateful," he continued, swallowing hard, "because I know that if you hadn't been in Maxie's life many years ago, Maxie never would have been in mine." Flushed, Arthur took a sip of his wine. To Arthur's surprise, Cora buried her face in her hands, did not speak nor move until the flood of emotion ebbed.

At last, Cora raised her glass. "I'm speechless, Arthur. Your words fall on my heart like dewdrops on a rosebud." Cora put her goblet on the table, ran her finger around the rim of the glass. "Thank you," she whispered. Then, reaching across the table, she tenderly touched Arthur's hand; he wrapped it in both of his.

Dr. Leib watched this exchange in silence and turned away. In the corner of the opposite wall, he spied an oil painting. A young woman, her face hidden behind an open umbrella, pressed forward on a windy, deserted boulevard—Paris, perhaps. The wet pavement reflected the undulating yellow glow of street lamps; empty park benches glistened in the mist. The apposition of prismal light and opaque shadow evoked the imagined clicking of hurried footsteps—echoes of escape. Dr. Leib slumped, covering his eyes with his left hand. From across the table, Maxie watched, perplexed by his behavior. Turning back to the table, Benjamin Leib spoke to Arthur with tearful eyes. "Oh, the power of words, my boy! Some, like psychic scissors, shred the cloth of our being." He paused, took a deep breath. No one at the table moved. "So few words to mend the delicate patterns of our tattered souls." His eyes sought out the painting.

"In each case," Arthur replied, softly, "I believe there are only three."

"Unless, of course, the intractable arrow has found its mark," Cora added, cryptically.

"Then," Arthur decided, "there are only two."

Benjamin Leib coughed, drew himself up, sat erect. "Yes, only two. You're quite right."

Extracting her hand from Arthur's, Cora said shakily, "You forget that neither of you would be in *our* lives." She straightened in her chair, rearranged her napkin on her lap. Recapturing Maxie's attention, she cleared her voice. "Life is good, my dear. Be in it."

Maxie looked into her empty wine glass, struggling to find a response. Caught off balance in this viscous moment—a moment she did not understand—she thought she heard the familiar stretching sound of hope's elastic membrane being pulled tautly over the drum of possibility. Maxie twirled the stem of her glass between her fingers, did not question what she was being asked to ignore. "I'll try," she managed.

"So, now we'll order a delectable meal," Cora declared, her voice confident, decisive. Turning to her husband, she asked, "What do you think you'd like, darling? Oh, I see there is veal. You love that."

A waiter brought a large breadbasket filled with croissants and French bread. Four hands plunged in greedily.

***

Arthur's loud sneeze brought Maxie back from her memories. Blazing landscapes blurred past them; shadows and sunshine danced together on the primal Vermont hilltops. She had barely noticed the white wood farmhouses nestled in the hushed valley, their crimson roofs a statement of enduring passion, commitment. "Bless you," she said.

"You're missing them, too, aren't you?" Arthur said, reaching into his jacket pocket for a tissue. He handed one to Maxie.

Wiping tears from her eyes, Maxie nodded.

"You just want to hold onto them and not let go," Arthur said, hoarsely.

"I know," Maxie said, clearing her throat. "Each time we leave, my heart aches. For some reason, I worry that we won't see them again—for a long time."

"Separating isn't severing. We have to keep telling ourselves that."

"This must be how Ashley and Rachel are feeling too—at least I hope they are—out there, facing unknowns, unsure of themselves, yet knowing there's something real and solid to grab onto when things get shaky."

"Are you going to be—OK, Maxie? Arthur asked, concerned.

"I think so. But it's a strange feeling I've got—I don't know—as if someone were taking off my manacles and saying, 'You're free to go now.' In my mind, I hear myself saying, 'But I didn't do anything bad—it wasn't my fault.' And the voice says, 'Yes, we've always known that. You could've walked out of this long ago.' Arthur, I feel—free, but I'm still scared."

"The Jews were made to wander in the desert for forty years, Maxie, remember?"

"Because they hadn't known freedom before, they wouldn't know what to do with it."

Arthur took Maxie's hand and held it in his lap. "Freedom means empowerment. It's easy to abuse power when you've never had it. But don't worry—it won't take you forty years to feel more comfortable with it."

"I'm not ready to be tested. I'm still trying to get used to the *idea* of being free."

As they crossed over the border into Massachusetts, Arthur spotted the familiar markings of a roadside café. "Want some coffee?"

"Yeah. I need a bathroom too. Drop me off over by the rest rooms and meet me in the coffee shop."

In a quiet corner of the cafeteria, Arthur found an unoccupied table. Using paper napkins, he wiped up some spilled juice, cleared away cookie crumbs left on the seats, and set down two cups of hot coffee. Returning from the ladies' room, Maxie sat down, wrapped her hands around the steaming cup, and took a sip. "Coffee feels good. Did you get anything to snack on?"

"No, this is fine for now." Arthur had eyed the ice-cream menu, but resisted.

Looking at Arthur over the rim of her steaming cup, Maxie pondered what was to come next, now that the house would be quiet, empty. "Hon," she sighed, "everything seems to be changing—so quickly. I've got sea legs already. Aren't you suddenly feeling a lot older?"

Arthur wore that uniquely pinched and drawn expression that revealed a weariness, a reluctance to contemplate more challenges, more worries. "Yes, I guess I do. But as long as *we* stay the same—to each other, I mean—everything is going to work out. Change is good. You've said so yourself. You just need time to get your footing, that's all."

"But aren't we changed *already*, Arthur? Some things are bound to be different, don't you think?"

"Of course, but we'll deal with them together—just as we've always done." Arthur fidgeted, wrapped a napkin around his index finger like a bandage. As he gazed out the restaurant window, on the highway streams of cars whizzed by, their headlights on in the early dusk. "Maxie, I don't want you to take this the wrong way—you know I love you very much—but, well, I *want* things to be different for us."

"What things, Arthur?"

"Listen, nobody knows as well as I do what you've been going through and I really don't mean to minimize your—pain. But, hon, your life can be happier now. You can start to think about the good things again. I want to come home after work, open the door, and hear you playing the piano, or maybe singing along to those Anne Murray tapes you used to love. I want to hear you laugh again and watch you clown around—remember how the kids used to love it when you did that slinky dance in the kitchen?" Arthur smiled, remembering.

"That was before I knew—what I know now, Arthur. How can you expect me to just pack it all away in a suitcase, stuff it in a closet, and forget?" Maxie reached across the table, put her hand on Arthur's arm. "Give me time. I promise I'll try to be a better wife, a better mother."

"Maxie, I didn't say I wanted a better wife—I said I wanted a happier one. When you're in pain, I am too. Can't you see that?"

Remembering Cora's words at Chambly, Maxie said, "No one is responsible for another's happiness. We can't expect that from anyone, not even each other."

"Yes," Arthur agreed, turning back to face Maxie, "but sadness seeps out of you and into everyone you touch. It's impossible for you not to affect the people who love you the most."

"I didn't know I was bringing everyone down," Maxie huffed. "Let's go home. I can finish my coffee in the car."

"You think I'm being self-serving, don't you?" Arthur insisted.

"No, you said what you had to—I know it wasn't easy for you. Come on, let's get out of here."

Arthur followed Maxie to the front door, looking back over his shoulder to the table where they had been sitting, thinking he had left something behind.

***

Walking into the dark, eerily quiet home that had just days before resounded with nerve-jangling telephone calls, the ins and outs, the comings and goings at all hours by old friends, new friends, and dates, Maxie and Arthur felt the palpable, unsettling reality of being alone. Maxie scurried around the house turning on the lights, the stereo—flitting nervously here and there in a vain attempt to fill the void. Arthur occupied himself with a huge pile of mail that had accumulated over the weekend. Sifting through the pile of newsletters, magazines, advertisements, and bills, Arthur found what he dreaded most. By a cruel but consistent irony, Sarah had sent a Rosh Hashanah card. To Arthur, the card was nothing more than Sarah's part in a deal she made with God every year—she did what was expected of her; He wrote her into the Book of Life. As Maxie checked the answering machine, Arthur stood at the kitchen desk, frozen, envelope in hand. Silently, he cursed Sarah Kahn for reopening the wounds, as this card most assuredly would. Maxie had not had her new resolve tested yet; this was no time to find out about her courage. *Damn that woman!* he thought. *How can I not show this to Maxie? She'd never forgive me for keeping this from her, even though I'd be doing it to protect her. I feel for Cora Leib—it must have been this hard for her too.*

Arthur's thoughts were broken by Maxie's playing of the messages. Ashley had called to say, "Hi! My allergies are ferocious, but otherwise everything's fine. Please call soon. I miss you guys."

"Arthur, did you hear Ashley's message? She's . . . hey, what's the matter?" Observing that Arthur's face had gone pale, she put her hand to his cheek. "Don't you feel well?"

"Huh? Oh, yeah, sure," Arthur said, absently, nervously.

Maxie spied the envelope in his hand, saw him compulsively turning it over and over, bending the corners. She caught sight of the script and recoiled. "Arthur, that's from Sarah, isn't it?" Her legs began to weaken.

"I've been trying to decide whether or not to let you read it. Are you going to open it?" Arthur hoped she would not.

"Of course, I'll open it," Maxie said, trying to sound brave, biting down hard on her bottom lip. "Let's see what witless drama she's whipped up for me this time."

Arthur reluctantly handed Maxie the envelope; she was making her way to the wine cooler. "If you really need that, I'll get some for you. Maybe you should sit down first."

"Yes, please. I do need it." Maxie made her way to the kitchen table and extracted the card from the envelope. It read: "For Daughter and Her Family at the New Year." Ornately outlined in gold, symbolic images of the holiday adorned the cover; the generic message inside was impersonal, all-purpose. It was the hand-written note that stung: "I'm just back from six weeks in Rhode Island—Toby made me stay longer because my pressure has been high. Toby wouldn't let me call you from her phone. Please don't be angry. Hope to hear from you. Love to everyone—Mom."

"Did you forget about reversing the charges, Mother?" Maxie asked aloud. She took a sip of the wine Arthur had poured for her. Sitting restlessly by her side, he chewed mercilessly at the inside of his cheek. "Stop doing that, Arthur," Maxie scolded, slapping his hand away from his face.

"What was that for?" he asked, stunned.

Maxie slid the card over for Arthur to read; he did not comment on the message. Instead, he rubbed his cheek where Maxie had slapped him. Gulping down the wine, she turned to Arthur. "Now, it's my turn to send a card. After all, it is the New Year, and I wouldn't want to be derelict in my duties, would I?"

Arthur cautioned, "Can't you just let it go? I mean, just let it die a natural death? If you don't respond, if you don't snap at the bait, she'll get the message."

"Not the message I have for her," Maxie retorted, pouring more wine into her glass. "This time there will be no doubt about any future cards."

"Maxie, you told me you felt free. A free person does not need to drink so much."

"One gets rather parched in the desert, Arthur."

"So, now you want to be *back* in the desert!" Exasperated, Arthur raised his eyebrows, put his hands on his hips.

"No, I just need to think. Why are you being so harsh with me?"

"I'm concerned that you're going to make things worse by answering. Act free, Maxie."

"'Live Free or Die,' is that it, like the license plate says?" Maxie slurred her words.

Arthur rose to open the cabinet where they kept a large bottle of aspirin. Letting the water run in the sink, he took out a glass, filled it, and turned to his wife. "I still think you should just throw the damn card out. Throw her out with it. Please, Maxie, *do* something about this obsession!" Arthur's stomach growled loudly, upset.

"So, that's what you think this is all about? Obsession? Well, I can't do that, Arthur. I've got unfinished business to take care of." Maxie waved the card in front of her.

"So finish it now. Throw that miserable card away. It's the right thing to do."

"You said after Philip's funeral you'd never tell me what the 'right thing to do' is."

"You're not listening to reason."

"And you're lecturing me again."

Swallowing the medication with a gulp of water, Arthur struck back. "You've drunk too much again. And you're not thinking straight. I can't talk to you when you're not making sense. Goodnight." Arthur retreated to the bedroom, wanting to say more, sure it would fall on deaf ears.

Maxie stayed at the kitchen table, feeling dismissed and stung by Arthur's accusation. To prove him wrong, she poured herself another glass of wine and savored each anesthetic drop. *Maybe I'm drunk on delusion,* she thought. *Well, it's better than being sober on illusion.* After finishing off the bottle, Maxie stumbled up the stairs to the bedroom feeling heroic. She took pleasure in the lovely headiness—a self-congratulatory pat on her psyche. She *was* going to do something; she had made her decision. Embracing herself from within, she smiled triumphantly. It was already apparent to her that future trips to the lake were going to be more peaceful.

***

Maxie slipped into a somewhere beyond consciousness, adrift in a wind that howls like a baying wolf, where the night—like a giant, yellow-eyed claw—scoops you up from the wreckage of your failures, holds you in the black of its embrace, kisses your lips with a hunger wet with promises. A stranger—faceless, disembodied—speaks, his voice an echo, swirling in a vacuum of time and space. Maxie reaches out in her dream, desperately trying to grasp the ethereal figure; but it steps back from her reach, hides in the cold, dark shadows, challenged.

"Maxine," the voice calls to her, "your quest for truth has brought you much pain. Are you prepared to pursue its logical conclusion?"

"Who are you? Why do you invade my dreams?"

"I come to tell you that truth is not a singular concept—it is a kaleidoscope of fragmented ideas—free-floating, random. These geometric configurations of truth change with every twist and turn of fate, and fall into some haphazard pattern that shows itself to you in beautiful new mosaics. Truth is misunderstood when it lacks context." The voice was gentle, earnest.

"Why can't I see your face?" Maxie pressed. "How do I know you're telling me the. . . .?"

"I am one of many faces, Maxine. I am a matrix of many disguises. My face, it may be said, is consistent with the moment."

"I'm confused. Are you saying that there is no truth—that I won't recognize it when I see it? Is truth so ephemeral that it can't be seen, cannot be captured?"

"Certainly not," the voice corrected, "but you can know only *your own* truth—you cannot experience nor can you define it for others. When you come upon *your truth*, do not think of it as a treasure chest filled with lucid gems and priceless pieces of antiquity. Do not anticipate an epiphany. Your enlightenment will require great inspiration. It will test your creativity to reconfigure, to redesign, to sculpt a future with new dimensions, new possibilities."

"I can't possibly know how to do all this! Teach me; show me what I have to do." The shadowy figure began to evaporate. "Stop! I need you to explain. Please, don't go!"

"I will tell you this, Maxine: it is your turn to tell the truth. You are not yet free."

The voice was gone; it was morning. Maxie awoke to find Arthur long gone to work. With remorse, she thought about their argument the night before. *I was abusive and irresponsible. He wants me to act free, but I'm still a wandering Jew.*

•25•

Sarah Kahn shuffled into the den and switched on the night table light next to the sofabed. Soft shadows clung to the walls, innocently lazing about in discreet corners. A gentle breeze filtered in through the vertical blinds, causing them to sway—their movement, not an altogether unpleasant happening in the otherwise stifling condo. Nighttime had once again spread its veil of peace on Sarah; she could breathe, exhale without sighing. Clicking on the television set, she settled into the sofa but was unable to focus on the anchorman. *Hell,* she thought, *it's only bad news anyway.* She scanned the room, trying to avoid looking at those things that reminded her of Philip. In one corner of the room was Philip's unoccupied rocking chair, a large Lincoln rocker in which his absence was conspicuous. For over fifty years, she had yearned for the day when she would hear the music, feel the rhythm of his death in the soles of her feet, lift her skirts, and dance herself into a frenzy.

Alone now, for four months, Sarah felt let down, cheated. Philip's death was anticlimactic; her life as a widow was not as she had envisioned it. The lonely widowers, rumored to be waiting at her door, begging for a date, had not shown up. After her husband's final departure, his last gift to her, Sarah tried to cleanse herself of memories. New bedding, new carpet, new wallpaper helped to erase his having been there, helped to wash away the stains of his last statement of defeat. "Please, God, don't take me yet—I'm not ready!" he had entreated. The reply had literally scared him to death. Her place was comfortable and quiet, now that the rasping and choking sounds had stopped. She still refused to sit in Philip's rocking chair. It was where he had plunked himself down on the day they moved into this place; it was where he stayed, immobilized by resignation. "Well, here we are, at the last stop on the road, Sarah," he had declared. He ate in the kitchen, slept in his bedroom—Sarah used the sofabed—and rocked in the den. Sarah had other plans. She learned how to play golf, joined the clubhouse group for breakfast and lunch, and, until Philip's last miserable year, went out to play mah-jongg at least two evenings a week. It wasn't heaven, but it was better than anything she had known back home.

When Philip was alive, Sarah's loneliness flowed into the spaces of her heart the way wetness seeps into the pores of a dry sponge. Things had always seemed that way to her—sucked up. Now, she was saturated with a loneliness she had not expected. As her eightieth birthday neared, Sarah wanted a present no one else could give her—to forgive herself.

Rising from the sofabed, Sarah walked out onto the small, enclosed patio and studied the darkening sky. How random the stars appeared—how vast the space in which possibilities traveled. For her, however, there had been only one choice; her survival had depended on it. She had not wanted to lose Maxie so completely, so irreversibly. Yet, there was something inherent in Philip's death that made it so. Reconciliation and friendship did not seem to be the logical results of their years of mutual exclusion. Watching the early fall sunset, the pungent reds and purples mixed with golden amber, she took in the visual sedative with greed. For Sarah, the superficial sufficed. Matters below the surface only caused her discomfort; reflection made her squirm. For Sarah, interior landscapes were like mazes—there were tricky twists and bends, turns, and detours along the road with no red lights to tell her when to stop. With no reliable landmarks to guide her, she tripped up at every intersection. In this respect, she had a lot in common with Toby; decisions left her stumbling, off balance. Toby and she were kindred spirits, held fast by a holy alliance of dependency. Like two tipsy drunks trying to make their way in the dark, they held onto each other and relied on the other's equally distorted vision to see them home safely. To Sarah's dismay, Maxie wanted to see things much too clearly.

From the clubhouse, muffled sounds of enjoyment drifted up to her balcony; she tried to imagine a cause for their gaiety.

"Fools, stupid asses, all of you! What do you know?" she spat, slamming her fist down on the porch railing. "Do you really think you're all that different from me? They'll come for you too—don't you worry about that!" Sarah's shouts ricocheted off the stucco walls, assailed her own ears.

"She hates me," Sarah whispered to the stars. "And I hate myself for hating her."

No, you don't, her conscience corrected.

"She's the devil's child, not mine," Sarah insisted. "A bad seed. I hate myself for letting her try so hard, for so long, to love me."

Her worst mistake has been in trying to make you love her. Conscience, wise beyond its years, knows all about selective interpretations.

As the night began to envelop Sarah in its cobalt chill, she stepped inside, closing the slider behind her. On the way to the kitchen for tea, she ran her fingers along the border of a Parsons table set next to the adjoining wall. Arranged in careful order on the table were framed pictures of her family. Among the dozen or so displayed, there was only one of Maxie, Arthur, and their children. ("Don't send me pictures without frames," she had warned. Those that had come unframed had been stuffed into a drawer, forgotten.) Picking up the one of Maxie's family, she touched the faces of each grandchild.

"I wouldn't know you if you showed up at my door. What do you look like now?" she asked the picture.

You could know—if you really cared.

"What I don't know won't hurt me," Sarah bluffed.

It hurts them, old woman.

"They'll understand—someday."

And who will explain?

"Time," Sarah sighed, replacing the picture on the table, behind all the others.

In the small, neat kitchen, Sarah poured fresh water into the white enamel teapot and set it on the electric burner. At the table, she waited for the water to boil. The quiet she had sought for so long descended like a boulder, pinning her down with its awful weight. Huge, fiery tears began to spill from her eyes, burning her cheeks as they flowed—dropping one by one onto the tabletop, melding into a salty puddle. Sarah fumbled for a tissue in the pocket of her housecoat; finding none, she lifted the edge of the tablecloth to her face. *I must be getting old,* she thought. *Tears are for old fools who think they can rewrite their stories. I am old, but I'm no fool. I know she'll find out one of these days—and when she does, what will there be to say? Should I have told her myself? No, for however long the charade may last, at least she'll think there's hope.*

The whistling of the teapot shook Sarah out of her vulnerability. Relieved, she rose to fish out a tea bag she kept in the tiny pantry. Inside the cupboard were two boxes of bran cereal (Maxie had told her it could lower her cholesterol), instant coffee, small cans of tuna packed in water (Maxie had advised against the salt), a few boxes of instant pudding, some spaghetti. For a woman who ate little, she kept her shelves amply stocked. Filling her mug with the boiled water, she darkened it with the tea bag, draining the bag by wrapping it around a spoon, and squeezing out the remaining liquid. She sweetened the tea with saccharine. A sardonic grin formed on her lips as she recalled how often Maxie had cautioned her about the ill effects of artificial sweeteners. It was Maxie who had taken her to doctors in Boston when she had felt the lump in her breast; it was Maxie who had made the appointments and paid all the bills for the doctors, the lawyer, the psychiatrist. Yes, her daughter had certainly tried.

Taking a few sips of the tea, Sarah sat back in her chair, recovering. The steamy tea soothed her; it calmed the jittery feeling that had crept under her skin, into her gut. She held the mug up to her cheek, grateful for the warming comfort it gave her and inhaled the herbal bouquet that spiraled up toward her nose. The momentary lapse into sentimentality had dented her armor but had not penetrated it. The knowledge that she had not succumbed to weakness allowed her to shake off the impulse to call Maxie, to have it out with her, once and for all. The unopened letter with the "Love" stamp still lay on the table. Pride had paralyzed her reason, snuffed out her curiosity. Stuffing the letter into her letter-holder, she rose to turn off the kitchen lights, checked the locks on the front door and made her way to the bedroom. She was so tired of being tired. Once in bed, she pulled the comforter up to her chin and lay perfectly still, wishing with all her heart that she could make the whole damn thing go away, if only she knew how. Sarah, devout fatalist and true believer in the irrevocable, worshipped at the altar of inertia; she sought absolution in the catechism of denial. For her, life fell back on itself like a downy blanket, concealing imagined lust, fantasized passion, real deceit; it hid the dust of past mistakes in its pleated design, in the patterned folds of a geometric guilt. The fibers of her own duplicity convinced her that she was covered; yet, they did not keep out the cold, the shivering of her sadness. To the silent reproach of her conscience she made it clear: "What's done is done," she averred. "I pay my own price. Good-night, Papa."

•26•

Rising early, Maxie thought about what she would tell Dr. Weissman. She was anxious to share all that had transpired since their last session. She wanted him to be proud of her—to be able to tell at a glance that her trip to Montreal had been an empowering experience. It was important that he acknowledge what she believed to be her new, stronger self. "I am woman; hear me roar!" she shouted to her mirror, carefully choosing her favorite beige slacks and pale-blue silk blouse. Maxie applied her makeup with particular attention to detail—her lipstick complemented her light olive complexion, gave warmth to her hazel eyes. To her long, dark eyelashes, she carefully applied accentuating strokes of the mascara wand. Satisfied with her appearance, she straightened out the bathroom, made the bed, dusted the desk and bureau. Giving the room a nod of satisfaction, she grabbed her handbag and went downstairs. *The kitchen is as I left it! How remarkable*! *I could learn to like this,* she mused. Before leaving for her appointment, she stopped to call Susan.

"Hello?" Susan answered.

"Sue. We're back. Just wanted to say 'hi' and to see if you'd meet me later for coffee," Maxie said, trying to conceal the lightness she was feeling.

"Maxie, you sound so—so different. How did the weekend go?"

"I'll tell you all about it later, Sue. In a word, incredibly."

"Sure, I can meet you. How about 1:30 at Joe's?" Sue was very curious to know what happened, but she knew not to squeeze for information—there were too many tender areas.

"That's great—1:30 at Joe's. See ya later." Maxie hung up the phone and reached for her car keys, taking one last glance at herself in the dining-room mirror. For once, she saw herself as she knew she looked to others—an injured child, a twisted visage of helplessness. When looking into a mirror, Maxie saw a face, one she knew to be her face but one that had always seemed featureless, unconnected to herself. At night, with eyes closed, she often tried to reconstruct her image, conjure some facsimile of herself. Struggling, she would think of the collection of photographs that Arthur kept of their trips and family celebrations, unable to recreate more than a blurry outline, a one-dimensional likeness. Of course, she had no trouble at all calling up the sculptured features of Arthur's face, his deep-set eyes, his firm, assertive jaw, the crease that ran vertically down his left cheek whenever he flashed his easy, boyish smile. The contrasts of Rachel's gray-blue eyes, set against her fair complexion and dark hair, were so easily remembered. Ashley's broad, embracing smile, her hazel eyes that danced mischievously, her infectious laughter that made her whole countenance so radiant and alive were there to contemplate, even in her absence. Alden—tall, enigmatic, dark and handsome, with curly brown hair and eyes as dark as late summer cherries—she brought to her mind effortlessly.

Why, then, could she not picture herself? She had once heard a story—a secret, really—about one of Sarah's older sisters, Frances, who "got very sick for a while," and had to spend some time in a hospital. When pressed for more information, her other aunts simply replied, "Oh, she thought she had no face. We thought she was losing her mind because she kept touching her face and screaming,

"My face! It's gone!" Maxie had been told by her aunts that she must never mention this episode to anyone, especially to Frances. Could it be, she wondered, that her aunt had been trying to convey the same consternation that she, herself, experienced? Forcing another long, hard look into the mirror, she was shocked to find a sad, chastened child, begging for her attention. "I will love you," Maxie said to the child, "I will protect you. Don't be afraid anymore." Wiping tears from her cheeks with the back of her hand, ignoring the streaks of mascara, she bent to retrieve her car keys from the floor where they had fallen. She secured the house and left for her appointment with Dr. Weissman.

***

Had anyone asked, Maxie would have said that light-years had passed since her last appointment with Dr. Weissman—that the moon had slipped into silent passage, waxing, waning, carrying her through space as she clutched the pendulum of change. It had been merely two weeks, but Maxie arrived at this Monday morning's session amazed that she did not feel afraid. Like some latter-day Delilah, Maxie believed she possessed the power of discovery. Sarah's fortress was crumbling, indefensible.

At exactly ten o'clock, Dr. Weissman opened his office door, greeting Maxie with an unaccustomed, jaunty air. He was dressed, she thought, rather fashionably in a lovely black-and-white silk-blend sports jacket and a white-and-black striped shirt with a natty charcoal-and-silver tie. He had had what was left of his hair styled differently. Black tasseled loafers finished the new look on a man who had never given much thought to appearance. A puckish grin, one that Maxie had not seen on his lips before, gave credence to her suspicions. He had to have a greater purpose in mind, Maxie reasoned. Looking younger and more attractive, affecting distinction and self-assurance that was commensurate with his professional prominence, had to mean that there was a "significant other" in his life. She had heard that his first marriage had failed and that he had let himself out to pasture. Today, he seemed leaner. Perhaps he was working out or eating a more sensible diet. In any case, he knew that she was appraising him; the twinkle in his eyes revealed his amusement.

"Good morning, Maxie, I'm glad to see you looking well. How are things with you? How was your weekend in Montreal?" His smile was warm, and she made a valiant attempt to return it. She settled into the armchair, signaling that she had much to relate. She told him about Sarah's letter and the extraordinary emotional exchange with Cora Leib at Chambly. Then she talked about Sarah's New Year's card, ending, finally, with the confrontation she had had with herself that morning. When she finished her long, uninterrupted monologue, Dr. Weissman continued to sit silently, deliberately, for what seemed to Maxie like hours. Her nonstop, hyper presentation over, she sat, unnerved by the silence. To fill the void, she forged ahead. "You know, Doctor, Sarah refused to have any baby pictures taken of me. I asked her about it once, and she told me that she didn't want any reminders."

"As I recall, you were in a full body cast," Dr. Weissman stated.

"Yeah—bilateral hip dislocations. 'Defective.' The 1945 poster child for plaster of Paris."

"Maxie, you're sounding bitter again. It must have been quite difficult for Sarah to care for you."

"She didn't—Belle did. Sarah took care of Toby." The animus in her voice was replaced by flat affectation She studied her long fingers, rubbing each one as if it hurt.

Making that tent-like gesture with his fingertips touching lightly, Dr. Weissman leaned forward and spoke softly. "Maxie, I'm going to ask you a few questions. I shall do so delicately, but I want you to think about them with honesty, and with as much clarity as possible."

"Of course," Maxie answered nervously. "What are they?"

"Maxie, did your father Philip ever make any sexual advances toward you? Did he ever approach you in a way that you might today characterize as sexually threatening?"

"No, I've already said that Philip was always reticent about physical contact. Toby and I wished he *would* touch us, hug us—anything to make a connection. He rebuffed *our* advances." Maxie was relieved that the question was so easy.

"Now, Maxie, let me ask you an even more delicate question. Did your mother Sarah ever do anything to you that now, as an adult, you might characterize as sexual?"

The question had the effect of a swift uppercut to Maxie's solar plexus—her breath truly punched out of her. A death-grip of panic wrapped itself around her throat, choking off vital air to her lungs. The demons howled as searing pain charged into her lower abdomen; she doubled over from the assault.

"I feel dizzy and faint, Doctor Weissman," she gasped, holding onto the arms of the chair for support.

"Maxine, you're hyperventilating. Take some deep breaths and let them out slowly. I'm sure you won't faint. Now, try to calm yourself. You're not going to pass out. Let me get you some water." Dr. Weissman stood, padded quickly to the water cooler. He opened a window. Fresh air flowed into the office, chilling Maxie's perspiring body. Trickles of moisture ran down her spine; droplets formed above her upper lip. Now she was trembling. Dr. Weissman returned with some water in a paper cup and handed it to her. He pulled his chair out from behind his desk and positioned it closer to Maxie's as he waited for her to regain her composure. The trembling abated; but Maxie kept feeling the clenching, the squeezing in her chest and abdomen. She recognized these spasms.

"When you are ready to continue, Maxie, tell me what you are feeling. Is there something you remember? Please don't be afraid. It can only help to say the words—the ones you've guarded with your life."

Maxie stared at Dr. Weissman's kind and gentle face; his now somber, gray eyes told her that he understood her anguish. Yet, there was something urgent about his appeal, something earnest in his coaxing that convinced her to whisper her confession.

"When I was nine or ten years old, Sarah started giving me enemas. I remember that I asked her why I needed to have them. Her answer was that my pediatrician, Dr. Browning, had said that I was 'not regular enough.'"

"How often did she administer these enemas?"

"At least twice, maybe three times a week," Maxie said, without blinking. "She'd wait until Philip went to his bed. Then, she'd summon me into the upstairs bathroom. I'd have to lie naked across her knees, as she. . . ."

"Go on."

"As she inserted the end of a long, black-tipped hose into me. I remember the orange plastic bag that hung suspended from the shower curtain on a clothes hanger—it hooked into the top loop of the bag. I would watch the bag slowly deflate as the soapy water flowed down the tube and into my body."

"What did your mother wear when she did this?"

"I don't know. I can only remember the hurt as she kept thrusting the tube."

"*Kept* thrusting?" Dr. Weissman asked.

"Yes. Slowly at first—then with a quick, forceful motion."

"Did she talk to you during this time? Did you let her know she was hurting you?"

"She would just say, 'Just a few more seconds, Max.' The warm purgative would, of course, produce its intended effect of pressure and urgency, but she wouldn't let me off her lap—even if I pleaded." Maxie held her stomach, rocked violently back and forth in her chair, reliving past sensations.

"What happened when she did let you off?"

"She just walked out," Maxie sobbed.

"No good-nights?"

"Nothing."

After a brief pause, Dr. Weissman asked, "What do you think Sarah was doing, Maxie?"

Maxie did not hesitate. "She was raping me, Doctor. Philip had raped her, she was raping me—first my body, and, forever after, my mind." *And she has continued to fuck me ever since,* Maxie told the stranger from her dreams.

"For how long did this continue?"

"It must have gone on for a very long time. I'm not really sure. On the morning that I came downstairs to announce that I'd begun to menstruate, Sarah got up from her seat at the kitchen table and slapped my face so hard I lost my balance."

"Why did she do that?"

"She said it was an old, superstitious custom. She informed me that as of that moment, I was among the cursed."

"Did you ever tell anyone about these enemas, Maxie?"

"My sister Toby had to know. We shared a bedroom."

"Did she ever have to be given enemas?"

"No. Just me."

"Did you think that was at all unusual?"

"No. By the time I was thirteen, everything in my home life seemed convoluted, sick. Nothing made any sense. I never felt safe."

"When you say 'safe,' do you mean *wanted?"* Dr. Weissman asked gently.

"I—I just didn't—yes, that's it—wanted. I just couldn't understand what it was all about. I made excuses to stay late after school—I immersed myself in my studies. My goal was to get out of that house. When I finally did get out, I realized that what Sarah called my 'stomach ailments' were really my desperate cries for help. I can see that now."

"Are you all right, Maxie? Tell me how you feel right now."

"Dreadful."

"Maxie, it's not the truth that hurts, but rather the discovery of the malice of intent. Protracted sadness, such as you've experienced, is like a necrotic disease that assaults the flesh of the inner being. It requires a strong dose of psychic medicine—some powerful intervention—to reverse these ravages. I believe you have been given such a dose." Moving his chair closer, he looked deeply into Maxie's eyes. "Open your arms, embrace that child you saw in the mirror this morning. Fill her emptiness with your love."

"Doctor, after reading Sarah's letter at Chambly, I thought I was going to die. Then I felt very strong, infused with resolve not known to me before. Now, I don't know *how* to feel."

"All I'm saying is to be good to yourself. Learn to enjoy simple, innocent things. This is all very new to you, Maxie. As time goes on, you'll see how much easier it will be. We all slip and backslide trying to move forward."

They had already talked beyond the scheduled hour, and Maxie, feeling the polar effects of the old pulling and the new pushing, smiled at Dr. Weissman and said, "I guess I'm still going to need your help. Confidence will come, I suppose, when I begin to act with courage. You know, years ago, Cora Leib used to prod me with just one phrase: '*¡Ánimo, hay que adelantar con ánimo!*'—'Spirit, one must go forward with spirit.'"

"That's a splendid note to end on today," said Dr. Weissman, rising from his chair to open the door for Maxie. "It's also very good advice. Remember, call me if you need me."

***

Maxie left Dr. Weissman's office armed with a plan, never more impelled nor purposeful. She understood now why she never saw the face of the stranger in her dreams—*I am the stranger,* she decided. Pulling out of the parking garage, she turned right onto Beacon Street and weaved her way through the busy lunch-hour pedestrian traffic to Harvard Street. With surprising luck, she found a parking space and maneuvered her car into it. After feeding the meter, she crossed the street to a card shop and began her search for an appropriate New Year's card for Sarah. There were many cards, all effusive with love and inspiration, all thanking the Almighty for the blessings and rewards of having such wonderful mothers, fathers, siblings, or stepparents. Maxie worked hard—reading, rejecting, reading, rejecting. None seemed impersonal enough. At last, she found a generic card that expressed all-purpose wishes for health and happiness in the coming year. Maxie bounded for the cashier, not wanting to lose her momentum; she did not want to betray her promise of the morning. She paid for the card and a stamp, and hastily left the store. She heard someone calling her to return for her change, but she had other, more urgent things on her agenda. Turning left, she walked briskly ahead to a coffee shop, ordered a large hazelnut, and sat down at a small boutique-style table nestled in a far corner. The shop was busy and full of chatter, clipped and constrained by the lunchtime work reprieve. Maxie cleared all the noise from her head as she took a pen from her purse and opened the card. She took long, slow sips of her coffee, mentally composing her message. When she was satisfied that as succinctly as possible she had come up with a fitting declaration, she began to write:

"Dear Sarah:

"There is a simple, ineluctable law of human nature which states that a life is not something you give, only to take away at discretion.

A life is not arbitrarily disposed of, as if it were a cheap, worthless commodity. So, this time, I am going to save you the trouble—I am taking *myself* away from *you*—permanently. I have unearthed your 'secret,' which really isn't a secret at all, as much as it is an excuse for your cowardice and shame. As you prepare to celebrate your eightieth birthday, my present to you is the knowledge that you are free—let's consider ourselves divorced—free to live out what remains of your life unencumbered by memories. I wish you health and peace.

Your daughter,
Maxine

"P.S. Just one more thing: You really piss me off!"

Maxie recapped the pen, tapping it gingerly on the little bistro table. Sipping her coffee, she reread the words that seemed to have flown straight from her heart to her hand to the paper. It said, unadorned by qualifiers and useless platitudes, the raw, truncated truth—*my truth,* she supposed. *Not Sarah's—not anyone's. I discovered my own now.* She brushed aside misgivings about causing Sarah a heart attack, slipped the card into the envelope, addressed it, and affixed the stamp. Had she paid attention, she would have seen that the stamp she purchased was brightly decorated with bold, red lettering that said "LOVE." *Oh, well*, she sighed. *Sarah can think about that one too.*

Outside in the bright September sunshine, Maxie took a deep breath, then walked without hesitation to the corner mailbox into which she pitched the card and shut the pull-down door. She heard the sound of the card as it fluttered down inside the box and hit the bottom. In her mind, the heavy iron bars rattled as the huge gate to the lair clanged shut.

***

Exhausted, hyperventilating, Toby sat on her mother's wicker bed, trying to calm herself. Stroking the floral chinz spread with a loving hand, resting her tear-filled eyes on the neatly tucked pillows, she felt shipwrecked, adrift on angry waves of grief. She had lost track of the days after the funeral. Was it three? Four? Alone in Sarah's apartment, dressed in black linen slacks and a respectful beige blouse, Toby sat, powerless, listening to the ticking of a small, antique clock on the night table, studying the photograph of her family positioned beside the clock. In the picture, taken many summers ago in her backyard, everyone smiled for the camera, even Candy, the dog, lying indolently at Toby's feet. For a few minutes Toby played with her wedding band, turning the diamond-studded ring around her finger, hypnotized by the repetition. Early afternoon sunlight poured into Sarah's bedroom, caught the facets of the diamonds, stung Toby's eyes with its clarity. Then, in a sudden surge of loathing, Toby snatched the framed picture from the night table and hurled it against the bedroom wall. "Goddamn you, Stuart!" she wailed. Shattered glass fell to the rose-colored carpet, each jagged shard cutting deeply into the scabs of her memory.

Maxie, away at school, never saw the bruises, never witnessed the black eyes, the split lips, the abrasions. Toby was getting so overweight and clumsy, Sarah had said, she seemed to be forever walking into doors and falling down. Six years separated the sisters in age; decades of disavowal kept them apart, splintered by mutual suspicions.

For all that it obscured, Toby's darkness was more than an absence of light; it was a silence she wore like a shroud. A cinereous nighttime of the spirit became the refuge into which she furtively crept.

"Darkness, sweet darkness, please keep me safe," was Toby's mantra invoked nightly; it was her prayer for salvation, her petition for mercy. How fervently she wished she could tell her only sister about the beatings, about the reasons for her constant state of fear. She yearned to confide in Maxie, to tell her about Janice. Could Maxie explain why evil endures by simply eluding scrutiny? Would her alienated sister understand that Stuart, a chiropractor and president of the local country club, could not abide a revelation that he perceived as emasculation, an excruciating whack of truth to where his whole sense of worth and definition resides? No, she could not tell Maxie of Stuart's discovery of her love for another woman. The total warmth and acceptance she had found outside the frigid wilderness of her marriage had provoked a rage so great that he had picked up their seventy-pound dog, Candy, and had hurled her down a full flight of stairs to the tile foyer below. What would Maxie have said if Toby had told her that, like a crushed bug, Candy had lain dead, legs splayed in every direction? A goulash mix of guts and blood had trickled from her contorted mouth, forming a sticky, viscous puddle. Candy's eyes had fixed on Stuart in horror.

Toby studied the scattered glass on the carpet, her eyes blurring with tears, her heart as shattered as the pieces before her. A single crystal lay on its side, propped against the baseboard, reflecting a sharp, intense light of late afternoon sun. Toby cringed, remembering how petrified she had been on that gruesome day, how hopelessly she had looked around the room for an escape. Stuart had locked his gaze on his wife, immobilizing her with a terror she had not seen unleashed before.

"You lousy bitch," he seethed, "you filthy, fucking bitch!"

As Stuart approached her, hands clenched, crimson rising steadily in his face, eyes ablaze, Toby took faltering steps backwards. He struck her with all his fury, with all his insensate wrath, with all his two hundred forty pounds of indignation. Toby flew through the air, crashing into the oak and glass stereo cabinet. An imported Daum crystal vase teetered, hesitated, then fell to the wooden floor, perplexed by a peculiar sense of its own waste.

"Stuart, no! The kids, Stuart—they'll be coming home soon!"

Stuart pounced on his wife, pulling her hair, mercilessly ramming his knee into her crotch, spitting in her face. Silently, Toby absorbed each blow, each bolt of pain; she felt each one distinctly, acutely. Toby wanted to remember always how it felt as every strand of her hair was being yanked. She wanted to remember always the revulsion of his sputum on her cheeks as it commingled with her own salty tears. Most of all, she wanted to savor the arc of anguish as it shot up between her legs, delivering an everlasting wave of contempt. Suddenly, abruptly, he stopped his vicious attack and was eerily quiet. He was thinking now; maybe that was a good thing. Toby certainly hoped so. Getting up in slow motion, Stuart looked down on Toby with disgust.

"All right, my queer little precious pervert. I'm gonna let you live, but you'll live in a hell every day of your life, wishing you were dead. You're gonna go on pretending that you're still madly in love with me, your husband. We'll continue living in this house, going to the club, playing golf, and acting fine and dandy—lovey-dovey, as they say. If you make one goddamn mistake, if one time I hear her vile name mentioned, or see signs that you've been together, you're as dead as that fucking dog. Keep your dirty secret buried six-feet deep, or you'll find yourself down there with it. Got that, Toby? Geez, I should've guessed—you're just like your mother, the sexless slut!"

No, Stuart, I'm not just like my mother; I'm not sexless. My mother had no one to love her. She chose not to love.

The dog officers came in a large, white van with bold lettering. Candy was taken away in a dark-green rubbish bag; her lifeless form was too heavy for just one of them to carry. Of course, they inquired about the circumstances of the tragedy. Stuart explained that his wife had gotten carried away while playing with the dog and had thoughtlessly thrown Candy's ball over the top of the wrought-iron railing. Instinctively, the dog had leapt over the railing, had sailed through the air in pursuit of the ball, and had plunged to her gory end. His wife, Stuart added, was so devastated, she was in her room, crying her eyes out.

"Pitiful, just pitiful," the officer said, completing the necessary report, buying into the pretense. The cue from Stuart's patient was undeniable.

"Yes," agreed Stuart, "isn't it?" He was on his knees, attempting to wash down the blood that had splattered the wallpaper and woodwork. "Listen, Roger, why don't you come down to my office on Wednesday. I'm sure I can do that spinal alignment you need for a very reasonable fee."

"Sure thing, Doc. Nice of you to see me on your day off," Roger smiled as he left the house.

Toby had tried in vain to convince her children that she had not killed their dog. Three months later, Janice died of a drug overdose. Toby, unable to attend the funeral, bought a gun. If nothing else, she would count the days to some distant but inevitable time when she would have the last word, when somehow she would find a way to make up for her cowardice. *Why should I expect my children to forgive me when I can't?* she confessed.

Still sitting on Sarah's bed, her soul a thin, translucent shell, Toby winced, shuddered. "It has to end—somehow, it's got to end," she said aloud, slipping off her wedding band, stuffing it into her pants pocket. Unable to force herself to do what she had come for, Toby felt overwhelmed. It was all too much, too soon, touching the clothes, the perfume bottles, the jewelry Sarah had worn last. Willing herself to stand, every bone in her body aching with loss, she walked into the kitchen. Wednesday's *Miami Tribune* lay on the table, still opened to the section on horoscopes. Sarah had circled hers in red ink. A half-filled mug of tea remained, the teabag wrapped around the spoon that lay on a folded paper napkin. Placed against the wall to the right of Sarah's chair, Toby spied the bright-yellow, plastic letter holder in which her mother kept unpaid bills, shopping lists, letters. Sitting down, Toby reached for the holder, deciding to sort the bills. The rent check had already been filled out and placed in an envelope; the gas and phone bills were filed vertically as reminders. As she thumbed through the papers, Toby found an unopened envelope, what appeared to be a card. In the upper left-hand corner, in bold red letters, followed by an arrow pointing to Maxie's address, Sarah had written: "RETURN TO SENDER."

Toby stared at the previous Monday's date clearly postmarked and figured that the card must have arrived on Wednesday—a week ago. What now? Indecision shook Toby; her thoughts cracked and peeled off the walls of her brain. Did Sarah forget to mail back this sealed card? Was it her mother's last wish? Should she, dutiful Toby, carry out that wish?

Chilled from the air conditioning, Toby rose from the table, her legs heavy, unsteady. She held onto the table until her dizziness subsided, then dragged herself through the dining room, past the family pictures, out to the patio. Needing the warm comfort of the Florida sun, she stood at the black wrought-iron rail, lifted her face to the sunshine. In the bright darkness behind her closed eyelids were the words to a poem Maxie had written in high school:

"If I were crabgrass, and found myself among
A thickly crop of tulips, none but yellow,
I'd spread my leaves like a singer filled with song,
Turn toward the mighty sun, and bellow
HERE I AM!"

"What a silly, stupid poem, Maxie," Toby had said. "Only someone like you would think of yourself as crabgrass."

Maxie had said, "Exactly. No matter how close to the ground I'm lying, my skin cold and wet, something inside me keeps screaming, 'UP! UP!' I can't live on my hands and knees, Toby. I can't stand looking down all the time." It was the last time they had spoken, the last time Toby had allowed her sister to touch her own terrible loneliness.

I lied, Maxie; I really did love your poem. Only now I understand it . . . you better. Squeezing her eyes shut, Toby clutched the rail. *And I lied about Mom too. I just pretended not to know what went on in the bathroom—pretended to be asleep when you got into your bed, crying softly, so you wouldn't wake me. I stay out of your life because I'm too much of a coward to be in it. I need you to hate me, Maxie, as much as I do myself. You don't realize it, but you're the lucky one. You're not afraid of what you are.*

Opening her eyes, still holding onto the rail, Toby looked out over the grounds of the condominium complex. She heard the thunk-thunk sounds of tennis balls served and returned in the court below. She watched sneaker-clad, gray-haired men and women run by in their orange-and-black or iridescent-aqua jogging outfits, smiling, gesturing, waving to friends. By the swimming pool, in the shade, other women—old red-headed women with folds of cellulite and sagging breasts—played bridge and canasta. Toby could hear their laughter, smell their fear. "So let me tell you about my grandson," crowed the one whose rhinestone frames slid down her aquiline nose. All things are possible in the end, Toby decided.

"I'll do nothing," she said, resolutely. "It's the least I can do." Minutes later, satisfied that for once she had made a decision, irrevocable and hers alone, Toby turned, reentered the apartment. At the kitchen table, she picked up Maxie's card and threw it into the trash. "I can't bring you back, Janice." Toby's sorrow burned in her chest, a poker stoking flames of regret. "But I feel your strength in my broken, coward's heart." Toby cradled herself, rocking gently to the warm, rhythmic sound of Janice's voice remembered: "The only thing that lies between now and nothing is hope. Move toward it, with courage."

The wall phone jangled with impatience, rattled twice more with insistence. "Give it up, fool!" she said, guessing it was Stuart, a twisted smile on her face. Ignoring the now furious ringing, Toby wiped her hands on her slacks, sighed, looked around the apartment. Opening the door to the refrigerator, she began the task for which she had come. "Clean it up, girl," she said, "clean it up." The phone continued to ring.

PHOTO BY JUDITH LIPSKY

About the Author

Georgene Weiner was born and raised in Waterbury, Connecticut. She received her Bachelor of Arts degree from Boston University and taught Spanish in Boston-area schools. Ms. Weiner has authored poetry and short stories. *Rape Seed* is her first full-length novel. A devotee of classical music, she is a pianist and singer who has also appeared in community theater. Mother of three, Ms. Weiner lives near Boston with her husband and is currently writing her second novel.